6|13

D0819530

3.15
Lexile: _____

AR/BL: _____

AR Points: _____

abandon

Also by Elana Johnson

possession
surrender

abandon

a possession novel

elana johnson

simon pulse

new york   london   toronto   sydney   new delhi

SIMON PULSE
An imprint of Simon & Schuster Children's Publishing Division
1230 Avenue of the Americas, New York, NY 10020
First Simon Pulse edition June 2013
Copyright © 2013 by Elana Johnson
All rights reserved, including the right of reproduction
in whole or in part in any form.
SIMON PULSE and colophon are registered trademarks
of Simon & Schuster, Inc.
For information about special discounts for bulk purchases, please contact
Simon & Schuster Special Sales at 1-866-506-1949 or
business@simonandschuster.com.
The Simon & Schuster Speakers Bureau can bring authors to your live event.
For more information or to book an event contact the
Simon & Schuster Speakers Bureau at 1-866-248-3049 or
visit our website at www.simonspeakers.com.
Designed by Angela Goddard
The text of this book was set in Berling LT.
Manufactured in the United States of America
2 4 6 8 10 9 7 5 3 1
Library of Congress Cataloging-in-Publication Data
Johnson, Elana.
Abandon : a Possession novel / Elana Johnson. — First Simon Pulse edition.
p. cm.
Summary: Jag, Zenn, Vi, and the rest of the Resistance are determined
to take down the Thinkers, but there is a traitor among them,
who could cost them their cause—and their lives.
[1. Science fiction. 2. Rules (Philosophy)—Fiction. 3. Brainwashing—Fiction.
4. Insurgency—Fiction. 5. Love—Fiction.] I. Title.
PZ7.J64053Abj 2013   [Fic]—dc23   2012051441
ISBN 978-1-4424-8482-5 (hc)
ISBN 978-1-4424-8481-8 (pbk)
ISBN 978-1-4424-8483-2 (eBook)

For Adam,
who continually teaches me that it's not about doing
what's easy, it's about doing what's right.

abandon

Jag

1.

Secrets are hard to keep—especially if your girl-friend can read minds.

"She shouldn't be a secret," Vi said, tossing me a pointed look over her shoulder as she straightened the blanket on her bed.

"*She* is not a secret," I argued, *she* being my ex-girlfriend, Indiarina Blightingdale.

"You did not mention her," Vi said, turning to face me. "Until I asked you about her—and I only asked you about her because she's all you think about!" By the end of her sentence, she had started to yell.

I suppressed the desire to roll my eyes. "I've had other

girlfriends, Vi. Do I need to detail my relationship with each one of them?"

She narrowed her eyes as if she knew I'd only had one girlfriend—Indy—before her. "Only the ones you still have feelings for." Her voice echoed off the low-hanging rocks of her bedroom and down the hall. No way everyone in the hideout couldn't hear this conversation.

"I do not have feelings for Indy." I deliberately kept my voice low.

Vi curled her fingers into tight fists. "She's all you think about." She cocked her head to the side, as if reading my thoughts right now. I wondered if she'd already discovered that I used to have a schoolboy crush on her sister.

"You don't have to listen if you don't like what you hear," I shot back. "And I'm only thinking about her because I'm worried about where she is. It's been two weeks, Vi." I swallowed back the fear that accompanied the thought of Indy being dead somewhere. "Only she knows what's happened in the Resistance while I've been . . . gone."

Her fists unclenched, and she closed the space between us with three steps. "Where were you? You know, while you were 'gone.'"

I thought about Indy. I remembered the way our eyes

would meet across a crowded room. I thought about how she knew exactly what I needed, and when.

Vi shoved me in the chest. "Stop thinking about her."

"Stop asking me about where I've been." I stepped close to her again, leaning against the archway as if it would lend me strength to endure this argument.

"You're only worried about her because you still have feelings for her."

"Not true," I growled, our faces only inches apart. "I'm worried about Thane, too, and I can't stand him."

"Thanks a lot." She pushed past me, striding toward the makeshift tech lab, where my brother Pace was standing in the doorway watching us. "So glad to know you hate my father."

"You hate him too!" I yelled after her, refusing to give her even an inch. She disappeared into the tech lab, and the fight left my body. I retreated to the hole in the wall I called a bedroom, but I couldn't figure out how to stop thinking about Indy.

See, Indy and I had gotten together on my fifteenth birthday, almost two years ago. And not only because she was an amazing leader in the Resistance. She wasn't hard to look at either, you know?

I'd been leading the Resistance for three years and didn't have much time for girls. Sure, I fantasized about Ty—the

Seer I had worked with to develop my voice talent. But Pace had claimed her as his as soon as he'd met her, and I'd kept my childish imaginations to myself.

Indy, along with her brother Irvine, had come to a surprise party Pace had planned for my birthday. Not that it was really a surprise. Pace had to get special clearance to leave the tech facility, and since our house was his permanent address, I got the confirmation before he did.

At my party she'd sauntered up to me, slid her arm around my waist, and put her hand in my back pocket. She smiled at me and motioned with her head toward the backyard.

Like I wasn't going to follow her. I'd have followed her to Freedom when she looked at me like that.

Indy had to take her hand out of my pocket to go through the back door, but I quickly caught it in my own. I was game for whatever she had in mind.

We held hands as we walked toward the back hedge. Indy looked killer under the summer moon. Her pink hair shone fuchsia, and her dark skin and eyes glowed in the soft light. She wore low camouflage pants with a black tank top that lifted just enough to show a strip of bare skin. Her hand was rough and warm in mine. It fit just right, and when she gave it a gentle squeeze, I couldn't even remember my own name.

"Happy birthday, Jag," she said.

I grinned like I'd won the electro-sweeps instead of surviving fifteen years without dying. "Thanks, Indy."

"So. We going back next week?"

"I guess," I said, shrugging one shoulder. She wanted to talk about work? What next? The weather?

"Jag, that thing you did with your voice last week was cadence."

I shrugged again. I hated talking about my talents. It's not like it actually took any special abilities to use them. They were just part of me. I tried to find her feelings, but I came up blank.

Indy cut me a look from the corner of her eye, a knowing smile playing on her lips. "Nice try," she said. She slipped her hand out of mine and moved it up my forearm. Her bright yellow fingernails traced a pattern near my elbow.

I tried not to shiver, but it didn't work. I couldn't blame the weather—the night was perfectly warm. *I wish I could call on the wind to come cool me down.*

I couldn't, so I choked out, "What does that mean?"

She slid her hand back to mine, and heat crept along my skin wherever she touched. "It means that I felt you looking."

"Looking for what?" I asked.

"How I feel about you."

I suddenly found the hedge in the neighbor's backyard fascinating. "Oh yeah?"

"Yeah. I blocked you out."

I glanced at her. "How?"

"Something Irv invented. Nasty tech when you swallow it, but after that it's dead useful."

Stupid Irvine. He's forever inventing something to keep the Thinkers out. I'd always supported him, but now that I couldn't use my empathic ability to find out what this incredibly hot girl thought about me? Not so much.

Indy traced her nails up to my elbow again. She took hold of my arm and pulled me toward her. "Let's walk, man."

"Sure." I stuffed my hands in my pockets. She laced her arm through mine, and we walked to the front of the house and down the sidewalk.

I wasn't sure what to say. I'd been on many excursions with Indy, eaten dinner with her tons of times, seen her first thing in the morning after she'd woken up on my living room floor.

But now? Words failed me. My imagination ran wild. How her mouth would feel against mine. What she would taste like.

"You're quiet for someone with a voice," she teased.

I grunted. Like I was going to screw anything up by speaking.

She removed her hands from me and put a couple of inches between us. "So. I got a question for ya."

"What's that?"

"When are you gonna kiss me?"

My mind went blank.

"It's not like I wanted to get you alone so we could discuss tactics." Her voice sounded far away, like it came from deep within her throat.

"Oh, well, I—"

"You're adorable," she said, stopping at the end of the street under an orange light.

Heat rushed to my face. "Adorable" was worse than "cute." Ty had called me that two weeks ago during our training session. I was still pissed off. I wasn't a puppy.

"Take it back," I commanded with my voice control all the way up.

She blinked, her eyes glassy, her jaw clenched. Then she smiled. "Ah. The tech doesn't work against your voice. I'll tell Irv."

"You do that," I said, striding back toward the house. *You're an idiot*, I scolded myself. Here I thought Indy liked me, but she was just testing tech for her brother—one of my best friends and an amazing technician for the Resistance.

"Jag!" She caught up to me in a couple of steps and pulled

7

on my arm to get me to stop. "Wait. You haven't answered my question."

I glared at her. "I am not a-freakin'-dorable."

She threw her head back and laughed. The sound was all wild abandon, and her throat looked mighty enticing. But she took one look at my face and sobered.

Leaning in, she smiled. "No kidding. You're freakin' hot."

"You're—"

She stole my lame comeback with her lips. I forgot why I was mad. Indy tasted like salt and apples. Her body was soft, yet hard, against mine. Her skin felt electric, like the pleasurable buzz of tech, under my fingers.

When she pulled away, I could barely breathe.

"Hot," she said again, burying both of her hands in my back pockets.

I didn't feel so hot when Gunner burst into the tiny hole I called a bedroom and pulled me from memories that felt like they had happened two lifetimes ago. "Jag, she's here."

I didn't have to ask who *she* was. I followed him into the corridor, both of us sprinting toward the common chamber.

"Indy," I called, searching for her pink hair. I recognized some of my old team from the Resistance. Their faces had hollowed. They looked like they'd been to hell and back. Maybe they had been.

"Indy?" I asked. The crowd parted, and there she stood.

"Jag." She moved toward me, and I was so cracking happy to see her alive that I didn't notice the way she had her fist cocked back.

Zenn

2.

The notification of Indiarina's arrival reached me last. I'm not gonna lie, I'm pretty sure Jag wanted it that way. I always got assigned the worst schedule—one that would keep me sleeping during the day and as far from Vi as possible.

That, and I'd volunteered for the traveling team. Over the past two weeks I'd only been on the ground for four days. Gunner and I spent a crazy-ton of hours flying hoverboards. We'd hit the cities in the Southern Region first since they'd been under relaxed control during the past eight months for breeding and talent recruitment.

The Thinkers there were receptive. Soft.

Weak.

When I'd touched down yesterday, Jag had immediately assigned me to the farthest post during the third night watch. I saw Vi for about an hour each day, always at meal times, always with a group of people. Always with Jag.

Insider Tip #1: Always do what the boss says. This is how you gain trust.

I let Jag rule over me. I let him think he was keeping me and Vi apart. I let him believe I was crazy-mad about my assignments. It wasn't like he modified them because of my complaints.

I wasn't truly playing both sides anymore, and though Jag and I weren't exactly best friends like we used to be, I wanted to regain his trust. And so I endured my difficult schedule, and hours away from Vi, and anything else he mandated.

When the runner came to alert me of a group coming in fast from the west, I knew it was Indy. And that Jag would call a meeting, never mind that my vision-screen read 2:53 a.m.

The runner, Saffediene, kept a steady stream of chatter coming over my cache. I let her talk, grunting in agreement or providing one-word answers when she asked a question. The closer we flew, the tighter my stomach clenched.

"We've been waiting for Indy for weeks," Saffediene said, flying close to me and touching my elbow.

I glanced at her, trying to figure out why she was grinning at me in the middle of the night as we flew toward the cavern that doubled as a Resistance hideout. The system of caves was about the size of my standard-issue house back in the Goodgrounds. But it was underground. With rock walls that oozed water. All things considered, I preferred standing guard in the middle of the night and crashing during the day. That way I didn't have to talk to people I'd rather avoid. I didn't have to watch Jag whisper with Vi and thread his fingers through hers.

"Uh, yeah," I said, looking away from Saffediene. "We need to know the whereabouts of Thane Myers."

"His last known location was the Goodgrounds," Saffediene said, her hand still on my arm. "Same as Indy's."

"Yeah," I confirmed. Thane was crucial to our survival. We didn't need him on our side. Not with us. But we needed him to act as Informant on Director Hightower. We needed his eyes and ears inside the Association of Directors. Without Thane's inside surveillance, we'd be crippled.

Sure, our Insiders included Starr Messenger. She's freaky-talented, but she's still a student. Trek Whiting is more experienced, but nowhere near climbing into the Director's back pocket.

As Gunn liked to remind Jag, we needed Thane—badly.

The knot in my gut turned into an iron weight as soon

as I landed outside the cavern, which was part of a series of shallow mountains. The entrance was concealed by a rotted tree stump that stunk like a million unpleasant things all rolled into one. Despite Saffediene's serious strong will, she was only a wisp of a girl with long blond hair. She struggled to push aside the stump before strolling into the cave. I lingered outside, relishing my last few breaths of fresh air.

I didn't really like being trapped underground. Fine, I hated it. To me, there was nothing worse than sleeping in a cage—talking, eating, breathing inside a box with one entrance and no exit.

I squared my shoulders and took one last lungful of unrecycled air. I arrived in the main chamber just in time to see Indy punch Jag in the mouth.

I couldn't help but smile.

Ten minutes later I sorta "loved" Indy for punching Jag. And by "loved" I mean "hated." The air in the cavern already reeked of everyone's breath and body odor, our stockpiled food, earth, metal, and murky water. Why not add some blood?

I didn't know why Indy had slugged him—and I didn't much care. Of course Jag didn't offer an explanation.

After Vi had glared Indy's face off, and after Pace had bustled Jag down the hall to the infirmary, I escaped to my hole of a room, where somehow the stench had already permeated. I yanked my notebook off the crude shelf and began scribbling. Anger simmered under my skin. Communicating with Jag would be simpler if he'd get fitted with implants. But he's as stubborn as he is smart, and he won't allow a technician within fifteen feet of him.

Everyone living in the cavern used their cache for conversation. Jag's voice echoed off the walls everywhere he went. But now that an implantless Indy had arrived with her team, talking out loud would become normal again. I sorta "loved" her for that too.

Falling back into being Jag's second-in-command came naturally for both of us. I had half a dozen items on his to-do list when I sensed someone coming down the hall. I tucked away my anger, loosened the grip on my pencil, and pasted on my Insider face. I'd gotten pretty good at thinking and feeling one thing while portraying something completely different. Fine, I was damn good at it. I'd been doing it flawlessly for four years.

Besides, I knew who was standing outside my door. "Hey, beautiful," I said without looking up. "Jag stop bleeding?"

"You sound tired," Vi said, ignoring my question.

I allowed myself to look at her. The sight of her made me ache. Because I could only look.

Not touch.

"I'm always tired," I said. Vi wore a pair of men's jeans that hung off her bony frame and a faded blue T-shirt. In the wild we scrounged for whatever food and clothing we could find. "The Director of Mountain Dale donated some clothes," I said. "Nothing's arrived yet?"

A sparkle entered her eyes. "Don't I look good in these?" She gestured to her outfit.

She'd look good in anything. Or nothing. "Absolutely." I moved toward her as she took a tiny step into my cramped quarters.

"Zenn—"

"Don't," I cut her off. I pretended to be someone I wasn't in every relationship I had. I wouldn't fake it with her anymore. We didn't need a cache—or words—to communicate. She could read my every thought.

While my voice was more developed than my mind control, I could catch the gist of most people's inner thoughts.

Especially Vi's.

I focused on the ground as I felt her inner conflict, her inability to make decisions, even simple ones. I'd like to think it was just a side effect of Thane's extreme brainwashing, her crazy-controlled life, or that making choices was a new thing for her. But all that would be a lie.

Vi just sucked at making decisions. Especially hard ones.

"I love you," I whispered, looking directly into her eyes. "It is what it is. I can't change it. I don't want to change it." I took a deep breath and prepared to say what I should've said long ago. "I can't change you, either. I don't want to. Not anymore." I gathered her into my arms and was more than a little surprised when she let me.

For the first time since Jag had picked us up outside Freedom, I kissed her. I could lie and say it didn't mean anything. But I was done lying. Kissing Vi was earth-shattering every—

single—

time.

The memory of her smooth, warm skin kept me sane during those long hours on my hoverboard. The smell of her hair gave me energy to talk to one more Director, endure one more sleepless night.

I'd do anything for Violet Schoenfeld.

She pulled away first. "I just came to tell you that Jag's ready to start."

I nodded, trying to bottle up my emotions before any more spilled out, revealing too much.

Vi traced her fingertips over my eyebrow. "I love you, Zenn Bower." She turned and walked away, leaving her next words unsaid but screaming through my mind.

But I love Jag Barque, too.

Jag

3.

Two weeks ago, the night Gunn and I had rescued Vi and Zenn, Gunn had pulled me aside after everyone else had gone to their holes to sleep.

"Starr Messenger gave me this." He held out a blood-crusted chip. "I haven't been able to watch it," he said. "My wrist-port shorted out."

I didn't need a cracking wrist-port to watch a microchip. "Let's go see my brother."

Pace manned the tech development for the Resistance in the second-largest cavern in the underground safe house. Since Ty's death I don't think he'd slept more than a few hours at a time. He hadn't said as much, but I knew. His eyes told me things his mouth couldn't say.

When Gunn and I showed him the chip, he pulled out an e-board. "Let's see. From Starr, you say?"

"She's the hot contact," I told him. "I've dealt with her for years," I explained to Gunner. "She used to send messages every week."

"Every week?" he asked. "For how long?"

I shrugged. "Three years? Close to that. I wouldn't know every intricacy of Freedom without her."

"Here we go," Pace said. The projection screen above the e-board brightened with Starr's face. She'd done something funky with her hair. I liked it.

"Gunner," Starr's voice said, and it echoed weirdly from the projection. "I'm sorry about Trek."

I cut a glance at Gunn, who frowned. "That's what she starts with? Trek Whiting?"

Pace paused the vid. "Trek is a genius," he said. "He's our communications guru in Freedom."

"Oh, sure," I said. "Trek. Love him."

But Gunn did not. He wore a sour expression and rolled his eyes. "So the guy can falsify a feed. Big deal."

But it was a big deal, whether Gunn liked him or not. "What's with you and Starr and Trek?"

"She's my match, and they're together."

"Oh, well," I said, the pieces aligning. "So you don't like him."

"He's not my favorite person," Gunn confirmed. "But I'll deal. Keep going."

Pace started the vid again. "Trek and I are still fully on board with the Resistance. When you get somewhere safe, make sure Jag Barque watches this."

I leaned forward as the camera cut away from Starr. The image vibrated and the screen went dark. One breath later, a new stream started. This time the camera wasn't in Starr's room.

"That's a laboratory," Gunner whispered.

"Where?" I asked, scanning the long rows of counters in the vid.

He didn't answer as the image zoomed in on one workstation. A man sat on a high stool, a piece of tech clutched in his hand. He wore a white coat, gloves, and a pair of protective goggles.

"Who's that?" I asked.

"Don't know," Gunn said. "Most of his face is covered by those glasses." The three of us leaned closer, anxious not to miss a thing.

The man—not much older than Pace—fiddled with his

tech instrument. He glanced at the camera—right at it. "My name is Cash Whiting," he whispered.

Gunn jerked away from the screen, and Pace paused the vid. "What?" Pace asked.

"Cash is Trek's brother," Gunn said. "He's—well, Raine drained him and, uh, now he's dead."

I raised my eyebrows. "She killed him?"

"No, no," Gunn said. "Zenn's report said Thane did."

"Why don't I have that report?" I asked.

Pace put his hand on my arm. "You rescued Zenn two hours ago, bro. Give him five seconds to sleep before he downloads every report he's filed in the past eight months."

"Fine," I said. "But no one gives *me* five seconds to sleep."

Pace smirked. "I can give you some meds that will give you as long as you want."

I waved him away. "Where did Cash Whiting work?" I asked Gunner.

"Evolutionary Rise," he said. "Raine told me about an Alias list. His name was on it, with 'Insubordinate' behind it. And 'Deceased.'"

I nodded my understanding as Pace restarted the vid. Cash leaned over his station, and the camera showed his view, as if it were perched on his shoulder.

A tray lay in front of him. He poked at something liquid

and pushed the end of his tech instrument. Blue dye seeped into the tray, brightening little rectangles one at a time until they were all showing.

"Administration of DNA," Cash whispered. "From someone with voice talent." He covered the tray and placed it in a chamber at the back of the counter.

I sucked in a breath. I knew what the scientists did in the Evolutionary Rise. Entire floors had been dedicated to creating genetic copies of talented people.

"Whose?" Gunner asked, his pale face almost gray. "Whose DNA is that? There aren't many voices in the world."

I knew what he was really asking: *Is that my DNA?*

I put my hand on his arm. "I don't know."

On the video an alarm rang, and we all jumped.

"Time to see if Batch 4395 can support life," Cash said, almost like he was making a video journal for his scientific records and not for us. Maybe he was.

"The embryos have been grown in the dark," he continued. "The temperature was kept two degrees below normal standards. They've been starved of the DNA needed to create a voice box—until they receive this application of DNA from Subject 261."

Cash removed the tray, and I leaned even closer to the p-screen. "Upon application, the embryos are warmed in an accelerator for three minutes and fifteen seconds. If life is sustainable, the blue dye will be purple, and physical evidence of life will be visible to the naked eye." Cash removed the lid.

He gasped.

I yelled.

Pace stumbled backward.

Gunner swore.

There, on the projection screen, purple overwhelmed every other color. The embryos had already begun to grow, the rectangles I'd seen before rounding into fetuses, pushing against each other and the edges of their containers.

Cash Whiting's face filled the screen. Fear lined his eyes. "This experiment is a success. Subject 261 will be brought in for DNA donation. The army will be grown in thirty days."

He glanced over his shoulder, and I saw the movement in his throat as he swallowed. When Cash turned back, he set his mouth in a thin line of determination. "I will destroy them, and all my notes. Starr, get this out to the right people. If They can replicate my procedures, the Resistance will never stand a chance."

The screen went dark, leaving only silence hanging over everything.

"Dammit," I said. I paced away from the e-board and

rubbed my hand along the back of my head. Starr spoke again, drawing me back to the p-screen.

"He destroyed them all, as well as his notes. He died for his actions. Hightower has doubled the personnel in the Evolutionary Rise. We don't have much time."

"No kidding," Gunner said, his voice haunted and hollow.

"I will be available to cache with you, Gunn, beyond the wall," Starr continued. "Trek will send Pace the coordinates and times. We'll keep you updated on any news from inside the Rises, especially the Evolutionary Rise." She looked down for a moment. When she met the camera again, her eyes sparked with power. "We can still win this. Do not lose hope."

Then the screen went black. I blinked, and a violent shade of purple imprinted on the backs of my eyelids.

"Destroy it," I whispered.

"Jag—" Pace said.

"Destroy it," I repeated. I stood up straighter and pinned Gunner and Pace with a glare. "The three of us know. No one else needs to be burdened. We'll use this knowledge and Starr's intel to our advantage, but we don't need to freak people out."

"They'll quit," Gunner said, leaning against the stone wall. "Won't they? They'll just quit if they think we can't win. If they know how close They are to successful cloning."

"Yes," I said. "No one breathes a word of this to anyone. Am I clear?"

"You got it, bro," Pace said. He snapped the chip out of the port and brought a rock down on it. The shards flipped through the air.

"I want Raine out of that city," Gunn said.

"It's one of my top priorities," I said. "But let's wait for Indy to come in before we go storming Freedom."

My jaw hurt. Indy packed a mean punch. I totally deserved it, but *ow*. I wanted to throw a wicked jab at her like I used to when we were younger. Then we'd end up wrestling and laughing like we used to, and she'd forget why she wanted to murder me.

Like she used to.

None of that happened. Number one, we were too old for that now. Number two, I left her behind without instructions for the Resistance, and then I got myself thrown into prison in the Goodgrounds. Number three, I'd taken her brother—not her—with me, and neither of us had seen him since. Number four, when I'd returned to the Badlands seven weeks later, I had a new girlfriend. Number five, the cavern was now filled with people, and Indy and I needed privacy to say all that needed to be said.

And then there was the whole her-being-in-love-with-me thing. I certainly couldn't encourage that.

Especially because of the whole Vi-glowering-in-the-doorway-with-her-arms-crossed thing.

So I'd taken my punch like a man.

That had happened a half hour ago. While I was bleeding, I had called an emergency meeting with my most trusted. Indy and her team were now resting in the infirmary—which was really just a tiny cave with two cots shoved against the wall. Our techs worked miracles in there, using whatever supplies they could find to make sure we all didn't die.

And, damn, Indy looked terrible. Her dark skin appeared bleached and her hair did not. The truth? The pink was totally faded. And she obviously hadn't been sleeping much.

Not that I could blame her for that. There isn't time for sleeping.

"So," Vi said, snapping me out of my Indy-focused thoughts. She was scowling. I kept forgetting that she can see just about all my thoughts, including the ones about Indy.

But if Indy's gorgeous—and she is—she still had nothin' on Vi. I tried to arrange my mouth into a smile when Vi dialed her glowering down to a glare, but it hurt my throbbing jaw.

"So, Indy says Thane wasn't in the farmhouse." I punctuated the news with a deep sigh. "Which isn't good."

"Where is he?" Zenn rubbed his eyes and blinked real fast.

I'd woken everyone up in the middle of the night, but Zenn had come off his watch. He looked pretty bad too. Some things couldn't be helped. Gunn yawned, and his eyes were bleary with exhaustion.

I'd never actually gone to bed last night, so yeah. I didn't feel sorry about waking them up.

My brother folded himself into a chair next to me at the rickety table. "Is he dead?"

Vi stiffened at the mention of her possibly deceased dad, and I threw Pace a shut-the-hell-up look. "Way to be sensitive, bro," I said. "We don't think Thane is dead. Indy says there was plenty of blood in the farmhouse, footprints and such, like someone carried him out. Just no body."

"Director Hightower got him," Gunn said, real quiet-like, the same way he says everything.

"I don't think so," I said. "No doubt he ordered Thane to be collected, but the better bet is the Director in the Goodgrounds sent a crew."

"Who's there now?" Zenn asked, sliding me a paper across the table. I didn't even look at it. I couldn't stomach the sight of his neat handwriting, detailing the fifteen billion things I had to do in the next hour. Sure, he'd immediately taken his place as my second-in-command, but come on. A list every time I saw him? So unnecessary.

"Director Shumway," Pace said. "A real piece of work."

"No wonder Indy and her team were all busted up," I said, more to myself than anyone else. I'd heard of Shumway, which meant he wasn't exactly on my side. Or even close to crossing over.

"We'll need the whole group for this," Gunn said, pushing himself away from the table.

"Probably. But we can spare a few hours, I think." My jaw popped with every word. I rubbed it but still heard the click-ing when I said, "Let 'em sleep till five."

"You got me up to say let's wait until five?" Pace grum-bled as he stood to leave. I should've felt annoyed, but all I could muster was a yawn.

I should've been more concerned, probably. The fact that Thane was MIA was about as bad as bad can get. Without him, all we had was Starr, and she spent most of her time in the Education Rise trying to gather intel without proper codes and clearances.

I thought briefly that losing Thane might actually be a good thing. I wasn't even sure he was who Gunn said he was, and twelve years of hating someone doesn't just evaporate.

I'd ordered his location and pickup. That had to count for something. Too bad the bleeder wasn't even there.

I cradled my head in my hands as Zenn left, huddled close with Gunn. My to-do list stared back at me from the table. The top item? *Assign interrogators for Indy's team.*

Which seriously needed to be done, but for the first time in a long time, I didn't want to be the one to do it.

Under that, Zenn had written, *Get implants already.*

Hell to the no. I'd refused—over and over—to have my wrist ported up so I could see someone's memories, or a vision-screen enhancement layered over my perfectly func-tioning sight. And getting an implant?

Never.

I didn't want that tech up in my brain. No way did I want someone to be able to contact me at any time about anything. Or people to track my location just because I activated my cache to tell Vi she's the most beautiful creature I'd ever seen.

"I'd love to discuss the subject of implants, just so I can convince you that Zenn's right about them," Vi said, gently putting her hand on my elbow and helping me stand. "But first you need to sleep."

"I'm fine." I almost added "babe" like I used to. But Vi and I weren't quite back to that level yet, even though we'd spent nearly every waking moment together for the past three weeks. She was still stuck in her whole Zenn-loves-me-and-has-saved-me-so-many-times loop. And our argument about Indy hadn't been fully resolved yet.

"I'm fine." Besides, I have the Resistance to run.

"You're such a liar," she said. "Let's go."

"Jag, let's fly."

I jerked awake, my heart beating a rapid rhythm in my chest. Gunn stood in my doorway, his fingers twitching in anticipation. "Cache convo with Starr."

I moaned. Raked my fingers through my hair, which felt like wet straw. My eyelids scratched over my eyes. I needed more sleep—and a shower. "Time?" I asked as I pulled on my shoes.

"Five forty-one," Gunn said. "Starr said six fifteen. I let you sleep as long as I could. Zenn's filling everyone in about Thane and Indy."

"Perfect," I said, though it was anything but. I liked Zenn; I did. I just didn't like him anywhere near Vi.

"Come on," Gunn said. "She only has eleven minutes." He left, and I scrambled after him, hoping we'd make it to the sector in time.

We didn't. When we touched down near the southwest wall of Freedom, Starr only had seven minutes left. She stood beyond the towering wall, in the gap between it and the techtric barrier—the second and last defense keeping Freedom's Citizens in and everyone else out.

When anything touched the barrier, an alarm shrieked. Enforcement Officers would then converge. The person who'd breached the wall usually didn't make it past the barrier. The hundred-yard gap between the wall and the barrier made sure of that.

But Trek used his wicked tech skills to bring down sections of the wall, so Starr could get out for these little chats without detection.

Gunn and Starr each had a cache, a device implanted in their minds they could use to communicate mentally, even with the barrier between them. Everyone had a cache in Freedom—which was why I would never get one.

Starr had a limited number of minutes away from her duties inside the city, and she didn't like it when we were late. She was also one of the smartest people I knew. She could get inside your head without even being in the same room.

Starr Messenger was true Thinker material. She'd been my contact in Freedom for almost three years. I'd only met her a handful of times, but I'd seen her face next to her reports—sent like clockwork every week. She liked organization and detailed lists and punctuality. So I didn't have to use my empathic ability to figure out she was raging mad that we were late.

Not that I could hear her. Gunner didn't speak out loud either. He just stood there, inches from the techtric barrier, gazing at Starr on the other side. At one point he raised his hand, and she lifted hers.

I felt the longing inside her. Guilt radiated from Gunn.

Until terror flowed from them both.

"What?" I asked Gunner. He didn't answer, just took a step closer to the barrier. If he touched it, that alarm would go off.

"What?" I asked again, trying not to control him with my voice but frustrated I wasn't included in the conversation.

I looked at Starr. Something fierce glistened in her eyes, making them shine like steel; power radiated from her shoulders. Yet fear kept the words silent. Well, that and the fact that I didn't have implants to hear her with.

"What?" This time I gripped Gunn's arm to get his attention.

"Director Hightower has Thane," Gunn said in his unnervingly soft voice. "He's using Raine to drain him. Tomorrow morning, eleven a.m."

4.

The day Vi tapped on my window changed everything. Well, if we're gonna be all technical, and I guess we are, the window tapping happened at night.

Which was why she got busted.

She was only twelve years old. The infraction didn't go on her Official Record, but it tattooed itself on my memory.

Vi shouldn't have meant anything to me. I knew her because she lived six minutes away in the City of Water, and we were in the same year at school. But our relationship shouldn't have progressed past us being two kids who were the same age.

I'd just turned thirteen, and I'd just returned from meeting Jag Barque in the Abandoned Area. I'd snuck in through the back door, returned to my bedroom, and checked my false transmission feed when the *tap, tap, tap* landed on the glass.

My heart pounded in my scrawny chest.

Maybe They'd been monitoring me. Maybe They knew I wasn't listening to the transmissions. I'd screwed up after only a few days of helping the anti-Thinker movement. The Resistance, my dad had called it.

Insider Tip #2: Don't hesitate. It shows weakness and indecision. Those who hesitate often have something to hide.

I took a deep breath and accepted whatever was gonna happen. I strode to the window and yanked it up, expecting to see a Special Forces agent with glinting black eyes and a fully charged taser.

Instead, I found Violet Schoenfeld. I could tell she'd been crying, even if the tears were already dried up. The full moon cast glimmers of white light in her brown hair.

"Violet?" I scanned the yard behind her. Empty. A hovercopter floated along the edge of the Centrals, a couple miles away.

"Zenn, I—" She cast a quick glance over her shoulder.

"You're gonna be seen," I whispered. "Climb up." I reached out to help her but drew back before we touched. That was against the rules, and the window was wide open so anyone could see.

Violet used to answer questions in class, used to show up to school with her panels done. She used to hang with the other girls during breaks. Then her dad disappeared. She'd withdrawn, and now that we'd moved into secondary subjects, she sat alone against the fence during breaks and hadn't turned in homework for months. She didn't speak to anyone except her sister Tyson.

I didn't even know she knew my name, let alone where I lived. Maybe she was searching for any window that looked like there might be someone awake within.

She struggled over the windowsill while I stood there and watched. I could've pulled up all ninety pounds of her with one hand. She straightened, and I towered at least six inches over her.

Her face was the color of uncooked rice. Her eyes were a mixture of blue and green, like the serene color of the lake. Her brown hair flowed freely over her shoulders, but it should've been secured in its customary ponytail or bun.

She was crazy-beautiful, even with tearstained cheeks. And then it hit me: A girl was standing in my room. In the middle of the night.

I'd been away from my transmissions for hours. My older

brother had developed tech that could simulate sleep patterns, but I wondered how Violet had managed to trick hers long enough to leave her house.

"I'm sorry," she murmured. "I shouldn't be here." She paced next to my bed.

I glanced at my brother, a decent sleeper, fifteen feet from us. "It's fine." I wanted to touch her shoulder, make her stop walking. Her squeaky shoes were going to wake my brother. "What's going on?"

"Nothing," she said.

"Nothing?" I repeated.

"Ty told me . . . It's nothing."

I folded my arms. "If it's nothing, can you stop pacing? You're gonna wake Fret."

She stopped and took a deep breath. "It's my mom," she whispered. "She hates me for not being Ty." Violet's voice began to rush. "And I just couldn't take it anymore. I had to get out. Oh, it's so late." She threw a glance at my bedside clock, her eyes wild. "I'm going to be in so much trouble."

"You're safe here," I lied, wishing it were true. But my smart house would rat her out if she didn't leave soon. Extra body temperature and oxygen usage and all that.

Violet moved toward the window. "You'll get in trouble," she said, climbing out.

"Wait!"

The hovercopter had already spotlighted her. The mechanical voice shouted for her to freeze. I shrank back into the shadows, terror thumping through my veins.

She sprinted toward the bushes in my backyard, but no one escapes from a hovercopter.

Like a coward, I slammed the window and drew the blinds. I peeked through two slats, watching the Special Forces agent interrogate her. She didn't cry. Her fists clenched and unclenched, and she accepted the citation without a word.

The hovercopter zipped away, and that's when Violet crumpled to the ground. Her shoulders shook with racking sobs.

Then I did what any thirteen-year-old boy would do: I dropped the shades and crawled into bed.

Saffediene Brown sat immediately to my right, frantically writing a report for Jag. Though we were the same age, she reminded me of myself when I first began serving the Resistance. She'd joined a month after I'd arrived in Freedom.

In fact, Saffediene had been my first recruit for the Insiders.

She finished writing, folded the paper, and put her hand on mine. I shook my thoughts away from Vi and that first night in my bedroom and jerked at the contact from Saffediene. She pulled her hand back and hid it under the table. Her eyes flickered to mine, a small smile playing on her face.

"Zenn?" she said, still watching me. Just like everyone else was doing.

"Indy and her team are drinking protein like there's no tomorrow," I said, stuffing my hand in my pocket as I stood. My skin felt hot where Saffediene had touched me. "They'll be on mandatory rest this week, and then we'll get them into rotations for duties."

I nodded toward Pace, who stood and started droning on about some new tech he'd invented that would eliminate the squealing in new implants. When Thane had first brought me beyond the wall of Freedom to this cavern, I'd barely recognized Pace.

The smile that used to come quickly to his lips now took longer. His eyes were dull, and Pace's long, silver hair didn't get washed enough, but I suspected that wasn't the only reason for its lackluster appearance.

When Tyson Schoenfeld died, a big piece of Pace Barque did too. I'd been present when she'd been killed, but the memories of those weeks are shrouded. I'd been brainwashed and medicated, with only moments of lucidity.

Thane had told me the story of Ty's death. It had aged

him too, though I didn't comfort him. The first time I saw Pace here in the hideout, though, I had gripped him in a hug that said more than *We're on the same team.*

It had said, *Please forgive me. I did what I thought was right. I miss Ty too.*

He'd understood, and he'd freely given his forgiveness—something Jag sucked at doing. I watched Pace now and noticed he'd revived a bit since Jag's return. I was reminded of when I first joined the Resistance, when Pace and Jag would embrace after months apart. They'd laugh about Irvine's seriousness and throw wads of paper at Indy as she snored on the couch.

I longed for the more carefree days of the Resistance, when the thought of battling the Thinkers only happened in our imaginations. It was easier then to feel like They were robbing the general population of their free will. I'd believed in the cause of the Resistance with my whole heart. No one should have to conform to a job, a marriage, a life they hated simply because someone with persuasive powers deemed it so.

So the Resistance fought talent with talent. They had Thinkers. So did we. They had voice talent. So did we. They also had vastly more personnel, many and diverse ways to find our strongholds, and untold resources.

We had Jag Barque.

Back before I turned Informant, me, Pace, and Jag would sit around the kitchen table in Jag's house, making grand plans and playing cards. Sure, we ran minor missions, sent messages, and attended training in Seaside with Vi's older sister, Tyson.

Ty had the unique ability to make you think you were the most important person in the world. Vi had worshipped her. I'd rescued Ty from the Goodgrounds, helped her through the desert to the Badlands, and passed her off to Jag. Pace had been there, and I still remember the first time he met Ty.

I was young—a few months shy of fourteen—and rescuing Ty was my first solo mission for the Resistance. But I recognized the light on Pace's face. I'd seen my dad look at my mom with that brightness that said, *The person standing in front of me could change my life.*

As Pace spoke now, here in this dingy cavern, it was clear that his easiness had been lost with Ty. He caught me watching him, and I half smiled. He seemed to understand what I was thinking and lowered his head slightly.

After Pace finished his update, Vi stood up and began assigning every member of Indy's team to one of our existing crew. I imagined how I must look, gazing at Vi the same way Pace had looked at Ty all those years ago. I couldn't help it.

"Someone to show them around, help them on watch, you know, orient them to our life here," she said.

And what a crazy-lame life we live inside this blasted cavern. I didn't say it out loud, but Vi cut me a hard look anyway.

After Vi sat, Saffediene got to her feet. "Gunner and I have assembled new two-person traveling teams for assignments in the Midwestern Region. You'll leave tonight." She listed off partnerships, and I glanced at her when she read my name with Gunn's.

Another trip to another unknown city. Half of me rejoiced. The other half died a bit more.

Before Saffediene finished her assignments, Jag burst into the cavern with Gunn two steps behind him.

"Cancel everything," Jag commanded. "Hightower has Thane, and we need to rescue him before eleven tomorrow morning."

Jag

5.

"I need you with Vi," I said for the third time. The meeting had broken up, and I'd gone from room to room giving assignments. Zenn had followed me back here to my quarters, breathing reasons he couldn't go to Freedom.

"You've been assigned to protect Vi," I said again. "You should be happy about that."

Zenn stood in front of me, his mouth a thin line of disapproval. I didn't get his hating-me thing. It's not my fault he defected, left Vi alone so she had to break rules to meet him, or that she got thrown into my prison cell.

I could've done without Zenn defecting. Everyone could

have. But I've never been sorry for Vi's rule breaking or that I had to "endure" jail time with her.

"We have an appointment in Harvest," Zenn said—for the third time.

"Stop trying to get out of going on this mission," I said, fighting back my voice power. "You want to play the hero, just admit it. Right now I need my hero in Freedom, to rescue Thane." I stripped off my filthy shirt and replaced it with a less filthy one.

"This has nothing to do with heroics."

"And," I continued, almost yelling, "everyone knows you're in love with Vi, and I'm assigning you to protect her."

His jaw tightened; his fists flexed. A bolt of satisfaction sang at the back of my throat. "It's what we both want," I said, stepping closer. He blocked the doorway of my bedroom, and I had forty thousand things to get ready for the mission.

"I can't go back there," Zenn said, his gaze dropping to the floor. The muscles worked in his neck. "You don't know what Director Hightower's like."

"Trust me," I said, "I do." Zenn had no idea what my life was like. Where I'd been for those eight months while he and Vi fell in love all over again. No one did.

That's how I liked it. Removing myself from everyone

and everything helped me keep people out. That way I could do what needed to be done for the Resistance.

No emotional attachments. That's why I didn't try too hard to explain anything to Indy and then brought her brother, Irvine, with me on the mission into the Goodgrounds. She didn't understand that, sometimes, being the leader of the Resistance required me to make difficult decisions. It was better to be completely detached from everyone.

"Except for Vi." Zenn didn't have to say it, but he did. The pain in his voice was poorly masked. He hadn't even tried. Sure, he was in my head, which annoyed me, but he was acknowledging something he'd rather ignore.

The fight went out of me. "Except for Vi," I conceded. "I'd change things if I could, Zenn. So many things."

I felt rather than heard or saw his defeated acceptance. An understanding passed between us.

"You might still make your appointment," I said. "We'll get Thane out, and you and Gunner can fly all night."

"Fine. But you get to tell Vi she's riding in the backseat on this one," he said. "She's gonna be mad as hell."

"Fair enough." I followed him into the hall, already dreading the argument I would have with Vi. "And Zenn, you are strong enough to resist this time."

* * *

I found Vi in her room, her face already closed to any discussion. I smothered a sigh and sat next to her on the cot. We both studied the floor. "So, we're going into Freedom."

"So I heard," she said. What she meant was, *I didn't hear it from you.*

"You've been assigned to Zenn. You guys will fly mid-pack and stay out of trouble." What I meant was, *I'm assigning you to Zenn. Ride behind him and keep your mouth shut.*

The silence in the room said it all. Her anger. Her defiance. Vi didn't like being told what to do.

"Do I have your permission to speak?" she snapped.

"Oh, brother," I said. "Say whatever the hell you want. It's not going to change my decision."

"I hate how you boss me around," she said.

I stood up. "I hate how you doubt all my decisions," I fired back. "I'm the cracking leader of the cracking Resistance."

She shot to her feet too. "I'm more than just another one of your Insiders. I'm your girlfriend."

My stomach clenched. Didn't she get it? That was exactly why she had to fly mid-pack and stay out of trouble. Sometimes her stubbornness amazed me. I glared at her a moment longer before heading toward the door.

"Stay with Zenn. Mid-pack." I left her simmering—okay, boiling—in her room. Zenn had been right—Vi was mad as hell. But you know what? I'd do what it took to keep her safe. Losing her was a risk I wasn't willing to take.

Gunner spent the afternoon detailing the layout of Freedom for the group. We didn't have customizable p-screens underground. So Gunn painted a picture of Freedom with words. He spoke in that way that commanded people to listen, using a Thinker's voice but not its brainwashing ability.

People listened to Gunner because of his quiet steadiness. I'd felt his determination and strength the first time I met him, even though I'd been strapped to a bed at the time. Now I could also feel the myriad of emotions teeming beneath his calm exterior. Because the girl he loved, Raine Hightower, was still trapped inside Freedom.

More than once he'd voiced to me that Raine's father wasn't afraid to do horrific things to his own daughter. Gunn never cried, but his desperation to get her out, protect her, never faded. I'd felt an immediate connection to him, because I felt the same way about Vi.

Neither of us could protect the people we loved, and it was killing us.

I listened to him talk about how Freedom was designed on a grid, and how navigating toward the tallest building shouldn't be too troublesome. Indy and Vi seemed the most interested. The rest of us knew the general layout. Gunn waved his hand, talking about Rise One situated in the middle of the Rise-canyons.

He paused, and I wanted to get up and clap him on the shoulder. Tell him to escape and have a good cry over Raine. Tell him to be honest with himself for a change. Instead I simply watched as he composed himself and said, "The techtric barrier presents the biggest problem."

"It's not a problem," I said. "It's a monumental issue." Everyone swung their attention to me. Beyond that, guards and seeker-spiders would likely present another obstacle. And Enforcement Officers equipped with tasers and various special talents.

"So how do we get past it?" Zenn asked.

I had no genius ideas, so we labored over how to breach the barrier without the loss of life and/or an earsplitting alarm.

"What about coming in over the water?" Saffediene suggested.

Even Vi, who'd been simmering against the wall for the better part of the meeting, gave her full attention to the newbie.

"The water?" Zenn asked, shifting closer to her. He favored Saffediene because she was his first recruit. He'd always said she was smarter than us all.

"Yeah," she said, taking a few seconds to think. "The ocean. We can fly straight east from here, over the water."

The tension in the room skyrocketed. Most of it originated from Gunner, though Vi didn't seem too happy about the flying-over-water thing either.

"What's the problem?" I asked him. I used to fly over the ocean, playing hoverball with my brothers.

"I don't know how to swim," Gunner said.

"Last time I was in the water, I passed out," Vi added.

I cocked an eyebrow—a story of Vi's I hadn't heard. It sounded like an interesting one at that.

"You won't be in the water," Saffediene said, glancing at Zenn. When his mouth twitched upward, she continued. "Just flying over it."

"Still," Vi said.

"The water is strictly off-limits in Freedom," Zenn said. "No one knows how to swim. The Thinkers set it up that way so the population won't try to escape. They don't even know what boats are." He kept his eyes locked on Saffediene as he spoke.

"We don't need boats," she argued. "We have hoverboards."

"We'll have two extra passengers. Maybe more."

Their volley caused exhaustion to press behind my eyes.

"It doesn't matter," I said, effectively cutting off Saffediene's retort. "Can we get around the barrier if we go over the water?"

"I think so."

"That's not good enough."

She crossed her arms and stuck out her hip. "Then, yes."

"Do you know? Or are you guessing?" Someone had to be a jerk, and more often than not that responsibility landed on me. I caught Vi's sigh, but I didn't apologize or back down. This was my job. Keeping people safe—running the Resistance— was more important than coming off as everyone's friend.

"I'm guessing," Saffediene admitted.

Raking my fingers through my hair, I exhaled slowly. "Well, a guess is better than throwing a stick at the barrier and hoping it comes down."

"Jag—" Gunner started.

I usually listened to every word he spoke, because he didn't talk unless absolutely necessary. But I silenced him with a glare. "We're going over the water."

"Jag—" Vi said.

"No questions," I barked. "Gather as many warm clothes as you can. Charge the boards. Pace, tether two extras to yours. We fly at dusk. Vi, I'd like a word."

I left them standing in the war room. I didn't wait to see if Vi would follow me. She would.

When she joined me in the alcove off the main room, her glower had become a cut-through-tech glare.

I didn't have time to soothe her. "Can you sense the barrier?"

"What?" she snapped. "Now you need my help? I thought I was to ride behind Zenn and keep my mouth shut."

"I didn't say that."

"You didn't have to."

I felt dangerously close to crying. Vi was mad at me. Zenn was uncooperative. Thane was to be drained. "I'm doing my best here, Vi. Please." I pressed my palms to my eye sockets.

Vi touched my elbow, and that's all it took for the tears to fall. I kept my hands up to cover my face. She yanked my arms down. "Don't you dare break down now, Barque," she commanded.

I looked at her through the water in my eyes. Her beauty made me ache. "I can't do this anymore," I choked out. "It's too much."

"No, it's not. We'll get Thane out. Raine too. Everything will work out fine. Yeah, I can sense the barrier."

"Not that. That'll work, or it won't."

She frowned. "Then what?"

I seized her in a fierce hug. Instantly the turmoil inside me began to quiet. I wished she wasn't my drug, wished I could find solace in myself. But I couldn't. Since the day I met Violet Schoenfeld, she'd calmed me from the inside out.

"You," I whispered into her hair. "I just want you to be safe. If anything happened to you . . ." I closed my eyes and leaned my forehead against hers. "I just need you to sense the barrier. That's all. Zenn will be there to protect you, okay?"

"I don't need Ze—"

"Yes, you do. Thane took you once. Made you forget. I can't go through that again."

"Where were you all this time?" she asked, in a classic Vi-topic-change.

No one needed to know where I'd been, what I'd gone through. If she thought she couldn't sleep now, Vi didn't know the depth of nightmares she'd have if I told her.

I clung to her a moment longer. "Zenn's flying mid-pack, but you guys will need to fly frontal with me until we make it around the barrier."

I ignored the flare of disappointment that rippled through me when I released her. The twinge of guilt when she stepped back, those changeable eyes of hers set on super-angry.

I'd taken three steps toward the war room when she said, "Will you ever tell me?"

I half turned back. "I can't."

"Can't, or won't?"

"They're the same," I said.

"We shouldn't keep secrets from each other," she said. "*You* told me that."

I bowed my head to acknowledge that she was right. Had I told her that? Yes. Should we keep secrets from one another? No.

"I love you," I said, and walked away.

Zenn

6.

Next to me, Vi flew silently, her left hand held out to her side as if she was letting her fingers trail along a wall. In essence, she was. Vi can feel tech, and the barrier created a wall she could "see" with her hands. She'd been careful not to make contact as she guided us.

In front of her, Jag rode his hoverboard as expertly as ever. Whatever had happened to him during his eight-month disappearance hadn't affected his flying ability.

Part of me admired that; another part wished he'd come back more broken. He remained as mysterious as ever, keeping people out and fortifying his barricades.

We'd been soaring over open water for fifteen minutes. Gunn rode in tight next to Saffediene, his face pinched with worry. I couldn't decide if it was because of the thirty-foot drop, the mission, or the fact that Raine was in danger.

But hey, she knew the risks of running missions with the Resistance. He did too.

I switched my thoughts to the insane half plan we'd concocted. Our mission: Fly to Rise One, bust in, take Thane and Raine, and hightail it back to the ocean.

Not stellar. Especially considering the length of the flight, and the fact that just because the sky had settled into ashy evening didn't mean there wouldn't be EOs out in abundance.

"Here," Vi said, her voice whipping away with the wind. "Jag! The tech is gone."

I slowed my board to a stop, as did everyone else. All eyes rested on Vi.

Jag inhaled, exhaled, before launching the rock he'd brought with him. Gunner cringed, expecting it to hit the techtric barrier and spark into jets of light.

Instead, the rock arced through the air, landing in the water a good thirty feet away.

Jag urged his board forward, almost at a crawl. He didn't fry to a crisp, much to my partial disappointment. The other half of me felt nothing but relief, especially when Vi glared at me with knowledge in her eyes.

"What?" I asked, though I knew exactly what.

We began the twenty-minute flight back to land, Vi still fondling the techtricity from the barrier. I watched the half smile form on her face, and it scared me. I didn't know what Jag had said to her, but that smile—that was Vi's way of sticking it to him.

I'd seen her direct it at her mother enough to know.

She caught me looking at her. "What?" she asked.

I shook my head even as I heard her think, *You can't put me in the middle of the pack, Mr. Leader of the Cracking Resistance.*

I wanted to fly closer and hug her. Tell her I'd never force her to do anything she didn't want to. Prove to her that everything I'd done was for her and only her. Instead I turned my face toward Freedom and quelled the roiling in my gut.

Freedom suffocated me, stealing the oxygen in the air and turning it into cement. The city lay still, as if holding its breath—as if it knew we were coming.

"Enforcement Officers," Saffediene said, pointing toward the Rises. Sure enough, the ultrawhite light of tech haloed the Officers as they swarmed through the streets.

More than fifty, maybe more than one hundred, all heading straight for us as we lapped over the last of the waves and flew above the sandy beach below.

"This is bad," I said to no one in particular.

"Evasive maneuvers," Jag called. "Find a spot to hide. Reconvene on the roof of Rise Twelve, midnight."

Then he disappeared down the coast and into the inky night, leaving the rest of us to save ourselves.

I watched him go, crazy-mad, until I remembered that he'd charged me with protecting Vi. Neither one of us could be taken again. I couldn't withstand the brainwashing—if I survived at all.

Now that Vi didn't have Thane's protective buffer, she absolutely couldn't be caught. With her powers, Director Hightower would strip her of her identity, mold her into a clone of himself.

"Vi! This way!" I flew along the barrier on the southern edge of the city. To my right the orchards were just starting to bud, and the branches would provide decent cover for a few hours.

The Insiders had a hideout in the Western Blocks, and that would be our destination. I crouched low, satisfied when Vi copied me. We flew at treetop level, dodging the occasional rogue limb that grew higher than the others.

"We need to get to the Blocks," I said.

If she didn't know what that meant, she didn't show it. One of the many things I loved about Vi. She was as unafraid as they come. Fiercely determined. And crazy-quick at improvising.

The faintest of sounds met my ears. I whipped around to find Saffediene and Gunner zooming behind us. Part of me rejoiced to see them and another part groaned at the large target the four of us created.

Shouts filled the air. The crackle of tasers followed, their super-hot light made it look like lightning had struck the orchard. I saw hoverboards with dark shapes flying in all directions.

"We've gotta get out of here!" I yelled to Gunn. "Block Twenty-Four!"

He waved his arm to show he heard me.

"Vi, let's get down under cover," I said. She nosed her board into the trees.

We flew.

Reaching the outer Blocks took forever. I thought for sure midnight had come and gone. At least we'd left behind the debilitating spark of the tasers.

We'd taken to the ground an hour earlier in an effort to

save the energy in our boards. I rounded the corner and entered an alley between two buildings, sure I'd see the familiar sight of Block Twenty—which had a tunnel to Twenty-Four.

I didn't. I swore under my breath, and Vi caught my eye. She couldn't help me navigate the city; she'd spent the majority of her time in Freedom under the influence of Thane's voice. Or mine. Or both.

Sometimes the guilt crippled me. Sadness pooled in my chest, right where my heart struggled to beat against it.

We both looked helplessly to Gunner, because he grew up in the Blocks and should be able to determine where we were. Saffediene kept her back to us, scoping out the possible danger behind us.

"Block Thirty," Gunn said, peering down the alley. "We're too far north." He twisted back the way we came.

"No," Saffediene said. "This is Twenty."

Gunner's face remained unreadable, except for the tiny muscle below his right eye, which twitched once. "I think it's Thirty. See the water tower? Those were built in the Upper Blocks."

Saffediene followed his pointed finger before pulling her sleeve down to cover her palm. She rubbed at something on the nearly pristine wall. The silver flaked off, revealing a patch of black underneath.

"Twenty," she proclaimed, as if the faux surface explained it all.

"I don't get it," Vi said, voicing my thoughts exactly.

"Director Hightower was having the Blocks re-teched. They made it to the mid-twenties before Gunn and Jag escaped, and he pulled all his people into security." She rubbed at the building again. "That black stuff is CoverAll. The Insiders marked all the Blocks concealing tunnels in increments of ten. It was my first mission."

"It could still be Block Thirty, then," Gunn argued.

"It could be, but it's not," Saffediene answered. She beamed at me, waiting for me to agree with her.

"How do you know?" I asked, hoping she was right. Then I wouldn't have gotten us lost.

"Like I said, the re-teching didn't get as high as Thirty. The buildings are black in the Upper Blocks, not silver. You'll see when we come out at Twenty-Four." She strode forward, her slight shoulders strong and sure, her blond braid bouncing along her back. "Can you disable this, Gunn? That silver stuff has recording capabilities."

"Know-it-all," Gunn muttered as he took up the rear position.

I didn't care if Saffediene annoyed him. I just wanted to get out of range of the building's recording capabilities. Our salvation came at the end of the alley, when Saffediene indicated the tunnel door.

Only darkness yawned behind it. I took a deep breath, hoping there'd be more oxygen inside this pit than in our Resistance hideout.

Hesitating, I reached for Vi's hand and gripped it tightly in mine. Her returning squeeze led me to believe that she was just as unfond of dark, enclosed spaces as I was. Finally, common ground.

I breathed again, and then again, wishing for another way to reach Block Twenty-Four. If only we had a transporter ring or—

"Go!" Gunn hissed. "I think I see—" The rest of his words ground to a halt as a strobing light filled the alley, and the reflective surfaces of the newly teched buildings flashed with the word "FREEZE."

I scrambled into the dark doorway as the alarm sounded. Vi, Saffediene, and Gunn squeezed in after me, and then we were all running blind.

Inside the dark, it's harder to hide. No one can see me, which allows me to see myself clearly.

I see how I tricked Vi in the Goodgrounds. How I brainwashed her to carry that tracker. A ring. The symbol of love.

I do love her. I love her so much it hurts. In the dark, that lays exposed too.

I see how I left Jag. How I told him I had other things going on in my life so I couldn't help his Resistance, when really I wanted to save my own skin. And get the girl.

I can't lie in the dark. I quit the Resistance because I wanted Vi to myself. I knew that if I continued working for the Resistance, her father would get his hooks into her. I couldn't risk her then.

I can't now.

The darkness reveals it all.

The slow hammering of my heart. The quick gasps of my breath. The fear in my footsteps.

I can't outrun myself in the dark. I've never been able to.

In the dark, I see how I helped Thane, even when I wasn't 100 percent sure he was good. I'm still not sure if he's on my side or with the Association. I hear my voice telling Vi dangerous lies. I see her glazed expression.

I see the adoration in her eyes, the adoration I don't deserve.

That causes a crazy-lotta pain to gather in my limbs.

And then we reach the end of the tunnel, and I'm gasping, and Gunner's talking, and Saffediene leads, and I take one look at Vi and see—

she knows.

She can see me. The real me. She knows what I've done for

her, and she loves me for it. I want to hide from the emotion in her eyes. I'm afraid of its truth; I'm terrified that it still won't be enough.

"Come on," she says, gingerly lacing her fingers through mine. "Zenn, come on."

I'd follow her to hell and back, and so I go.

Jag

7

Leaving Vi with Zenn took every ounce of my self-control. Still, I'd charged him with her care, and even if he'd abandoned me once before, I knew he'd never do that to her. His sorry-I-can't-help-you thing only seemed to apply to me.

And if the Enforcement Officers wanted me, the smartest thing to do was to separate myself from the others. That way no one would get hurt because of me.

I'd been separating myself for years.

Living in isolation had saved me countless times. Drawing on that independence forced me to learn how to survive.

Don't think about how Irv went missing. Where could he be?

Don't think about what the Greenies will do now that you won't wear the implant. What would they try next?

Don't think about seeing Mom and Dad die. Why did I beg to go to the market with them?

Don't think about Blaze alone in the alley in Freedom. How could I have sent him on that mission?

Don't think about enduring the endless flames of that dark capsule.

I shuddered, hot dread settling in my stomach. I would never feel a release from that heat. Never find a way to tell Vi about it.

Stop, I told myself in my most commanding voice. I definitely couldn't think about where I'd been while Vi was in Freedom. It was why I hadn't slept well in weeks.

Every time I shut my eyes, I was transported inside that capsule again. So I didn't sleep very much.

I aimed my board toward the ground at a way-too-steep angle. The Enforcement Officers coming my way didn't slow or change direction. And why would they? They didn't have independent thought. They'd been told to take me out, and they wouldn't stop until they did.

I didn't want to draw further attention to myself, so I buried my voice and pulled my hood over my head. I could take these guys with just a hoverboard.

I wove through them, bumping off a body here and a helmet there. They couldn't change direction as fast as I could, and I'd swooped past them before they realized I was even there.

Rise One loomed in front of me, but I cut a wide arc to the north, setting my sights on Rise Twelve. I wondered who was in charge now that Thane was gone. I wondered how much damage he'd done to the system I'd established years ago.

Could I have asked Zenn? Sure, but I didn't trust him the way I used to.

Could I have asked Indy? Maybe if she wasn't so busy punching my lights out.

I'd never trusted Thane as Director of Rise Twelve. Every-thing he'd done since I met him screamed *Informant!*

Then when I became the leader of the Resistance—and my brother Blaze died in the alley so close to Rise Twelve—I wasn't sure I could ever believe Thane again.

Yet here I was, risking everything to save him.

I told myself it was because he held Resistance secrets the Association couldn't have. With a determination I hadn't felt in a long time, I descended to the roof of Rise Twelve.

I had exactly two seconds to breathe and only one foot on the ground when a group of people leapt up from behind a flower bed.

"Who are you?"

"What do you want?"

"Kick the board over here."

I flipped my hood down. "Relax. I'm Jag Barque," I said in my most authoritative voice.

They all stopped talking. One guy actually relaxed against a bench.

A girl a few years older than me recovered first. "That's some voice you've got there." She spoke in a cool tone that gave nothing away.

I shrugged. "Like I said, I'm Jag Barque."

"*The* Jag Barque?" she asked. "Prove it."

She wanted me to prove it? "Jump up on the wall there," I said, and every person within hearing distance hopped onto the shallow wall that edged the roof. "Walk toward me."

Their mechanical movements made me wince. "Okay, okay. Get down."

They thumped to the safety of the roof. Slowly they came to their senses, watching me with curiosity burning in their eyes.

"I'm Jag Barque," I repeated. "Leader of the Resistance. Do you need additional proof?"

"No," the girl said, exchanging a nervous glance with the man next to her. She stepped forward. "I'm River."

"What's the status here?" I asked. "Who's in charge of Twelve?"

"My father, Mason Isaacs, with Starr Messenger as his second."

I frowned. "Thane said Starr would be in charge if something happened to him."

"She's still a student," River said. "Director Hightower appointed my father when Assistant Director Myers went missing. Starr is still second."

I knew the Isaacs family. Blaze had smuggled them out of Northepointe several months before he'd died. "Is your dad around?"

"He's at Rise One with the other building Directors. Word is there's a threat to Associational security." River gave me the up-down. A slow smile stretched across her face. "I guess they were right."

"I have friends out there. What's the word on your safe houses?"

Before she could answer, an explosion tilted the sky. I fell to my knees, my arms automatically covering my head.

As I regained my feet, River moved to the edge of the roof and faced north. "That was our last hideout," she said. "I hope your friends weren't heading to Block Twenty-Four."

Somehow I thought that's exactly where they'd be going.

"Send a rescue team," I said, joining her at the wall. I gripped the edge until my finger bones hurt.

I couldn't lose Vi. Not in an explosion I hadn't seen coming. Not in the dead of night while I lingered on a rooftop and couldn't help.

"Who should we be looking for out there?" River asked. I got the impression it wasn't the first time. I couldn't tear my eyes from the plume of smoke spreading into the sky.

"Jag, who—"

"Violet Schoenfeld," I said. "Or Zenn Bower. Or Gunner Jameson."

"If they were in that building—"

"Go," I said. "Just go."

Zenn

8. Block Twenty-Four had been compromised. The four of us stood on the fringes, staring at the smoke still wafting from the hideout.

One look at Gunner, and I knew not everyone had made it out. "What can you feel?" I asked, hoping it wasn't as bad as the smell of ash and plastic and wet, hot metal. I wondered if Trek had been inside. Or Starr. I swallowed hard.

He closed his eyes and shook his head. "Too much."

"We'll wait here," Saffediene declared. "We're not that far from Rise Twelve, and the danger seems to have dissipated for now."

My arms felt dissipated from my body. My legs too. My head. All of it—the EOs swarming in the streets, the spyware in the silver paint, the alarm, the darkness, the destruction of the Insider hideout—was just too much.

"We can't wait here," Vi said, glancing around. "Something doesn't feel right."

I snapped back to attention. "What doesn't feel right?"

She and Gunn turned. Vi cried out in surprise; Gunn shouted. I spun around and immediately raised both hands in a placating gesture.

A handful of people stood in front of us, their clothes nonstandard, their eyes watchful. One held a taser, obviously an older model he'd scrounged from somewhere—or taken off a dead body. The other four wielded "weapons" of rubbish bin lids or pieces of the blown-up building, as if we were the ones responsible for the detonation of their hideout.

"Wait, wait, wait," I said, my voice power employing without a second thought.

"Calm down," Gunn said, his voice on high too. "We're friends here."

The people exchanged glances. "Who are you?" a man asked.

"I'm Zenn Bower," I said. "And this is Saffediene, and . . ." Could I give Vi's name?

"Violet," Vi said, making the choice for me. "I'm Violet Schoenfeld."

Weapons were lowered and glances exchanged. "It's them." The one with the taser stowed it in his jacket pocket.

"Them?" I asked.

"How do you know who we are?" Saffediene asked, showing her strength by speaking without so much as a waver in her voice.

"Jag sent us," the man said. "I'm Newton." He named the others, but I got hung up on River Isaacs.

"River," I said. "I know you. How do I know you?" I studied her tangle of brown hair. Her nose sat too small in the middle of her face. Her eyes, round and alive, reminded me of someone. She had a few years on me, but I had to look down on her. She carried strength in her body, and I knew she was no lightweight.

She gripped my hand in a crazy-firm handshake. "Zenn Bower. You saved my family a couple years back."

All eyes focused on me, but none felt heavier than Vi's.

"I—I—" I didn't know what to say. I remembered now. Mason Isaacs. His wife had been taken and coerced. He needed passage to Freedom, and Blaze and I had provided the service. River looked like she'd aged ten years instead of three.

"How's your dad?" I finally asked.

"Director of Rise Twelve," River answered. She cast her

eyes around the wreckage behind us. "Come on, we're not safe here."

She and her band of rebels faded into the shadowy alley. Saffediene moved with them, easily hiding herself among the darkness. The girl had mad sneaking skills.

Gunn and Vi stood deathly still, gaping at me.

"What?" I asked, stuffing my hands in my pockets in an attempt at nonchalance.

"Interesting," Vi said. She made to follow the others without removing her laser gaze from my face. "Very interesting."

"What does that mean?" I asked Gunn, who'd hopefully picked up on Vi's feelings.

"I think," he said, "it means she's sad she doesn't know everything about you."

"What the—"

"I lived with you, and you're still a complete mystery to me. Don't worry, Zenn, it's part of your charm." Gunn flashed one of his rare smiles before leaving me alone with my despicable self.

Upon arriving at Rise Twelve, Jag immediately put everyone to work. Leave it to him to show up unannounced and take over. He was a natural-born leader. Some say it's his charisma. And by "some," I mean "girls."

I say it's because of his crazy-powerful voice talent.

No matter what it is, everyone obeyed him. Not that he really commanded. But he spoke with authority, and as much as I hated to admit it, his ideas usually had merit.

"Got that, Zenn?"

"Hmm? Oh, yeah." I tried to focus on the convo, but we'd been over it before: use my voice if I had to, stay close to Vi, blah blah blah.

Jag didn't buy it for a second. "You weren't even listening."

I looked at the midnight horizon over his shoulder. "Was too."

"Gunn." Jag glanced at him.

"He wasn't listening." The traitor ratted me out.

"How do you know?" I asked. I'd been burying my emotions for years. I didn't want them exposed for anyone to feel.

"You don't argue when you're right," he said.

"Whatever," I mumbled. At least he couldn't smell my guilt.

A few minutes later Jag sent Pace and Saffediene back across the ocean sporting backpacks filled with supplies, which only left me, Gunn, and Vi to bust Thane out of Rise One.

"We'll attract less attention with a smaller group," Jag said. "River doesn't have more fake IDs anyway."

"Who's going to tether the boards?" I asked.

"Yeah, that," Jag said, and I knew I wouldn't like whatever

came next. "Pace took your board. He left his for you—with the tethered boards."

I glared at the ocean, as if it was to blame for this.

"Your board was the only one not voice activated," Jag continued. "I had no other choice."

Right. Or it was just another clever way for Jag to stick it to me.

Ten a.m. found me changing into standard-issue clothes and clipping a fake ID to my collar. I descended to the lobby, where the rest of the rescue team waited.

"Nice," Jag said, examining us in Freedom's finest. "We look official enough."

We took to the streets with River's team of three at ten thirty a.m. The few people out walked in straight lines, black suits glinting in the weak March sunlight. I was used to the silence that permeated the streets of Freedom. If people spoke, they used their cache.

Insider Tip #3: Follow the rules of the city you're in. If you don't know the rules, keep your mouth shut.

I glared at Jag, hoping he wouldn't speak out loud. He must've gotten the message, because he kept quiet the whole way to Rise One. We walked right up to it and past a huddle of Enforcement Officers. River held the door open, and we filed toward the ascenders in the back of the lobby.

I couldn't believe how easy everything was going. Adrenaline surged through me, making my nerves jump.

I swallowed hard when we arrived on the seventh floor. The air felt charged, yet eerily abandoned, as if the whole operation had been moved somewhere else since we'd been gone. Lab seven, though the largest, certainly wasn't the only place in Freedom where heinous acts went down. Maybe we were in the wrong room.

But the two doctors standing guard at the end of the hall suggested differently. They'd already drawn their weapons and aimed them in our direction.

Gunn and Jag sprinted toward them while Vi squeezed her eyes shut. Even though my mind control wasn't very developed, I knew she was keeping the guards frozen and silent.

Then Gunn and Jag said in tandem, "Release the weapons. Open this door."

The guards put down their tasers, punched in the codes to open the door. Vi and I joined Gunn and Jag, and we took a collective breath as the glass slid sideways.

Inside the lab Raine already had her hand cemented to Thane's. The walls blared with color that almost formed images.

"Damn," I said.

Jag

9 *This is a trap* circled through my mind. Everything felt too easy, despite the fact that Raine's hand was already glued to Thane's. A sense of unease skittered over my skin.

"Zenn, Gunn," I said so softly I wasn't sure they heard me, but they both sprang into action.

"Release her," Zenn commanded the lone technician in the room. He didn't move. Zenn's fingers curled into fists. "Release her. Now."

The technician held his ground, his dark eyes glinting with defiance. He thrust out his jaw. "I won't. You can't brainwash me."

Zenn cocked his fist back and punched the technician in the face. He crumpled to the floor, leaving Zenn's path to the counter of supplies unobstructed. I heard Gunn talking somewhere nearby. I heard metallic clangs and a shout. I heard a girl scream.

But I couldn't tear my eyes from the two men seated at the silver counter: Regional Director Van Hightower and the General Director of the Association himself, Ian Darke.

Vi had to leave, now. I glanced at her, silently pleading with her to turn and return to River, to Rise Twelve, to safety. She spared me a half-second glance before returning her attention to her father.

"Ah, Jag Barque," Ian Darke said, drawing my attention from Vi. Everything blurred along the edges, the same way it had when I found myself in that impossible situation in the Goodgrounds almost a year ago. Then, there had been so many voices. So many tasers. So many green robes. I'd managed some major speaking damage—until They silenced me.

Now, only Van and Ian stood before me, but I felt just as unsettled, especially with Vi still here.

Darke smiled and threw his arms wide, as if welcoming me home after a long absence. "So glad you could join us."

I didn't know how much time we had, but I knew it wasn't long. Maybe not even minutes. Could I speak, though?

Nope. I just stood there, staring at him. Thinking, *So this is who I've been fighting for years.*

I mean, I've always known it was Ian Darke. His profile in the Resistance is legendary. He's powerful—and power hungry. His file is rivaled only by Van Hightower's. If possible, he's even hungrier for control, and rumor is he'd do anything to unseat the General.

"Hello, Ian," I finally said. Around us, the images on the walls began to wash into grays.

"Jag," Ian said, his voice scraping against my eardrums. "No cache, I see." He *tsk*ed, as if I were a naughty boy who'd taken his feed out early.

"We just want Thane and Raine," I said. "No one gets hurt."

Van's laugh was maniacal. It echoed off the silver in the cavernous room and actually made Vi whimper. Zenn squeezed her arm, then quickly set to work helping a very weak Raine onto one of the spare hoverboards.

Please go, I begged Vi again, but she didn't look at me.

"Take them," Ian said, waving his hand dismissively. "We got what we wanted."

What? Or who? I thought, my hands tightening into fists. A distant, barely audible pinging echoed in my head. Thane's drain couldn't have been completed; we hadn't been late.

"Everything you wanted?" I asked, molding my voice into

coolness. If I could keep Van and Ian talking long enough, maybe the no-one-getting-hurt thing would actually happen.

"Except you," Ian said.

You, you, you, echoed in my mind. I forced him out, the anger burning through my body with enormous heat. I took a breath to quench the fire inside.

"How'd you get in my building?" Van asked.

"Your city is not as secure as you think it is." I'd deliberately left River and her team down in the lobby. No need to compromise their identities if I didn't have to.

Van's eyes narrowed. His chest rose in self-importance. "I've destroyed all the Insider hideouts."

I crossed my arms and shrugged with one shoulder. "That you know of."

Rage transfigured his features, and I took a step backward at the change in him.

"You will not leave here alive," he growled.

"Oh, I think I will," I said, but my heart jumped as if it might be on its last beats. Just like in the capsule.

I schooled my thoughts, shoving the disturbing reminder of imprisonment to the back of my mind.

Ian snapped his fingers, and a door in the back of the lab clicked. "I've heard you have no stomach for confined spaces."

My breath wisped against my dry throat. I raised my chin in

a gesture to Gunn to get the hell out of there. He'd secured an unconscious Thane to a hoverboard. Zenn mounted his board, and the tethered trio started to rise toward the air duct at the back of the lab, as per our plan. We'd assumed Officers would be arriving on scene via the hallway before we could exit that way.

Gunn held Raine's hand, his eyes never leaving her face. Vi followed Zenn, a heavy dose of worry coming from her. At least she'd gone with him. I didn't want to think about what would happen to her if she got caught.

As I remained alone, I logged the direction Zenn steered his board. The ceiling loomed three stories above me. Every wall except the one behind me glared back with metal surfaces. The single door in the back of the lab now bulged with white-coated technicians waiting for the code to be entered so they could swarm inside.

From her position near the ceiling, Vi threw me one last look over her shoulder before the glass wall behind me exploded.

I landed on top of Van, his hot breath searing my face. I scrambled away from him as a team of silver-suited Enforcement Officers entered the room from the hallway. One of them handed Ian, then Van, a pair of sound-canceling headphones while I wiped blood from my forehead and felt an ocean of pain coming from my back.

Trapped, trapped, trapped, I thought. *No way out. Can't get out.*

I stumbled toward the back of the lab, pulling my folded hoverboard from my pocket.

Trapped, trapped, trappedtrappedtrapped.

"Expand," I croaked. The board did nothing, as it didn't recognize my voice when it was filled with particles of glass, dust—and fear.

I jabbed at the buttons and leapt on the board as the first electro-spheres dropped at my feet.

"Up!" My board shot toward the ceiling, which I rammed with my skull. My back arced when the techtricity hit me, and my board faltered.

Go, I said in my head. *Go.*

Maybe I said it out loud. Maybe I didn't. But my board went. I'd fallen to my stomach, and that suited me just fine as my board careened only six inches from the ceiling. There was so much pain in my back, it felt like it had caught fire.

Out, I pleaded, the edges of my vision turning dull. My head felt heavy and soft. Voices shouted below me. Electronics sparked, sending bright bits of techtricity into my path.

Blood dripped from my chin, pooling on my board. I felt so, so tired.

Trapped, I thought as a very solid wall loomed closer. My mind looped on that thought. *Trapped, trapped, trapped.*

Through it all, I heard Ian's voice. "You'll never get out of here alive."

Was he right? Maybe. But he didn't have to be so arrogant about it.

Out, I thought. "Please," I said aloud.

I managed to maneuver the board along the perimeter of the room. Below me, smoke curled, men shouted, and electrospheres continued to discharge. No escape presented itself in the next corner, so I made another right turn. Soon I'd be back where I started, and I knew what waited for me there.

Up ahead I spotted the air duct. Zenn had already removed the vent. Two feet from the opening, my board bucked. A new pain radiated from my thigh. I lifted my body enough to peer over the edge. A grappling spider spread its legs, hooking itself to my craft.

Ian would then reel me in like a bloated fish. Cage me in that capsule again. Death would be better. My breath clogged my lungs. I couldn't think clearly; I'd lost so much blood.

"Deactivate," I said, brushing at the spider with my hand. "Dislodge."

The spider obeyed my voice, retracting its legs before the green lights of its eyes winked into darkness.

A small—possibly pointless—victory. My board now vibrated because of the damage, my thigh was bleeding, and I'd passed the air duct.

I looped back around and positioned myself below the opening. An electro-sphere landed on the board next to my head. I snatched it up, intending to launch it right back to the floor.

Instead I held it. Felt the humming tech beneath the ball's aluminum surface. If I timed it just right . . .

I checked my position again. Straight up to freedom.

I dropped the e-sphere. Said, "Up."

My board obeyed, and the sphere detonated about five feet below me, sending a shock wave of techtricity in all directions.

Including up.

I rode the wave through the duct system as far as I could. After that I twisted and turned and doubled back inside the ventilation system until it spat me out into the too-bright sunshine.

Oxygen greeted me, and I couldn't suck it in fast enough. I expected EOs to be hovering, but a commotion on the ground had drawn them all away.

I recognized River's tangled hair in the fray before I nosed my board toward the ocean. Clever girl.

I did not have the strength to sit up. Or speak. For now, breathing was enough.

The soothing sound of the ocean called at me to sleep. *What can it hurt?* I thought. I closed my eyes against the malicious sunrays bouncing off water.

I thought, *I'll just rest for a minute.*

I thought, *It's a twenty-minute flight anyway.*

I thought . . .

10.

After our return to the hideout, Vi had attended to Raine, who'd lost consciousness on the flight.

Then Vi turned her attention to her father. Neither of them looked good, but at least Vi was alert, which was more than I could say about Thane.

Now she chewed her nails as she paced the length of the war room. Back and forth, back and forth. I couldn't watch Vi anymore, worried about her beloved boyfriend. I returned to the hospital nook, where Pace was working over Raine. "How is she?"

Gunn wouldn't leave Raine's side, and he didn't glance

up when he answered. "She thinks she's Arena Locke." His sigh came out in bursts. "She seems to remember me, though. She called me by my name. When I said her name was Raine Hightower, she . . ."

"She's been Modified," Pace said. "It'll take time." He put his hand on Gunn's arm and gently pushed him back a step so he could administer meds to Raine. She lay on the bed, her eyes closed. Her skin looked like white plastic, and her hair like translucent strands of wire.

Raine and I may not have seen eye-to-eye on some things, but she was a dedicated Insider. A friend to Vi. A friend to me. "What can I do?"

Pace stepped back and Gunn filled the empty space next to Raine. He stroked her hair and leaned close. "Your name is Raine Rose Hightower," he whispered. "I'm Gunner Jameson, and I love you."

Pace swallowed hard and wouldn't look at me. "Gunner is going to stay here and tell her what her life used to be like. Sometimes the unconscious mind can recover more than when it's awake." He returned to his medical tools, leaving me with Gunner and Raine. I'd spent the better part of the last two months with them. My chest felt so tight. What would I do if that were Vi?

I knew what I'd do. I'd do exactly what Gunner was doing.

I'd hold her hand and tell her I loved her and beg her to come back to me.

"Gunn," I said. He glanced up. "Come get me if you need me."

He nodded and returned his attention to Raine. I strode back to the war room, catching Vi's hand as she paced past me and looking her in the face. She opened her eyes in surprise as I leaned forward. I didn't want to kiss her—fine, I did—just get close enough to achieve some measure of privacy.

"I love you," I whispered, in case she had forgotten, or didn't know, or just needed to be reminded. She didn't say it back, but her icy demeanor melted a little. She searched my face for an answer I couldn't give, and then collapsed into my arms. I comforted her without words while the minutes ticked by. I wondered how long we'd have to wait for Jag to come back. If he came back at all.

Vi pushed away from me, anger in her features because of my thoughts. "He's going to come back." Vi extracted herself from my embrace and resumed her pacing.

"Maybe someone should fly out and see if they can find him," Saffediene suggested from her position at the table.

"I'll go." I practically leapt toward my hoverboard. I couldn't stomach staying in the cavern for another second, with Vi's anger and the equally awful and exciting promise of becoming Jag-less.

"I'll come with you," Saffediene said. I didn't care. I just had to get out—now.

After flying for twenty minutes over open water, my nerves had settled. But now my gut was rolling with uncertainty. Jag had been missing for an hour and a half. He could be anywhere. He could be dead.

Saffediene voiced my thoughts. "We should've seen him by now. The barrier should've ended back there."

I slowed to a hover, turned, and searched the distant city skyline. Dark clouds engulfed the sky, blotting out the sunlight we could've used to recharge our boards.

"Where are you?" I whispered. True, the General Director was in Freedom, and no one had been expecting him to be so far from his stronghold. But Jag was notorious for being able to get out of any and all situations.

But he got caught in the Goodgrounds, a doubtful voice said in my head. *And who knows where he's been for the past eight months.*

He certainly hadn't been on vacation. When Gunn and I busted him out of his holding cell last month, Jag was covered in blood and could barely stand. He'd also refused to say anything about his whereabouts or what had happened. Anyone else would have to report, tell every little detail. But not Jag.

He lived with his demons, just as I lived with mine.

But where was he now?

"Wouldn't Starr alert Gunn if Hightower or Darke had him?" Saffediene asked.

"Yeah," I said. "If she could."

The city stood serenely against the storm clouds rolling in, all smoke from the explosion erased. Seconds became minutes became who knows how long. I half expected to see Jag come careening from one of the tall buildings, but he never showed.

"There," Saffediene said, pointing out toward open water. "Come on!"

She launched her board farther out to sea. I followed at a slower pace, scanning the endless water and finding nothing. We flew toward something only she could see. "Can you see him now?"

I couldn't. But I trusted Saffediene.

Finally, after another few minutes, I saw a flash of light on the horizon. "Is that . . . him?"

"That's him," Saffediene said.

The glimmer got bigger and bigger, until I could make out

a hoverboard holding a white blob, which became a board with a bleeding, unconscious Jag riding it facedown.

The blood was dry, the hoverboard stationary.

Jag looked dead, what with the whole back of his white jacket shredded and plastered with dried blood.

A hot wind blew over the ocean, unsettling me further. Wind should be cool, refreshing. This wind stank of death and the promise of horrible things to come.

"Jag," I whispered, silently pleading for him to take a breath, wake up, anything.

Saffediene hovered next to him, her fingers pressed against his neck. Tears streamed down her face, her hands fluttered from his shoulder to his back, and she hiccupped when she turned to me. "Zenn, help him."

I snapped to attention, tearing my eyes from Jag's limp body. I descended next to her and slapped her frantic hands away. "Let me," I said. "Let me."

She sobbed, but withdrew her hands enough for me to see the gentle rise of Jag's back. Relief flooded me. "He's alive. But he needs help."

I didn't know how much charge I had left in my board, but it couldn't be much. Jag's board was dead in the water, literally hovering inches above the waves, and Saffediene's board probably had less charge than mine. Even the weather was against us, as the clouds continued to block the sunlight we needed to recharge. I cupped my hands around the charge light, and felt my stomach lurch.

The red light blinked, which meant I had less than 10 percent of reserve power.

"Let's go," I said, quickly pulling Jag's board onto the front of mine. I shifted to a sitting position so I could assess his wounds while we flew.

"My board is almost dead," Saffediene said. At least she'd composed herself. I didn't know what to do with crying girls. Non-crying girls either, for that matter.

"Mine too." I opened the emergency first aid kit from my board's storage compartment and set to work cleaning the dried blood off Jag's face. "I'm gonna use the wind. Tether your board to mine."

She followed my directions as I found the head wound a few inches behind Jag's hairline. It looked like a clean cut. Pace could stitch him up when we got back to the cavern. There was a flesh wound on Jag's leg to tend to. The series of slices on his back spoke volumes about why he'd passed out.

Jag also bore burnt tracks along his arms. Black streaks spiked over the back of his hands, like claws reaching for his fingers. He'd been tech-shocked.

I twisted to look over my shoulder, whispering under

my breath for the air current to come rescue us. It happily agreed, tousling my hair before wrapping itself around me, Saffediene, and Jag.

"Land," I whispered to the wind, meeting Saffediene's eyes as we began to soar across the water.

"So you can control the elements, huh?" she said, not really asking and not really accusing either, which I appreciated. We stared at one another for a few long breaths. Long enough for me to notice the smattering of freckles across the bridge of her nose. Long enough for me to forget I was a twenty-minute hoverboard ride from safety. Long enough for me to wonder why I'd never seen her properly before.

Then the moment broke. "Yeah." I cleared my throat and directed the northerly to take us away from prying Freedom eyes.

Vi launched herself at me and cried into my neck before bustling off to sit with Jag. She and Pace disappeared into the hospital nook, leaving me and Saffediene alone in the war room.

The cavern permeated sadness. It seeped from the very rocks themselves, clogging everything and everyone with melancholy. I inhaled slowly, but the thought of staying in the confines of this sadness choked me.

I turned and strode toward the exit, desperate to escape. Escape the cavern. Escape the sadness.

Escape my life.

Saffediene found me a half hour later, my back against a skinny tree trunk, facing away from Freedom. She sat down without speaking. She picked at the wild grass, and strangely, I didn't mind her presence.

"Gunner asked me to go with you to Harvest. We're leaving at dusk," she said.

"Yeah, sure," I said. *Whatever*, I wanted to add. The Director of Harvest could wait. Saffediene must've heard the pain in my voice, because she slipped her hand into mine.

Her skin felt startlingly cold; her hand was dwarfed by mine. I loved Vi, but this was the first meaningful human contact I'd had in a long time, and I didn't want to let go.

So I didn't.

We sat that way under the tree, palms pressing together, until the sun started its arcing descent to the west.

11.

Walls surround me on every side. Above, below, there is no escape. And it's wildly hot. So hot, my fingertips feel blistered from touching the metal several hours ago. Maybe they are, I can't exactly see.

There's only miles and miles of darkness; endless metal, smooth in every direction, maybe without corners, maybe not.

I can't tell anymore. I don't know how much time has passed. I made it all the way to the vineyards in White Cliffs before the vanishing tech had worn off. With the teleporter ring, I'd escaped scrape after scrape, always landing in an unknown city.

I could figure out my new location pretty fast. I mean, I have the entire Association memorized, and whenever I used the ring,

I always had the image of Vi in my head. I liked to think my destination had something to do with her.

The first time I teleported, back in early July, I landed on the beach. Violet loved the beach. I didn't know if she was on a similar beach at the time, but that's what I imagined.

That way, our separation didn't hurt so much. That way, my heart didn't feel like a fish out of water, flopping and useless.

The teleporter ring ran out of juice by August. Who knew that could happen? Well, me now, I guess.

I'd flung the ring at the approaching guard in Baybridge, nailing him in the left eye. That's how I'd made it out of that alley. Seemed everyone in the whole blasted Association was looking for me.

I spent the fall on the run, moving from one Midwestern city to another. No one would hire me—my skin held too much sun, and that called everything about me into question. Then officers/ guards/patrols would be summoned, and my picture would come up on every screen.

Forcing me to run again.

Sure, I relied on my network of Insiders every step of the way. I knew the hideouts. I knew most of the leaders, if only by name or picture. They certainly all knew me.

My hair went from black to blond to brown and back. An Insider in Northepointe provided me with eye enhancements in October. I got a work permit. I shoveled snow for months.

And I hate being cold. But the bulky suits—and hats—kept me off the radar. It's my mouth that always puts me back on it.

I choke inside the capsule. There's not enough air. They know it; they come fill it every few hours.

How long has it been? I don't know. I take another breath, but I can't tell if it's filled with oxygen or only my own exhalations.

There's only darkness—and the memories inside my own head.

I don't like remembering. It makes me feel weak, like I should've done something different—like I could've done something different, if only I had been stronger. Better.

Should've, could've, would've.

I've been buried alive. I try not to think it, but the horror is always there.

The capsule is so permanent.

The darkness is so heavy.

It'd be so easy to die.

My eyes are already closed. My body is already in the tomb. My girl is already gone.

At the thought of Vi, I force another breath through my body. Her face, fair and fierce, floats in the recesses of my mind.

I can't give up on her. On us. She's sustained me through difficult situations before, maybe she will this time too.

I can't feel my feet now. Or my fingers—even the painful, blistered ones. I slump against the metal behind me. Hot, burning threads snake down my back, but I can't move. Don't even have the energy to whimper.

I'm dying, I think. They've won.

Pure, unadulterated fury accompanies that thought. I thrash against the darkness, but I can't clear it away. My eyes are open; my voice screams.

"They will not win!" I yell so loud my throat rips. "You will not win!"

Inside my metal prison, I'm met with only an echo. No one comes. No one comes. No one comes.

There is no rescue from this hell.

I clawed at something that had been put over my eyes. My heart pounded in my throat; I swung my free arm to feel the space around me, and I made contact with a soft body.

"Jag, it's Indy."

My head throbbed. I blinked, trying to see. Indistinct shapes hovered in the room; the lights were too dim to really see who was there.

The light meant I was not in the capsule. I inhaled. Oxygen existed here.

"Relax, bro," someone said. My brother.

"Pace." An endless depth of relief surged through me. "Help me."

"We're trying," he said. "You're beating us back."

My leg pulsed with my heartbeat. The skin along my back pulled, as if a thousand little teeth had found a home there. "What happened? Where's Vi?"

"She's here," Pace said. "She just stepped out to get a bite to eat."

"You're all busted up," Indy said. "Pace has been attending to your injuries."

Little by little, my vision cleared. I felt a bandage on top of my head; my fingers brushed another binding on my thigh. Indy and Pace knelt in front of me, worry etched into their eyes.

"My head hurts," I complained.

Pace chuckled. "I bet it does. Just a sec. I'll drug you up again." He stepped out of the hospital alcove, leaving me alone with Indy.

I couldn't catalog all the body parts that hurt. "Hey," I said, looking at Indy and trying not to cry.

She inched closer, one hand held tentatively toward me. When I didn't punch her in the face, she threaded her fingers through mine. Her chest rose with a deep breath. "I was so scared."

Those four words said it all. Indy had a whole I-never-get-scared thing going on. And she usually didn't. I choked back my own fear—my own memories—and gathered her into a hug. Fire erupted along my shoulders where she touched me. I gave a strangled moan.

"Sorry," she murmured, removing her hands, but not moving away. "Your back is sort of shredded."

"Explain," I said.

"Vi's been in here, bawling for hours."

"That's not an explanation."

"She shattered the glass in the lab, thinking it would debilitate the Directors, buy you guys time to get out. Zenn and Raine and everyone escaped, but *you* were also debilitated. Took a lot of glass in the back. Pace worked on you, picking out shards for hours."

I felt shredded inside and out. I held Indy tighter, finding comfort in the way she smelled like grass and something sweet. Her touch was tender, familiar.

"I'm sorry," I said, apologizing for everything. For not knowing where Irvine was. For leaving her behind in the Badlands with a weak promise that we'd talk when I returned. All the things I'd never said, but should've.

Should've, could've, would've.

"I know," she whispered, her lips skating along my ear.

"Irvine . . ." I said into the recess of her neck.

She stiffened just the slightest bit. "No word," she said, and this time she let her mouth linger on my earlobe. She planted tiny kisses down my neck and across my jaw.

I let her. I shouldn't have. I knew I shouldn't.

Two inches separated her mouth from mine. "Jag," she breathed.

"Indy," I whispered. "I'm sorry."

Tears filled her eyes. She knew "I'm sorry" meant *I'm in love with Vi, and I'm not going to screw it up by kissing you.*

When I said "I'm sorry," she heard *Please don't make this harder than it needs to be. I will always love you, but in a different way.*

And my "I'm sorry" also meant *I will find Irv.*

She understood all of it. Acceptance replaced the adoration in her dark eyes. Before she could move away, someone coughed.

"Vi, wait," I called, stumbling into the hall. My back seared with pain, and my leg didn't fare much better. She disappeared around the corner in the direction of her room.

I hobbled after her, waving away Pace's protests, the needle he held in his hand, and the pull of bandages up and down my back.

I turned the corner to find Vi standing in the doorway to her room, her arms folded tightly. "Vi, come on."

She moved out of my way so I could step/hop/collapse onto her bed. My breath hurt going in and coming out.

"I didn't know you and Indy were still, you know, *together*," she said.

"We're not. It was a long time ago."

"Jag, don't lie, okay? Just tell me if you still . . ." She let her words trail off, the pain evident on her face.

How could I make her understand? "Vi, anyone and anything that happened before I met you feels like it happened in a different lifetime, to another guy." I longed to draw her close, wrap my arms around her, and feel her cheek pressed against my chest. She stood so stiff, so unyielding. Typical Vi.

I stood, closed the distance between us, and reached for her anyway. She resisted for a second before allowing me to gather her into an embrace. She clung to me, and I held her, and we breathed together, as if neither of us had the strength to stand alone.

I know I didn't.

She lifted her face toward me, three words lingering on her lips. I memorized the way she looked at me with love.

I spoke first. "I love you."

"I hate it when you say exactly the right thing." Her

mouth lifted in that whimsical way that said, *I don't hate it; I love you too; kiss me, please.*

So I did. It felt exciting, like kissing her for the first time. I wanted to show her how much I loved her. I wanted her to know she was the reason I'd survived the past eight months, the endless hours/days/months in the burial capsule.

She broke the kiss, gasping. Her eyes widened with terror. "That was real? That—you being buried alive—that was real?"

I simply stared at her, confused that she knew about the capsule. I hadn't told her. I hadn't told anyone.

So how did Vi know?

12.

I stood at the end of the hall, watching Vi kiss Jag.

Of course I knew she loved him. I knew they must've been kissing all that time they were together in the Badlands, in the desert, while I was out on watch.

I'd just never had a visual of it until now. Fine, I'd seen them kiss in the transport the night Vi and I had escaped from Freedom, but that was a reunion kiss. An I'm-so-glad-you're-still-alive kiss.

This was so much more.

I turned away, half expecting to throw up and half expecting to throw a punch. I stormed past Saffediene with a clipped, "Meet you outside," and practically flew toward the exit.

She joined me a few minutes later, stuffing a sheaf of papers into her knapsack. "You ready?"

As ready as I was going to be without saying good-bye to Vi. "Ready," I said.

We'd never gone on a mission of this magnitude before. I'd recruited Saffediene after spending just one class period with her. Her quiet strength had been a dead tip-off. She'd stopped clipping in of her own volition about four months before I found her.

She reminded me of Vi in a lot of ways. Except she was nicer. And she didn't kiss other guys.

I swallowed the bitterness in my throat. Why would I care who Saffediene kissed? I didn't.

"Let's go," I said. We kicked off together, climbing through the darkening sky until we achieved the optimum hoverboard cruising altitude.

"Fully charged, with a spare pack," Saffediene said. "We should be there by dawn if we fly all night."

I grunted in response. One great thing about these missions was that we couldn't talk out loud because of the stealth required. Of course, the cache could always be used for mental conversation. But Saffediene somehow sensed that I wasn't in a talking mood, and she stayed silent.

After ten minutes, the silence was almost as damning as the darkness.

"Tell me something," I blurted.

"What?" she asked.

"Anything," I said, desperation clawing at each syllable.

"Okay, um," she said. "My mother begged me not to join the Insiders." Her voice drowned out the one in my head that could only moan *Vi*.

"She said there was only heartache here. No matter what argument I made, she insisted we'd never win."

"Is that why you joined? To go against her?"

Saffediene paused. The rush of the wind filled my ears.

"No," she said. "I have a good relationship with my mother. I just didn't believe her. I think we can win."

A scoff rose in my throat, but I muffled it before it could escape. Her words didn't carry any trace of doubt. I settled onto my board, my mind churning with crazy-scattered thoughts.

In the end, I had to ask myself some questions: Did I believe we could win? Was I fighting on the right side? Was a free government better than a functioning one?

I honestly didn't know.

And that unsettled me more than the hot wind. More than seeing Vi needfully kiss Jag, tangling her hands in his hair.

I used to know. I'd joined this Resistance four years ago to make a difference. Fight the Thinkers. Make my own decisions.

Part of me believed that could still happen. Another part felt so pessimistic, I wanted to turn around, then turn myself in. And a third part simply didn't even know which way was up anymore.

"What do you think is better?" I asked. "Free or functioning?"

Saffediene cut me a quick look out of the corner of her eye. This was dangerous territory, but I honestly wanted to know what she thought.

"A government that allows for freedom is better."

"But you don't know that," I argued. "You've never lived with that kind of government before. You've seen the vids." We all had. War. Protests. Killing in the streets. Hunger. Mismanaged finances and resources, and an energy crisis had brought us to the brink of extinction.

That's when the Thinkers had stepped in. The images from the vids marched through my mind's eye the same way the Thinkers' armies had torn through communities. Brainwashed against brainwashed, brainwashed against freethinking, it didn't matter. The free-thinking didn't go down without a fight. The Resistance started the fires that spread across the earth—at least according to the Thinkers. The memory of crackling flames mingled with the moaning wind as I flew; I was an active member in that Resistance.

On the vids the smoke had cleared much faster than it did in real life. And there'd been very little real life left. The Thinkers blamed the Resistance for the Association's polluted state, and They took freedom away. The people thrived—fine, they lived—without their will to choose. But the water was clean, the air was pure, and people felt safe inside the city walls.

We'd watched vid after vid of the benefits of controlled life. I'd watched, but the sound of those raging fires always drowned out all other sound. To die like that . . . No wonder people had traded freedom for survival. And the Association had done a crazy-good job of making themselves out to be heroes.

"Yeah, I've seen the vids," Saffediene was saying. "They don't say the *only* way to function is without freedom. Who says things didn't function before? I'm sure the lives They show on the vids weren't always so chaotic."

I appreciated that we could discuss this without emotion. Everything with Jag was so black-and-white. Right and wrong. Good and bad. With Saffediene, gray existed.

"Have you ever considered that They only show us what They want us to see?" she asked. "That not all of it was real?"

"The fires were real," I said quietly. I'd trekked back and forth between the Goodgrounds and the Badlands plenty of times. Those buildings didn't cripple themselves, and I'd taken enough science courses to know it took a crazy-hot fire to melt steel.

Saffediene touched my arm, drawing me out of the memory of the crackling flames. "Don't you think everyone would want the ability to choose for themselves, the way you have for the last few years?" She peered at me, as if trying to see something under the surface. "I would. I do."

"Yes, but at what cost?" I desperately wanted her to reassure me.

"We've already traded freedom for safety. We've given up everything. I think it's time to take some of it back." She hugged her knees to her chest and watched the horizon.

I let her words play in my head. It felt like I'd given up everything. I just didn't know how far I was willing to go to get it back.

Dawn streaked the sky before we reached the outskirts of Harvest. Saffediene smiled at me as she stood on her board and stretched. Her hair was scattered over her shoulders where it had come loose from her braid.

We touched down a few miles outside the city, and I

positioned the hoverboards to soak up as much sunlight as possible. She rebraided her hair as she gave me the lowdown of what we needed to accomplish.

"Director Benes is sympathetic to the Insiders, having been one himself for years. He's a lot like you, Zenn," she said without looking at me. "He played both sides until he was promoted to Director."

"Hmm." I thought back over my years of service. I *had* played both sides incredibly well.

"You know, Zenn, if you're worried about which path is right, you could always go back undercover. You could make the necessary changes we need—from within."

My heart stuttered. "I can't." When she asked why, I didn't answer. I was done playing both sides. It sucked more out of me than anyone knew, except maybe Starr Messenger.

Back in Freedom, when I couldn't sleep, I'd fly to Rise Twelve. Starr was almost always there. We'd talked countless times about the energy and dedication it took to play both sides. People couldn't understand it unless they lived it. Jag didn't appreciate the sacrifices people like me and Starr made: friendships, relationships, grades, sleep.

"I haven't been able to tell Gunner anything legit for years," Starr had said one night. Gunn and I had just started sharing a flat. "I probably could've loved him."

What she didn't say was that she'd fallen in love with someone else—someone on the Inside, someone who knew her secrets, who knew where she went at night, someone who'd helped her out of sticky situations.

She didn't say who it was, but she didn't need to. Trek made sure everyone knew he and Starr were together. He devoted hours to the defensive tech at Rise Six, where she lived; he configured feeds for Starr first; he looked at her the same way Pace used to look at Ty. The way I look at Vi. The way she looks at Jag.

Thane had made the most sacrifices out of anyone on the Inside. He'd left his family years ago. His daughters. He'd given up his whole life to enact change from within.

I wasn't willing to do that. "I can't," I told Saffediene again as I settled myself on the ground to catch a few minutes of rest. "I can't go back undercover."

She studied me before continuing. "Benes hasn't sent out a transmission since his appointment almost six months ago. What we need from him is"—she rifled through her knapsack and pulled out a leather booklet that would fit in my back pocket—"to reprogram the tech generators with this code." She sat next to me and tilted the book so I could see it. I saw a jumble of letters and numbers comprising some sort of password.

"We'll shut them down on our way in, and then he'll reprogram them—he's the only one with clearance."

"Sounds great," I said, the usual thrill of doing something dangerous—something that would make life harder for the Thinkers—starting to seep into my system. "How long do we have?"

"Nine minutes from the time we deactivate the generator to when Benes needs to input the new code."

"So we'll need to comm him to explain everything first," I said, gazing at the city like it was an old friend. I half-wondered if I could stay here instead of returning to the cave where Vi kissed Jag.

"He's meeting us, actually." She blinked rapidly, a sure sign that she was checking her cache. "Fifty-six minutes from now."

"Even though we're a day late?"

"He's been expecting us," she said. "He goes to the generators each day."

"Wow." I lay down and looked up into the brightening sky. "How long has he been doing that?"

"Every morning since he took over as Director, I think. That's what Jag said."

"What else did Jag say?" My voice came out an octave higher than normal. If he was telling anyone important information, it should be me, his second-in-command. Or Indy. Now that she had returned, we shared the job. Plenty needed to be done, and Indy had an iron will as well as a way of sugar-talking people into doing what she wanted.

Except for Jag. He always did what *he* wanted, everyone else be damned. At least I knew Vi and I would be able to find common ground on that point.

Saffediene didn't answer. The silence between us weighed heavily now. I listened to the breeze cut a path through the prairie grass so I wouldn't have to think about anything Jag related.

After a while Saffediene's fingers traced a line up my fore-arm, gently moving my arm away from my body so she could lay her head on my chest. "You're wound too tight, Zenn."

All my muscles tensed at the sound of my name. It was so . . . different from when Vi said it.

Saffediene's body curled next to mine felt different too.

Different, but not bad.

I allowed myself to cup Saffediene's shoulder in my hand. "I'm sorry."

"For what?"

"Being wound so tight."

She hummed in her throat. "It's fine. You've got a lot going on right now."

I wanted to laugh, but couldn't. "I always have a lot going on."

"More now than before," she said. "What with Jag back and all." She must've noticed the way my body spasmed in anger. "I'm so sorry, Zenn. I know you love her."

I nodded, the back of my head sliding over the grit on the ground. She cleared her throat. "I'll give you some time." She started to get up.

"No," I said, my hand tightening. "No, stay."

She settled back down, and the silence surrounding us infused me with a peace I hadn't felt in a long, long time.

Director Benes paced on the roof of a short building inside the city limits of Harvest. His dark, gel-coated hair stood stiffly on his head. I couldn't decide if we could trust him or not. Which Benes were we seeing? The Insider? Or the Director?

I let Saffediene lead so I could catalog every detail. She spoke with the Director in professional tones. She explained everything. He asked questions; she provided all the answers.

"Mr. Bower will cut the power to the generators using the elements. That way you'll be able to cite a natural disaster as the reason for the loss of control. Then you'll need to input this code"—Saffediene tipped the journal toward the Director—"and we'll be on our way."

"And my city will . . ." Director Benes trailed off, his concern clear. He didn't glance around, a sign that he was not worried about anyone overhearing—and he wasn't hiding anything. I relaxed and stepped closer to Saffediene.

"The new code will allow you to cancel all recordings the Association normally collects. Essentially their data will be cut off." Saffedienc smiled a little, and I found myself staring at her mouth.

Director Benes drew my attention with a sharp scoff. "They'll send someone to fix it."

"Don't worry," Saffediene said. "Once you upload this code, we'll send them a prerecorded feed from our headquarters. They'll never know anything is wrong. All you might—*might*—have to explain is why the generator went down in the first place."

Nine minutes later, I'd caused a windstorm to take out the main generator, Director Benes had typed in the new passcode, rerouting the feed through our systems, and Saffediene and I had remounted our hoverboards.

I kept glancing down as we flew above Harvest. Flocks of people were all headed in the same direction. Excited herds of people. Something squirmed in my gut. Large groups usually spelled trouble.

I automatically slowed, craning my head to see where

they were all going, but the high-rises prevented me from finding their destination.

"Zenn?" Saffediene asked from next to me.

"All those people," I said, "where are they going?" I swung my board to follow them. Saffediene mirrored my movement.

We sank lower and lower into the streets as we drew closer to the crowd. I touched down in a side alley and leaned my board against the wall. At the end of the alley, the street opened up into a square.

Men and women stood on a raised platform to my right. They spoke into an amplifier so everyone could hear.

"Citizens! It is time to read the results of the vote!" cried one woman.

A vote? The word didn't hold much meaning for me, but unease squirmed inside.

The woman passed the amplifier to a man, and he read from an e-board. "The majority of the polled population in Harvest has voted in favor of . . ." He paused for dramatic effect.

I could practically taste the tension in the air. A couple of people sparked tasers into the air, because of excitement or nerves, I didn't know.

"Major Duarte as the next Director of Transportation!" the man concluded.

Half the crowd erupted into cheers.

The other half didn't. In fact they gravitated toward each other, pushing and winding their way through the celebrators until they'd formed a crowd directly in front of me.

Simultaneously they all pulled tasers from their pockets, activated them, and raised them above their heads, sending a battle cry into the air.

13.

Vi knew about the capsule. Somehow she knew. Words failed me. Vi searched my face for answers. I felt deflated and completely out of my element.

I always knew what to do. What to say.

The only other time I'd felt like this, I'd ended up getting buried alive.

So I started small. "Vi?"

Something foreign flashed across her face. Deception. I've seen it a thousand times on a thousand different faces. But never hers.

"I think you better tell me," I said as calmly as I could.

My uncertainty was giving way to frustration, which would bloom into anger.

She fidgeted, her fingers on my biceps flitting around like they didn't know where to settle. I felt a strange mix of longing, desperation and fear coming from her.

"I won't be mad," I coaxed.

"Yeah, you will." She closed her eyes. "I'm afraid you'll be furious."

Like that had stopped her in the past. I took her flighty hands in mine to calm them. "Guess I'm not the only one with a secret. Wait. That's not entirely true. You seem to already know mine."

"It's not my fault," she said, with a defiant plea. "I can't help what I can do."

"And what is that, exactly?"

She stood straighter as she took a deep breath. "I can sort of . . . well, sometimes I can . . . I don't know how to explain it. I mean, I can . . ."

I waited out her silence. I didn't know what she needed, so I couldn't give it to her.

She pulled back. It seemed to help, so I released her and sat on her bed. "Please," I said.

She shuffled backward until she crowded the doorway. I kept my eyes down. I knew her words would hit me hard.

"I can see inside your head," she said.

"That's not new knowledge," I said. *Nice try*, I wanted to add.

"While you're asleep," she clarified. "I can experience your dreams . . . as if I were you."

"What?" I whispered.

Her words rushed out, unordered, but each statement made it more difficult to breathe.

Things like "I saw Blaze die in Freedom" and "I know you watched your parents' deaths" and "Because you dreamt it, I saw Zenn leave the Resistance before I even knew he was in it" and the real kicker, "I know you were buried alive. I've experienced that capsule too."

I cradled my head in my hands, and cried.

Vi's seen me do the whole bawl-my-eyes-out thing before, and somehow it doesn't freak her out. I rolled onto my stomach, remembering all the nightmares Vi had voiced— even though I'd give anything *not* to remember.

Vi smoothed my too-long hair off my forehead, got me something to drink, and whispered her apologies.

I wanted them. I wanted her.

After a few minutes she said, "You know, Jag, you don't have to shoulder the whole Resistance alone. I'm not as fragile as you think I am."

"I know." And I did. Who else would have the guts to force her boyfriend to wear a vanisher, certain she'd never see him again? Who else would sacrifice herself for brainwashing so the one person she loved could go free?

Only Vi.

Her sacrifices weren't lost on me. I knew them, felt them, every time I thought of her. That's why it was so hard to put her in compromising situations. I couldn't. Wouldn't.

Shouldn't, couldn't, wouldn't.

"I was stupid," I said. "That's how I got caught. Stupidity. Surely you can understand why I wouldn't want to tell you all about it."

Vi's hand, refreshingly cool, wiped my tears. "You're self-ish," she said. "I want to know everything about you, especially the stupid things you do. Then maybe I won't feel so inadequate all the time."

I opened my eyes and looked at her. "You are anything but inadequate."

She seemed close to scoffing. "I've seen the way people look at you. The way they rush to obey everything you say. Between the two of us, you're clearly more important."

She rushed on when I opened my mouth to protest. "I'm okay with it; I am. I don't need to be important. Except to you . . . I want to be . . . I mean, never mind."

"Vi, you are the most important person to me. The very most."

She looked down. "It doesn't feel like it sometimes."

"When?" I challenged.

"When you don't talk to me, tell me what's important to you, let me in." She met my gaze, and I couldn't argue. "When you shuttle me to the middle of the pack."

"I don't want to burden you with the horrors of my life," I said. I was protecting her. No one should have to live through what I did. Most people wouldn't still be alive.

"I want those burdens," she argued, "if it means you don't have to carry them alone. And we both know you already have a lot of other crap to deal with."

I felt her sincere desire to help me. The authentic way she'd do anything to make my life easier. I loved her more, if that was even possible, because of it.

"Okay." I took a deep breath. "This is very hard for me."

She smiled, and my stomach flipped in a good way. "Start small. How did you get caught?"

Dread returned to my body. "I'd gone to Harvest. It was the end of January." I flashed back to that day: cold, with the promise of icy rain.

"I'd been working in Northepointe, shoveling snow on the maintenance crew. But Javier Benes had been appointed

Director in Harvest—and that was a huge win for the Resistance. He started out like Zenn, working both sides until he received his own city. He's what we'd been grooming Zenn to become."

Vi raised her eyebrows at this. "Interesting."

"What does that mean?" I echoed what Zenn had asked Vi a few times when she'd said that to him.

"It means I'm not sure who Zenn plays for. Are you?"

I rubbed the last of the salty tears out of my eyes and off my face. I had to admit it. "No, I'm not sure about Zenn either. I wish I was, but yeah. He's just like Thane. I trust him about as far as I can throw him."

"That's what Gunner said."

I nodded, lost in a tangle of trust and truth. "Insiders are the hardest," I conceded. "People like Zenn and Starr and River. People who seem to be on the side of whomever they're talking to."

"Right," Vi said. "But people like you, you're *so easy* to figure out." She laughed. It tugged on my heart, making me smile too. I couldn't remember the last time I'd smiled.

"At least when someone talks to me, they know where I am," I said. "I've always been Resistance, through and through."

"It's black-and-white for you," she said. "It's not like that for everyone."

"I know."

"Anyway, Benes Somebody was Director of Harvest?" she prompted.

I smiled again and took both her hands in mine. "Yeah. Director Benes was assigned Harvest, which was huge, because he was the first Insider to get that high in the Association. I mean, he was given command of his own city. He took the reins in October, but his inauguration wasn't until late January. He was the first Director in an Association stronghold who was completely Resistance bred. I had to go."

I remembered asking for leave from my job, which wasn't all that stupid, but implied I'd come back. I knew I wouldn't. I can't stand that kind of restriction. I should've quit, but that might have led to the investigation anyway.

"So I went to Harvest for the ceremony. Everything went smoothly. It was one of my finest moments, seeing Benes don those robes and accept an entire city. Thousands upon thousands of people we could free."

"Sounds like everything went well," Vi prodded.

"Yeah. Afterward we met, and he confirmed that transmissions hadn't been sent since he took over in October. I already knew, of course. Free people think and feel differently than the brainwashed. His city is filled with emotions people like me can feel."

"So where's the part where you were stupid?"

"I didn't go back to my job in Northepointe." I squeezed her hands. "You should know I'm just not that kind of guy. I can work, don't get me wrong, but I just don't think my place is on the maintenance crew."

"Now you tell me," she said, a wry smile gracing her beautiful face. Impulsively I leaned over and kissed her.

It still took me by surprise every time she let me do that. I'd have to try to do it more often.

"Continue," she said, pulling away. Was that a blush? I ducked my head to hide my smile.

"I didn't realize the crew chief in Northepointe would care when I didn't report back. I should've known he'd care. I *should've known* he'd file a report with the Director there. Kingston is ruthless, and the Insider contingency couldn't intercept the report before it was too late."

I sighed. "Kingston figured out who I was. See, I'm sort of wanted everywhere. Not sure if you knew that."

She nudged me with her shoulder. "You and me both, buddy."

I lifted my arm to put it around her, ignoring the aching fire in my shoulder and down my left side. I seriously needed whatever Pace had in that needle.

"I'd left Harvest by then, but had just arrived in Rancho

Port when all hell broke loose. Flight Cops were waiting for me at the border, as if they knew I was coming. It's impossible . . . but maybe not.

"It's so hot in the south, even in early February." I stopped, lost in memory of the absolute heat of the Texan Region and how I clung to the frostiness of shoveling snow for the first part of my entombment.

Underground, I remembered the way my breath would freeze my lungs together, little barbs of ice catching each other until I thought the air couldn't force the tissue apart. The sting of my fingers as they froze and then thawed. The way I used to think I'd rather endure a trial by fire instead of freezing to death.

In the capsule, it always came back to me thinking, *Well, you got what you wanted. Heat.*

So much cracking heat.

"Jag?" Vi snuggled in closer to my side. "How'd you get caught?"

I forced myself to focus on the here and now; the pressure of Vi's body against mine; the gentle rise and fall of her chest, the silky quality of her skin, the taste of her mouth.

"Jag?" She tilted her head to look at me.

I kissed her, desperate to ground myself. I knew my mouth

was too hungry. I needed her the way I had needed air in the capsule. I knew what it was like to go without both.

The touch of her lips softened my insides. She calmed me in her usual Vi-fashion. When we broke apart, I was happy to see she was as breathless as me.

"Like I said," I whispered, our faces inches apart. "They were waiting for me. Before I could do anything, I'd been silenced, tased, and cuffed. Blindfolded. Someone shoved a needle into my neck, and everything went quiet. Numb. Beneath me, the ground moved, but I couldn't even so much as twitch my fingers."

I drew a breath, as if I could summon strength into myself with such a simple action. "When the drugs wore off, they removed my blindfold and made me dig. I dug and dug and dug."

"No," Vi murmured.

"Yes," I said. "I dug my own grave. Someone stuck a needle into my arm. Their mouths moved, but I couldn't tell what they were saying. Everything was blurry, shapeless, mute. They uncuffed me before shoving me into the capsule."

"Stop," Vi whispered, but I couldn't.

"Then I was falling. I fell and fell and fell and it was so, so dark. The last thing I remember is the sound the dirt made as it rained down on the metal capsule." A shudder ripped through my body.

Vi wept openly now. I should've been able to.

Should've, could've, would've.

But I didn't. Telling her about what had happened actually released the burden from me. Who knew I'd feel like that?

"Thank you," I said, touching my mouth to hers again, this time softly. I waited for her permission to continue. She gave it, slowly exploring my lips with hers, as if she hadn't kissed me before.

"How'd you get out?" she asked when she pulled back. "How'd you get to Freedom?"

I was ready to give her all my secrets. I would've too, if Gunner hadn't burst into her room.

"It's Thane," he said. "He's awake."

Zenn

14. I grew up in the City of Water, where my father said I'd been able to manipulate the air since birth. There isn't a time I can remember that I couldn't control the wind.

My older brother had no such talents, beyond thinking for himself. My mother favored him, but my father doted on me. He counseled me on how to use my talent without detection; he introduced me to the physics educator at school; he took me to work with him and let me experiment in the wind machines.

My father also covered up the infraction with Vi. The house *had* alerted him, and the report would've gone on my official record since I was already thirteen.

He knew about the Resistance—because he was involved. He'd recruited me; he'd taught me the subtle art of playing both sides; he'd introduced me to Jag.

I adored my father.

He didn't understand my sudden withdrawal from the Resistance, but I blamed the failed mission during which Blaze Barque had died. I'd never confessed the deal I'd made with Thane Myers—he'd matched me with Vi in exchange for information about Jag. My first true test of living the Insider life.

I'd "left" the Resistance, but I'd never revealed anything of importance to Thane.

Insider Tip #4: Give information that is either already known, or that won't damage the other side.

Jag hated me because I'd quit, but I'd had no choice. Thane held more power than Jag knew—power to make my life difficult. He'd threatened my father; he'd threatened Vi.

I'd do anything to keep the two of them safe. The decision was easy: I defected. Jag could deal.

As I pressed into the alley wall in Harvest, I remembered that mission to Freedom when Blaze had disappeared. The fear felt the same, but the stakes were much higher now. I flattened myself against the wall as the battle cry became a roar. The taser-happy crowd surged forward, joined by more people from the alley behind me.

Saffediene cried out, and I turned to find her on her hands and knees. Anger boiled through me as I grabbed her hand and pulled her to a standing position next to me. I stepped partially in front of her to shield her from further danger.

"Our boards," she moaned, looking down the alley roiling with a steady stream of people. "No way they survived that horde."

I had to agree, but we had to focus on our most pressing problem: getting out of here alive.

"Who'd you vote for?" a man asked a mere half foot away, his taser sparking with blue techtricity.

I swatted it out of my face. "Get that away from me," I growled.

For a moment he looked like he might leave. Then he saw Saffediene. "Oh, I get it. *She* voted for Duarte."

"*She's* not even from here," I said. "Leave us alone."

His eyes glazed at my voice control, and he joined the fray of anti-Duarte supporters.

"We've gotta get out of here," I said quietly. "Come on." Saffediene's hand trembled as we ran down the alley together, away from the square.

I didn't look back, despite the screams that pierced the

air. Saffediene stumbled, but I kept her upright. As we hurried away, I realized that the scene in that square could've been one of the vids the Association showed students. *See what happens when Citizens are allowed freedoms?* I heard the slogans in my mind with little effort.

I didn't look back, even when the hovercopters arrived, blaring with instructions and popping with taser fire.

Free vs. functioning? looped through my mind.

Next to me, Saffediene wept openly, but I didn't feel the slightest bit like crying.

I didn't look back, because I couldn't stand to see the proof that humanity couldn't manage themselves. That they'd always need a Thinker.

That I'd been fighting for chaos these past four years.

At the end of the alley, our hoverboards were indeed gone. I mourned their loss for only a moment before I snapped my fingers, and a current of air stalled in front of me. Its edges shimmered in my vision, gray and then purple and then blue.

Saffediene wouldn't be able to see it, so I pulled her closer and said, "Hold on to me, okay?"

"Are you going to do that freaky wind thing again?"

"Yes," I said. "Hold on to me tighter."

She complied, facing me and wrapping both arms around

my waist, then burying her face in my chest. I lifted her onto the air cushion and whispered, "Up, please."

The wind obeyed, taking us straight up until we'd escaped the mayhem below.

"Wait," I said, and we paused to watch the scene below. It mirrored the vids I'd seen in the past. People were running here, there, everywhere. Hovercopters crowded the rooflines; officers shouted instructions through the amplifiers. The spark of tasers looked like lightning in the morning sunlight.

I couldn't believe it. This was what I'd been in favor of? Citizens killing other Citizens? Violence as a means to achieve a desired outcome?

No. I did not advocate those things.

My peripheral vision caught a movement in the sky. Director Benes floated on a hoverboard a hundred feet away, also surveying the chaos below. He met my gaze with raised eyebrows. His message was clear: *Tell Jag.*

Half of me wanted to stay and see if or when he might intervene. The other half couldn't wait to get away from the upheaval. Far away.

That half won.

Saffediene and I didn't speak about what we'd witnessed on the way back to the cavern. I expanded the cushion of air once we left Harvest so we could both sit comfortably. She could've chosen a spot far from me and passed the ride with only her own thoughts.

She didn't.

She sat right next to me, both her hands holding one of mine, talking about her life before the Insiders, her mom, her two younger brothers, her assigned educational track. She asked me about school, and how I met Vi, and if I had any siblings.

I told her everything. Everything about my older brother, and meeting Vi, and joining Jag, and when I defected, and how sometimes I ached to see my parents again.

She felt safe to me. Saffediene had become someone I could tell anything to, and she wouldn't judge or question me. She accepted who I was at that moment, and empathized with who I'd been in the past.

I'd never met anyone like her. When the night swallowed the last of the day, I realized why I felt so secure with Saffediene.

She had no agenda. She simply *was*.

I envied her. I lived my entire life according to an agenda, mine or someone else's. I couldn't tell them apart anymore.

And maybe that was my real problem.

15.

Vi and I stayed in her room for a few heartbeats, both of us staring at one another.

Thane, awake.

The rocks seemed to shout the question running through my head: *What will happen now?*

"Only one way to find out," Vi said. She laced her fingers through mine, pressing our palms together. Every muscle in my body protested as she helped me stand.

"I need meds," I complained, limping into the hall. Gunn had gone ahead, too agitated to wait. I should've asked him if Raine had woken up yet.

"She's with Gunner," Vi said. "And we can stop by the hospital alcove for meds on the way to Thane's room."

"Perfect," I said.

"Pace," Vi said, leaning into the hospital alcove. "Jag needs meds." She turned away as Pace fed the drugs into my system. Immediately, the ache in my head receded; the throbbing in my leg slowed.

"Thanks," I said. "How often can I have that?" The cuts along my back still pulled, radiating pain through my body.

"Come back before bed," Pace said, smiling. It was his big-brother smile. The one that told me he was in control, that I could confide in him.

"Where's Raine?" I asked, noting two empty beds in the hospital alcove. I'd need to get a report from her too.

"Everyone is in Thane's room," Pace answered. "Same hall as my room. Better hurry, or you won't get front-row seats." His words were filled with bitterness. I understood how he felt. All this time, Thane had been working against us.

For us too, but definitely against us. He'd killed Ty. He'd taken Vi and brainwashed her. Forced her to live in Freedom for eight months without any memory of her real life.

Who does that to their daughter? To anyone?

Zenn.

The thought came unbidden, but it rang with truth. Zenn had done the same thing. Could I trust him?

I didn't know.

Could I trust Thane?

Maybe, with time.

I could only wish/hope/pray that Zenn and Thane were on my side. I needed them badly.

Vi and I moved slowly down the hall. A nervous energy buzzed from Vi, but she stepped patiently with me as I dragged my hurt leg. We passed through the empty war room and continued down another narrow hallway.

A crowd had gathered at the end of it, and excited voices filtered back to us. My nerves felt spent. The thought of facing Thane exhausted me.

But I pasted on my leader-of-the-Resistance face and said, "Excuse me." The people in front of me stepped to the side, leaving me and Vi a path to the room ahead.

Indy grabbed and held my gaze. I couldn't feel her message with the whole team gathered around. Whatever it was, her look didn't broadcast anything good. Maybe she was still angry about the not-kissing we'd done earlier. I had left her without an explanation—again—when I'd hobbled after Vi.

A pretty girl with long white hair stood next to Gunn. The last time I'd properly seen Raine Hightower, she'd had her hand suctioned to mine. Gunn held her hand and whispered in her ear. Besides sporting skin whiter than the snow I used to shovel, she looked healthy. "Hey," she said when I stepped next to her. "I'm Arena—I mean, Raine."

She shot a fast look at Gunner, and his face said it all. Raine would need rehabilitation to recover the memories she'd lost.

"Hey," Vi and I answered at the same time, in the same sad/surprised voice. I wanted to kiss Vi again. I settled for squeezing her hand.

In the bedroom Thane sat on a cot, staring at me. His bare chest revealed the wounds Gunn had given him in the Centrals. The skin surrounding the mostly healed holes shone new and pink.

He definitely could've looked worse. His eyes flickered with fire, just as they always had.

"Thane," I said, trying to school my voice into friendliness. It didn't quite work.

"Jag," he replied in the same almost-neutral manner.

We were nothing if not committed to maintaining our we-don't-like-each-other vibe.

"Well?" he asked.

Oh, hell no. If he was here to try to make me look like a fool, that so wasn't going to work.

"Report. Tell me everything." And without taking my eyes off Thane, I said, "Gunn, be sure to record this."

I sensed his nod of understanding and waved my free hand at Thane to start.

His gaze lingered on my fingers entwined with Vi's, and I felt a ping of satisfaction at the anger twitching in his jaw.

"Report," I said again, just because I could.

Thane's report wasn't anything I didn't already know—at least the information he was willing to share in front of twenty people. I knew there was more; I could sense it. I briefly wondered if it had anything to do with the cloning experiment Gunn, Pace, and I had witnessed on Starr's microchip. I'd need to ask him as soon as possible.

Five minutes into his report, I wanted to sit down with a tall glass of water. I actually did just that, citing my injuries as the reason I couldn't stand.

Thane didn't stand either, and his report was bogus. When he finished, Pace grounded him from all Resistance activity for the next several days and ordered him back to bed.

"You too," Pace said as we shuffled down the hall to my room. "No flying, nothing physically stressing for at least three days, okay?" He stopped outside the infirmary and selected a needle from our very limited supplies.

"Not okay," I said. "There're five million things that need to be done." We had secured Thane, but he had no new information. We needed to proceed. Get more traveling teams out to the cities, get more Directors on board, plan the attack on Freedom. Maybe there were five million and one things to do. All I knew was I couldn't take a three-day break.

Pace administered the meds with a disapproving frown. "Gunn and Indy can take over for a few days. Zenn will be back tonight too."

My head felt fuzzy. "Where'd he go? Wasn't Gunn supposed to go with him?"

"Harvest. And Gunn asked Saffediene to go in his place so he could stay with Raine."

I nodded, and I swear my neck didn't have bones. What was in that needle?

"You have to rest," Pace said.

"I don't trust Zenn," I blurted. "Or Thane." I leaned in closer, as if we could share secrets in this tiny compound where we all slept on top of each other and every hallway echoed with conversations. "What about the clones?"

Pace slid my arm over his shoulders. "Come on, bro, time for bed."

I was beyond tired. I thought I might actually be able to sleep tonight too, because I'd told Vi all about the capsule and I didn't have to live with that alone and Thane wasn't going anywhere and—

My knees hit stone as my legs buckled. I heard Pace's voice, but it ricocheted from far away. I felt Vi's lips against mine, but that might've been my imagination.

I moved like I was in water up to my chest. Someone held on to me. Someone who smelled like meds and flowers. I heard a girl say, "Clones? What's he talking about, Pace?"

I tried to hold on to consciousness, but it slipped through my fingers like smoke.

Images drifted through my mind. Neat rows of flowers and white picket fences. Green lawns and laughing children. Families playing in the park and friends ordering coffee on Saturday mornings.

Freedom: what life would be like without Thinkers.

I finally submitted to sleep with a smile on my face.

16.

Jag lay in his bedroom, his mouth hanging half open, snoring. I knew the guy wasn't perfect, and now I had proof.

I stood watching him longer than necessary, imagining his mouth against Vi's. Gunner drew me out of that crazy-bad place.

"Zenn, Raine wants to see you. Oh, and we're leaving in the morning for Lakehead."

"Already? I just got back." I'd signed up for the traveling team, but I still wanted more than eight hours on the ground. A large part of me wanted to fly with Saffediene again. I wondered how obvious it would be if I asked to go with her instead of Gunn.

He clapped his hand on my shoulder. "Well, welcome back. Come on." He left me standing there, still staring at Jag.

I found Gunn in Raine's room. They sat in comfortable silence, clearly caching it up. I almost felt like I was intruding, until Raine's face lit up. She jumped up and hugged me.

Zenn, she chatted. *You look awful.*

Thanks a lot. Using my cache felt strange, yet perfectly familiar, especially with Raine. I still had a blip of fear about who would be listening before I remembered that I wasn't linked in to Freedom's network anymore.

No one was listening.

No one cared.

She grinned. *You know I mean that in a good way.*

Sure, sure, I cached, but I was smiling too.

Tell us about Harvest, Gunn's voice joined the convo, and my smile faltered at his choice of topics.

I didn't know what info to give about what had gone down in Harvest. Saffediene and I hadn't talked about the riot or if we were going to tell anyone. Our mission with Director Benes had gone off without a hitch.

Did the Resistance need to know about everything that

happened there? I didn't know anything about transportation disputes, and surely our people would be ready to fight the Thinkers when we needed them.

Everything went as planned, I chatted. Technically it wasn't a lie, so I didn't feel guilty, which is usually how people get caught lying. *Director Benes is solid.*

Raine looked more alive today. She at least knew my name. "How are you doing?" I asked her.

"Good," she said, reaching for Gunn's hand with her gloved one. "I can remember my name now. And Gunn's, and yours, and Jag's. Gunner's been quizzing me for hours." She smiled at him, but the edges quivered, like she might be embarrassed she couldn't recall the details of her life.

"That's great," I said. I wouldn't want to be shown pictures and be able to recognize the faces but unable to recall names. I wouldn't want my memory erased, no matter how painful some of it was. "What happened after you helped us escape?"

"Is this my official report?" she asked.

"Sure," I said. "I'm second-in-command. I can take your report."

She smirked. "Second-in-command. Zenn, please. You're not second."

"Third?" I joked.

"First," she said.

"Oh, no," I said, my voice full of mock seriousness. "Jag is forever first." The exchange almost called for laughter. Both Raine and Gunn knew how much I'd lost when we'd busted Jag out of prison. And neither of them pretend very well.

"I'm sorry," Raine said.

Somehow her apology boosted my mood. I wouldn't say losing Vi to Jag was okay, because it wasn't. Technically it sucked big-time. I shrugged. "Voices are never nobody, right?"

"Right," Gunner said.

"So, let's hear what you can remember," I said to Raine. "Gunn, you want to record it?"

"Sure," he said, and blinked to turn on his cache.

Raine suddenly looked like a shell of herself. "I remember the blood the most."

From there, she detailed how she'd held on to her father's face for as long as she could. How the sirens sounded like screams, how the rain came and erased so much more than the filth from her hands.

"The next thing I knew, I was attending class on the Fourth Level, and everyone was calling me Arena. The name never quite fit, but I couldn't remember anything else."

"What about Cannon?" Gunn asked. Cannon had been Raine's match and best friend in Freedom.

"Who's Cannon?" she asked. Gunn and I exchanged a glance.

"I can tell you later," Gunn said. "Let's continue with the report for now."

"I went to genetics and biology in the morning. In the afternoons I worked in the Evolutionary Rise in an analysis lab, or in Rise One with my guardian—" She cleared her throat. "I mean, my father—Van Hightower."

"What did you do in the Evolutionary Rise, specifically?" I asked. Gunner shifted nervously, a signal I'd grown to recognize when he was being secretive. He knew something about the Evolutionary Rise. I knew what the scientists were trying to do there: produce clones.

"The analysis lab where I worked was testing blood for abnormalities. Diseases I could barely remember the name of at the time. I didn't do very well there. And I was failing biology. I couldn't remember taking any bio courses before." She hung her head as if she should be ashamed. In her semi-Modified state, she probably was.

"You'd never taken bio," Gunn said. "You told me you were taking it next term." He squeezed her hand, and when she looked at him, hope shone in her eyes.

"I remember now. You showed me the stars." A smile played at her lips.

"Yes," Gunn said. "You asked me to—"

"Name an animal, and I'd tell you which kingdom it belonged in," Raine said. "I remember." The grin bloomed across her face, making her appear healthier. More alive.

"That's great," I said. "What did you do in Rise One?"

"Drains," she said, her joy over her recovered memories fading into seriousness. Gunner shot me a look filled with caution.

"How many?"

"I don't know. Sometimes every day."

"One or two or three a day?"

"I couldn't handle more than one. If I had to drain someone, I got the rest of the day off. I almost—" She swallowed hard. "I almost liked doing them." Her voice ghosted into silence.

"It's okay, Raine," Gunn murmured.

"I wasn't tied down," she said. Suddenly her eyes grew wide. She moaned like a frightened animal. "I used to be strapped down during the drains." Her eyes rapidly shifted between me and Gunner. "Didn't I?"

"Yes," I said. Gunn nodded, and a single tear trickled down Raine's cheek. She swiped at it and took a deep breath.

"I wasn't tethered during the drains as Arena. They didn't hurt as much. I—I liked doing them because then I could go home, get away from everyone watching me." Raine shivered. "Their eyes felt like razors."

"I love you," Gunner said, and he pressed his lips to her temple.

She leaned into him, gratitude in her eyes.

"Anything else you might want on the report?" I asked, a surge of loneliness and jealousy roaring through me. Gunner watched me with sympathetic eyes, but that only made me feel irritated on top of isolated.

She shook her head. "Gunner is going to tell me about the flight trials," she said. "He says I'm a good flier."

"You are," I assured her. Gunn's fingers moved up her arm, and I took that as my cue to leave. I'd have to corner Gunn later for what he knew about the Evolutionary Rise.

I'd never ventured into Saffediene's room before, but my feet took me there now. She had a curtain hanging on the wall. I stared at it, marveling at its normalcy, wondering if a window really lurked behind it.

"It's just for decoration," she said through the darkness. She pressed a button and a dim lamp flared to life. Shadows chased each other across her bed and concealed half her face.

"Hey," I said. "Can I talk to you for a sec?"

She shifted on her cot and gestured to the small space at the end.

I sat, suddenly nervous to be there. I didn't know why, but I thought the way Saffediene and I had been holding hands and lying in each other's arms may have had something to do with it.

"About what we saw in Harvest . . ."

"That riot," she said. Saffediene didn't like to sugarcoat things. She called it how she saw it. I remembered when she did that during engineering class. I'd taken it as another sign that she was thinking for herself.

"Yeah, the riot," I said. "I don't think we should detail that in our report."

Silence stretched so long that I squinted at her to determine what she was thinking. She twirled the ties on her quilt, her eyebrows furrowed.

"What's the purpose of keeping it a secret?" she asked.

"Maybe it's an isolated incident," I said. "Also, it has nothing to do with our mission. Director Benes is still solidly on board. I don't think Jag needs the complication of some stupid transportation dispute in a city hundreds of miles away." I shrugged in an attempt to look nonchalant. "I just don't think it's necessary. What do you think?"

Insider Tip #5: Always ask for another's opinion. That way, you'll never come off as the one making all the decisions.

She kept her eyes on the blanket for another few moments, then raised her gaze to mine. Her fingers went still. "I think Jag needs to know everything."

I wasn't sure, but I thought that statement held a double meaning. "Yes, eventually," I said. "But right now?"

"If Benes can't even solve his labor disputes, how is he going to send people when we need them?" she asked.

"Who directs the transportation department is a far cry from sending Insiders to help take down Freedom," I said.

She nodded, her attention back on the blanket. She seemed so forlorn.

"What else is bothering you?" Saffediene had been so in tune with my troubles with Vi, but I was surprised that I'd noticed she wasn't her normal self.

She exhaled, and seemed to further deflate. "You're going to Lakehead," she said, her voice hesitant.

"Yeah, so?" I asked. "It's a day trip. Though I'm sure I'll have some crazy-late watch assignment after that."

She smiled, but it came and went before it could truly settle on her mouth. I caught myself staring and glanced away.

"Yeah, so, I'll miss you." She met my gaze with a challenge. For the first time since I recruited her, I did a little bit of investigating inside her mind.

And oh, man. She—

"I like you, Zenn," she said. She shifted on the bed, and I shot to my feet.

"I should go."

Saffediene's eyes pinched as hurt crossed her face.

"Maybe when I get back we can . . . talk some more."

"Yeah, talk," she said, dipping her chin so I couldn't see her eyes.

"Uh, what about Harvest?" I asked.

"I won't say anything in the report," she said. "I'll file it tomorrow."

"Okay," I said, releasing a breath I didn't know I'd been holding.

I stood in the doorway, wanting to make this right before I flew away. No matter who stood in front of me, I'd always spoken the right words and known just the right thing to do to maintain their trust.

But this was outside my scope of Insider training. They didn't offer a course on how to deal with free-thinking girls who liked you.

Finally I said, "Saffediene?"

She looked up.

"I'll miss you too."

And that was the truth.

Jag

17.

I cross the border at a run, like I usually do. Entering the Goodgrounds has become easier over the years. A surge of satisfaction blankets me as I leap a small ditch and set my sights on the forest. I'd rather enter the city from the south, where there are bigger crowds to get lost in, but my reports say an armed contingency of authorities have been hovering in the Southern Rim.

Coming this way means I have to sneak through the Centrals—which have very little cover in mid-April. But whatever. I've snuck through the Centrals many times, and hey, this way I can distribute my tech along the way.

*I steer clear of the Fire Region, because the heat there com-
promises my tech. Instead I loop around the lake and head to
the market square, where people gather to receive their daily
supplies.*

*When I arrive in the hundred acres of cleared fields, my head
spins. Farmers display their goods—mostly the last of the winter potatoes and squash. Craftsmen exhibit their leftover cloth,
leather, shoes, and hats.*

*A flash of green cloth causes me to dart behind an empty
stall. The Greenies are here, checking cards and display permits.
I don't understand why. It's not like someone could sneak into
the Goodgrounds, start growing corn, and then show up to sell
it here.*

*There's no buying and selling in the Goodgrounds. The people
work the jobs they're told, and in return the Thinkers provide
them with necessities. This market is trade only, and the Citizens
are allowed to bring only whatever's left over after the government has taken what they need to sustain their population.*

*No, the Greenies are here to make an example of someone.
I'm determined that it not be me.*

*I slip down the rows of wares, pausing briefly at a teched-
out stand displaying silver spheres and cubes and all manner of
things I can't even begin to imagine.*

Pace could though, and he'd kill to get his hands on this

technology. My hands twitch, desperate to pilfer some of this and bring it back to him in the Badlands. Of course I'd have to hold on to it for a while, since I don't exactly know where he is at the moment. But he shows up from time to time, always looking well fed and happy to see me.

"Over here," someone says, and I tear myself away from the tech booth. The familiar voice came from between two stalls, and I don't even think before stepping into the space.

"Brother-man," Irvine Blightingdale says, shaking my hand. His engulfs mine, and looks twice as dark as my heavily tanned one. I quickly pull my long sleeves down to hide my incriminating skin after he releases me.

"Irv," I say, "how long have you been here?"

"Couple of minutes. I knew you'd get all trapped up in that tech." His shoulders shake with laughter, but no sound comes out.

"Yeah, well." I scan the area behind us, which is just the back of two more huts. "I was thinking that I could leave my wares in that stand," I say. "No distribution required. But there are Greenies here."

"Yeah, I seen 'em," he says.

"Did you gather what you need?" I ask. I'll be sending him to the Southern Region in another week or two. Irv is killer with tech, and the Resistance hopes he'll be able to find a place in a city to set up a safe house.

He leans closer and catches me off guard with his newly enhanced green eyes. I'm still not used to them. "Got it."

"Nice," I say. "Stage two in effect. Did you meet with Bower?"

"Stage two," Irv confirms. "And yes. Bower's a go. He'll join me down south in a few weeks." He looks over my shoulder. I follow his gaze, and shrink back into the shadows. Two Greenies stand in the market path, looking at palm readers and shaking their heads.

"Better get rid of that tech," Irv whispers. I scoot around the back of the stand after him and out of sight of the Greenies. My heart pounds, but I don't feel scared. The adrenaline is a sign that I'm doing something besides looking at plans and blueprints. Something besides sitting in meetings and asking people questions.

Something.

I try to assign myself to field missions, but it's been getting harder, what with bringing the Oceanic cities on board and increasing recruitment efforts across the Association. I can't be everywhere, doing everything.

But I can come to the Goodgrounds. No one's better at that than me. Not even Indy, though she likes to think so.

I smile at the thought of her, but it's almost sad. She'd broken up with me last week when she saw Sloan dancing with me. "With" isn't even the right word. More like "near."

I tried to explain, but Indy didn't want to hear it. She said my "killer voice" couldn't save me this time.

I'd assigned her to management duty while I took this mission, just to get away. That, and Gavin had said I'd find something here. Something huge.

I don't think she meant in the dregs of the trade marketplace behind an endless swath of booths. But I could be wrong.

In fact, behind these booths is the absolute safest place for me as the sirens start.

"Rendezvous one," Irv calls, sprinting into the fray of bodies scrambling down the path.

I run in the opposite direction, but stop short at the sight of two board-reading Greenies. They see me, and I reach up to pull my hat lower.

My hat is gone.

One of them, a bald one, raises his reader, and I'm pretty sure the resulting flash signals that he's just confirmed my identity.

I drop my backpack and kick it as far away as possible. They see every move. I spin and run in the same direction as Irv. His dark-haired head bobbing through the crowd is the last I see of him.

After a half hour of running and many random turns, I'm bent over, gasping. In front of me lie the tech canyons created by the tall buildings in the Southern Rim. I can get lost there. Waste some time in one of my Insider hideouts. Get back to the Badlands in a few days.

I've lost my tech, but that hardly matters now. I duck into the cleanest alley I've ever seen and slide my fingers along the smooth surface of the building on my left. I wonder how many people it takes to keep the Southern Rim so sparkly silver, so clean, so orderly.

I know it takes twenty-one Thinkers sending out transmissions, laying down proclamations, getting inside people's heads, to control the population.

A wave of disgust washes over me. I can't believe people once believed their lives were so bad that they willingly gave up control over them. But I didn't live during those wars; I didn't survive those fires; I didn't emerge from an underground bunker to complete nuclear devastation.

I could only strive to make things right now, centuries later.

I thought back to my time in Seaside with Gavin. She'd had a premonition about someone in the Goodgrounds. Whoever it is will tip the scale. Either for us or against us. You must find them. And soon.

I'd immediately thought of Zenn. But he was already against us. Sort of. Maybe.

I'd delayed my trip here last month, sending Indy and her

team instead. They'd found nothing. No one. Our contacts hadn't heard anything either.

Now, in the impeccably clean alley of the Goodgrounds, I think of Blaze again. He died in an alley like this in Freedom. My sadness suffocates me.

I try to shake away the thoughts of him. I shouldn't be so emotionally attached. It makes running the Resistance too damn hard. Because people are going to die, most likely because of a decision I'll make. I can't afford to be emotionally attached.

So it's probably a good thing Indy dumped me, I think.

Wrapped up in my thoughts about Gavin, and Blaze, and Indy, I get stupid. I'm not paying close enough attention.

I don't even realize I'm surrounded until it's too late.

I wake up, feeling my mattress shift. Someone's just gotten out of the bed in my holding cell. My bed. The bed I'm lying in.

Across from me sits a girl. The first thing I notice is her wicked-cool hair. It spikes all over, colored like the depths of night. I switch my gaze to her eyes.

Thinker eyes. Part blue, part green, and as sharp as my father's before he died.

But something isn't right. This girl doesn't seem . . . real. I can almost see through her.

"Who are you?" I ask, reaching for her to see if I can touch her or not. "What's going on?"

A mask of panic covers her face, and suddenly I know who she is and exactly what's going on.

I woke up coughing, the jerky movement sending pain rippling through my sliced-up back. My mind reeled with a different kind of disturbance, though. A whole Vi-was-just-in-my-head-witnessing-how-I-got-caught-in-the-Goodgrounds kind of disturbance.

The faintest of lights splintered the darkness covering my room. I blinked, trying to make my eyes see more.

"Vi?" I knew she was there, even if I couldn't see her.

"I'm sorry," she said. "I can't help it." Her voice pitched higher, and she started crying. I followed the sound to the chair near the doorway and pulled her back to the bed with me.

She snuggled against my chest. Like we fit, the pieces floating in my head suddenly clicked together.

She'd woken up and gotten out of bed—in real life.

The same disturbance woke me in my dream. And then I saw her—in my dream.

"Shh," I said, smoothing her hair. "So. Did you see it all?"

"Yes." Her voice sounded like a child's. Tiny/afraid/far away. "I can't help it," she repeated.

"I'm not mad." I held her until she fell asleep again, her breathing deep and even against my collarbone. I felt weary, but I didn't allow myself to sleep.

If I didn't, then Vi wouldn't have to witness my nightmares.

Zenn

18.

The buildings of Lakehead shimmered against the horizon, blocking the sun like a partial eclipse. My back hurt. My head too. My heart also sang with pain. Strangely, because I'd spent most of the last seven hours thinking about Saffediene instead of Vi.

Which hurt in a new, weird way.

Gunner made a great companion in that he didn't ask questions. He didn't feel the need for useless chatter either. But his silence had made the last several hours almost unbearable in comparison to the flight with Saffediene, her cool hands holding mine, and her perky voice telling stories about her life.

Half of me preferred Gunn's steady, sure approach to our missions. The other half longed to watch Saffediene rebraid her hair as she went over the finer points of our assignment.

"Hey," Gunn said. "Are you alive?"

"Huh? Yeah." I took in his disbelieving expression.

"Look, you've got to stop pining over Vi."

I glared. "I am not pining over Vi." But the way he just came out with it reminded me of Saffediene. Could I be pining over her?

He rolled his eyes. "I can feel stuff, Zenn." He wasn't like Saffediene in his specificity. Right now, I appreciated his "stuff" more.

"What do you know about the Evolutionary Rise?" I asked. He regarded me for a moment in surprise. "I can figure *stuff* out too."

"Ask Jag," Gunn said. I didn't want to ask Jag—and it annoyed me that Gunn knew something I didn't. I looked away.

Lakehead was a blip on the radar, a tiny city surrounded by lakes. Mostly a water filtration city, the people lived packed on top of one another in a narrow neck of land between two large bodies of water.

"The Director sent an e-comm several weeks ago, claiming

to have stopped all transmissions." Gunn flipped through his dad's journal, any apprehension about my question gone. "But I don't see how that's possible. For one, Indy said she never sent the software. For another, the Association would need to be fed a fake feed, and there's no record of that, either."

I slowed to a stop as we approached the border. "What does the journal say we need to do here? What's the mission?"

"Install the software, send the live feed," Gunner said. "Then we've got to find the…" He checked the book. "The West End Lakehead Treatment Facility and locate a man named Phillip Hernandez."

"At least we have a direction. There's got to be a million treatment facilities here." One loomed just below me, white curls of smoke painted into the ebony metallic surfaces of the one-story building.

"You're right. Super," Gunn muttered. "Well, let's get this done already."

No wasted words, no wasted time. Gotta love Gunn.

Half an hour later, we hadn't succeeded in even one of our objectives. The city was closed.

That's right. Closed.

The fences had been activated, creating a dome of tech-energy over the main group of buildings. Guards stood at every ground entrance. Gunn and I had retreated to a small stand of trees near one of the smaller lakes, about ten miles away.

Gunn pulled a cube from his pack. "What do you want to eat?"

I smiled, but didn't answer. The best part of being on the traveling team was the food-generating cube. We only had two in our possession as a Resistance, and we used them while traveling.

But it meant I didn't have to eat out of a can.

A moment later Gunn handed me a stack of toast as high as my head.

The wind rippled through my hair, whispering a word of greeting. The sun beat down on my bare arms, charging our boards with its rays. I took a bite of buttery toast.

Ah, this was the life.

"Can you do something about the dome?" I whispered to the breeze. It scampered away, leaving me too warm and wanting.

Insider Tip #6: Use what resources you have, as long as you can do it without detection.

Ten minutes later the dome went down.

Gunn and I managed to float over the city at four hundred feet, well out of range of any guards, even if they had vision enhancements. When we hovered dead center, I gave the signal to descend.

We landed on the roof of a medium-size building, where I fondled a cool westerly and said, "Thanks."

The air current zipped away, buzzing with pride.

Before we could even begin, the dome regenerated, trapping us inside.

"At least we can get two things done," Gunn said, folding his board and shoving it in his pocket. He looked to his right, then his left. "So, which way do you think we should go?"

Shouts filled the sky, and that same crazy-unsettling unease I'd felt in Harvest filled my gut.

"Toward that sound," I said, though every particle of my being wanted to get back on my board and fly far away.

Gunn looked at me, shock darkening his features. "What's going on?"

"I'd say a rebellion," I answered calmly. I felt it deep, deep down. And I wondered—again—if canceling the transmissions and providing the general population their free will was a good thing.

Free vs. functioning? If Saffediene were here, I'd ask her. But I didn't dare voice anything with Gunn, lest Jag hear about it and question my loyalty again.

I led, walking fast across the close-knit rooftops and

waving off Gunn's repeated questions. He'd see for himself soon enough.

After only a few minutes, we arrived on the scene. I blinked, activating the recording capabilities of my cache before I looked down.

Gunn and I stood on a ten-story building, looking down on complete mayhem. The open area was circular, with banners and flags waving every few feet. A celebration had obviously been interrupted, but by whom and for what reason I couldn't determine.

All I saw were crazy-mad people crying in crazy-loud voices about something I didn't understand.

A group of Thinkers stood in the middle of the fray, wearing bright-as-the-summer-sky blue robes, holding their hands out in the same placating gesture.

"What are they saying?" Gunn asked.

"I don't know." I listened, but the voices combined into a cacophony of anger and fear and desperation.

"Equal rights," a voice nearby said.

Both Gunn and I startled. A boy, not more than ten, stood on the roof about fifteen feet from us, surveying the madness below.

"Who are you?" Gunn asked, edging the tiniest bit closer to me.

"Stone," he said, still not looking at us. Like we didn't even matter.

"Equal rights?" I asked.

"Yeah, you know, like education and food and water and stuff."

"You don't have food and water and . . . stuff?" I asked. I liked this kid already.

"We used to. Everyone did. Everyone had the same stuff, actually. Same clothes, same rations, same houses. Now—" He finally turned to look at me, and I saw how sunken his cheeks were. "Now we don't."

"What happened?" Gunn gestured down to the open area. "What happened to make them act like that?"

"They woke up," Stone said.

Jag

19.

I don't want him here, I don't want him here, I don't want him here. I couldn't stop thinking it. Even when Vi smacked me in the chest and glared my face off.

Even when Pace gave me another dose of meds.

Even when "he" came over and said, "I can just go if you want."

"It's fine, Thane," I said. "I need the information you have."

"I reported two nights ago when I woke up."

"Sure, yeah, whatever. I need the information you have." I sat at the head of the war room table with only a small contingent surrounding me. Pace, Vi and Saffediene, and Gunn and Zenn, who needed to report on why they couldn't finish their objective in Lakehead.

My only consolation was that Indy had opted to stay back in the infirmary. I couldn't have handled her here too. I'd given her an assignment she was less than pleased with, but someone had to watch Thane while our plans moved forward, and I couldn't spare anyone else.

Her displeasure at my decisions reminded me so much of Vi.

"You've seen some of what I know already," Thane said, and I read between the lines. The cloning experiments. I nodded in unspoken acceptance. "I gave you everything else I know."

I swiveled in my chair. "Vi, if you would, please." I hated putting her in this position, but I couldn't read the joker's mind. I could, however, feel a massive vein of deceit flowing through the room. Nearly all of it emanated from Thane.

And the rest?

Zenn. The guy held a secret, and no one was leaving here without me knowing what it was.

I tapped my foot against the chair leg, waiting for Vi to excavate the information I needed.

"He knows what Van's plan is," Vi replied.

"Which is?"

"He wants General Director," Thane said stiffly, cutting a tight look at his daughter. She returned it in force. Ah, how I loved her.

"Keep talking," I said.

"I maintained Rise Twelve, as per Resistance instructions," he said. "Starr Messenger was supposed to take over, and she's a fighter. I left her a file that was only to be opened if I didn't return. I can only assume she gave it to Mason Isaacs when he was appointed Director of Twelve."

"And what was in the file?" I asked.

"Instructions for how to arm the Citizens of Twelve. How to bring in the Insiders. I knew that if I disappeared, Van would know I'd double-crossed him. He'd start with the Insiders. Van's biggest problem is his craving for power. He cannot tolerate people disobeying him."

"Hmm," I said. "Sounds like a common thread among Thinkers." I steepled my fingers under my chin, ignoring the pull of skin on my back. After two days of rest, my head and thigh were almost healed. But my back . . . Ouch. Pace had used sealant last night to keep two of the wounds together.

"We know he wiped out the Insider hideouts," Zenn said. "What's his next move?"

Thane looked at Zenn, and his jaw unclenched. I watched their exchange with interest. They both had a cache, they both served both sides, they both didn't have my trust. For all I knew, they'd been working together—against me—for years.

"You're in a room full of people," I reminded them. "Speak out loud. General Director Darke is in Freedom. What do you know about that, Thane?"

Zenn slid a piece of paper from my own notebook toward me in response. I didn't look at it.

"Van is looking for a replacement," Thane said. "And he didn't wipe out the Insiders, as I was telling Zenn. Isaacs was able to bring most of them in. The casualties were very low."

"Define low," Zenn said, clearly agitated.

"Less than two dozen." Thane delivered this news with calculated coolness. Typical Thinker. No emotional attachments.

I suppose I was just like them. "How do you know all this?" I caught Gunn's eye, and he nodded. The information so far had matched everything Starr had been caching us.

"I have talents too," Thane said. He didn't even blink. I knew his talents all too well. Voice and mind. A lethal combination.

"No," Vi whispered, but it sounded like a shout. She shook her head, looking from Thane, to me, to Zenn. "No."

"What?" I asked.

"No," she said again, more forcefully now.

"Violet," Thane said.

"Tell me," I commanded.

"Van Hightower is looking for his replacement," Thane said. "He believes his appointment as General Director is coming soon."

"And?" I prompted.

"He wants Zenn," Vi said, anguished.

I looked down at the paper Zenn had passed me. The note read, *Should I say yes?*

Voices broke out, but I sat silent, staring at Zenn's message. He sat silently too. When he caught my eye, he jerked his head toward the closest hallway. I stood up and followed him into the tunnel.

"Well?" Zenn asked.

I folded my arms. "What aren't you telling me?"

He held my gaze, unflinching. Classic Insider. But the pause before he spoke told me everything.

"I don't trust you," I said. "And this is why."

Still no outward sign that Zenn was withholding information. But he was. He had to be.

"Should I say yes?" he asked, sidestepping my question.

I raised one shoulder in a shrug. "If you want. I don't care."

"Think how much I could do in Freedom as Director."

It was exactly what I was thinking.

Zenn cast a glance toward the argument still raging in the war room. "Will it help Vi?"

"Vi doesn't need your help," I said. "She's safe with me." I said it to hurt him, and even cool-cat Zenn couldn't hide the pain/fury/anguish fast enough. I saw it. I saw it all.

It hurt me to hurt him. We used to be best friends once, united in our zeal to take down the Association. I'd fought from the outside, and he'd crippled them from the inside. My barricades softened, just for a second, but it was enough.

"I'm sorry," I said. "I shouldn't have said that."

"I would change so many things," Zenn said. "Starting with you and Blaze."

I cleared my throat, trying to scrape back my tears. I nodded.

Zenn copied me, and actually brushed his hand across his eyes.

"It's your decision," I said. "I'll support it." Then I returned to the war room, kissing Vi before I sat down.

I still didn't trust Zenn. A few tears and a couple of nice words didn't buy confidence.

"Zenn will choose," I said, effectively ending the discussion/argument/shout-fest. "Thane, what else?"

"Everything should be set inside the city," he said. "We've

still got Starr Messenger and Trek Whiting who are Informant. I believe Gunner's been receiving their reports."

Gunn nodded. "When I'm gone, Saffediene's been picking up the chats."

"Yes," Saffediene said. "But I'd like to request to be on the traveling team."

"Gunn?" I asked.

"She can have my spot." He looked down the hall. "I'd like to stay. . . . Starr likes to deal directly with me."

"Right," Zenn said, having rejoined the group. "I think Raine likes to deal directly with you."

I laughed with everyone else. In response Gunner handed his dad's journal to Zenn. "She does, actually. Can you be in charge of this?"

"When he goes into Freedom, I'll take it," I said.

Zenn fingered the leather-bound book, his eyes taking on a far-off quality. "*If* I go."

But I knew he'd go. Zenn wanted to matter. He always had—and what better way to matter than to hold an important government position? He'd definitely be going. It was just a matter of when.

Vi put her hand on Zenn's arm, and my stomach flipped. I didn't want her touching him, even if they were just friends.

"How's the tech, Pace?" I asked to distract myself, but I found it impossible. Vi's hand remained on Zenn's arm, and I couldn't look away.

"Coming along," he said. "We got some good stuff in Freedom, and I've been tinkering. We'll have what we need in a couple of weeks."

"Which works out well with the traveling schedule," Zenn said. "Last I checked, we still had six cities to visit."

"Maybe seven," Saffediene noted. "I don't think all the objectives were completed in Lakehead."

"True," Gunner said. "The city was in lockdown. We managed to upload the software and start the false feeds, and that's all. But those are the important things. The last objective came from the journal and doesn't have to be complete in order to launch the attack on Freedom."

"Will we have support in Lakehead?" I asked. "Will they send people?"

"Yes," Zenn said, too loud. He and Gunn wouldn't look at each other, or at me.

And there it was. The thing Zenn wanted to hide from me. No matter. I'd get it out of Gunn after Zenn left with Saffediene. They'd have another mission coming up soon, probably tonight.

"Next mission?" I asked.

"Cedar Hills," Saffediene replied automatically. "Zenn and I leave in a couple of hours."

"Fantastic," I said, almost smiling. "Let's go over assignments. Pace will run communication with all the cities we already have on board, letting them know our schedule. He'll also be equipping us all with defensive tech."

"You got it, bro," Pace said.

"Zenn and Saffediene will finish visiting the cities and compile the travelogue. We'll also need a list of supplies each city can contribute, and how many people they estimate sending."

Saffediene nodded, typing something into her e-board. Zenn watched me, his expression unreadable.

"Gunn and Raine will be in charge of maintaining contact with Starr to stay updated with events inside Freedom. Oh, and Zenn, you know Mason Isaacs and have a cache. Can you contact him before you leave this afternoon?"

As soon as the words left my mouth, I couldn't believe I'd *asked* him. I didn't ask anyone anything. I assigned. Zenn waved his hand in agreement.

I surveyed my group. "Excellent. Adjourned."

"Wait," Thane said. He'd been silent so long, I was happy to have forgotten about him.

"What?" I snapped.

"I just received a chat from Van Hightower."

Zenn

20.

"Impossible," I said, too quietly for anyone to hear. If Thane had indeed received an e-comm from Director Hightower, the Director would have to be close-by.

Very close-by.

Way too close.

Instead of questioning Thane, Jag simply hit a button, which caused a strobing blue light to fill the cavern. He began issuing orders: "Pace, get all the tech. Tell Indy to help you. Vi, stay next to me, see what you can find, and don't hold anything back." He spun, his eyes wild, but his voice calm. "Saffediene, Zenn, go to Cedar Hills. Gunn, get Raine and start evacuations. Don't leave any sensitive material lying around!"

People emerged from the doorways lining the war room, most of them in time to hear the end of Jag's directive.

Panic hung in the air, but no one acted irrationally. Saffediene linked her arm through mine. "I need to go to my room first!" she shouted over the many footsteps and voices surrounding us.

"Let's hurry," I said, a vein of fear snaking through me. Director Hightower would love to get inside my head if he could. I'd been branded a traitor because of my Informant activity, but my file in the Association listed me as rehabilitatable. I hadn't decided if I wanted to pretend to go through that. I didn't know if I could pull off such an act convincingly.

In her room Saffediene shoved her extra clothes and the contents of one drawer into her backpack before declaring she was ready. She followed me to my room where I did the same, leaving everything but my clothes, a blanket, and four memory chips I'd taken from Freedom.

They contained all my fondest thoughts of Vi. Things from the Goodgrounds before we'd left. Lucid moments in Freedom. My father had also sent a chip—an old, out-of-date model compared to the tech in Freedom—filled with vids of me as a child, my brother, our family.

I tucked the chips into my pocket and joined Saffediene in the hall. The blue light danced off the dark walls, washing her pale features in an eerie glow. She gripped my hand, her tension evident in her touch.

"This way." She tugged me away from the only entrance—and thus, the only exit—and toward the mess hall.

"What—?"

"Emergency exit," she said. Two guys from Indy's team were filling packs with canned food. They didn't look up as we passed. Part of me wished I could've at least said good-bye to Vi. Part of me wanted to march out the front entrance and confront Director Hightower. All of me was desperate to get away.

But as we entered a square opening I could barely fold my shoulders through, all I could think was, *This place had another way out and I didn't know?*

We flew south, away from the cavern, expecting the Director would approach from the north, from Freedom. Saffediene wanted to talk, and I let her.

"I wonder how Hightower found us," she mused. "I mean, we've been so careful. Flying in from different directions, meeting Starr in random sectors. And we're over a hundred miles from the border of Freedom. The orchards are a huge buffer as it is. . . ."

On and on she went. I grunted every now and then. Just thinking about how Director Hightower had discovered the hideout made me tired. Everything Saffediene said made sense though. I couldn't help but wonder if someone inside our ranks had narced.

Insider Tip #7: Suspect everyone. Trust no one. When things go wrong, assume someone has tipped off the enemy.

See, that's what Insiders do. We provide information to both sides. But as far as I knew, I was the only Insider at the cavern.

"Besides Thane," I said out loud.

Saffediene didn't miss a beat. "I suspect him too," she said. "Funny how Hightower shows up at our hideout within days of Thane's arrival, after we've been safe there for months."

She hadn't been there for months, but Pace and a small contingency had. And no one had been the wiser—not even me. At least until Thane had brought me outside the barrier a couple of months ago. We'd been sneaking tech and med supplies to the safe house during our "training sessions."

"Do you think Director Hightower put a tracker on him?" I asked. "Why didn't we check that?"

"Pace checked when we returned, remember? Thane was clean."

In my concern for Jag, I'd zoned out most of what had happened after we'd returned. "Okay, so there's me, and there's Thane," I said, ravenous to know who'd told the Director about our hideout.

"I used to live in Freedom," she said. "And Raine. And Gunn. Do they have special implants? Ways to track them?"

"I'm sure Raine does," I said. "She's the Director's daughter."

"Vi was probably marked in some special way too," she said. "Hightower went to great lengths to retrieve her."

I shuddered at the casual way Saffediene said "retrieve her" like Vi was a possession that could be lost and found. Saffediene had grown up that way, but still. Thinking freely for almost a year should've humanized her vocabulary.

Part of me liked that she didn't mince words though. She moved her board closer to mine. "Do you think Vi is carrying something unknowingly?"

"Anyone could be," I said. "Me, you, her. I guess it doesn't matter."

"Unless you think someone did it on purpose."

In my mind, images flashed with fire. The Association's vids had blamed the destructive fires on the Resistance. *They did it on purpose* mingled with the roar of flames in my head. I found myself contemplating that vid more and more. I'd always believed it to be false—and I still did. I wished I knew which side was telling the truth, though. Because I'd lied. All Insiders lie.

Pics of the Resistance members flashed on my vision-screen. I dismissed each as it came up.

Jag? Definitely not.

Vi? No way.

Gunn, Raine, Saffediene, Indy, Pace? None of them.

Someone still living inside Freedom?

Trek Whiting? Hell would freeze first.

Starr Messenger? The sun would have to go black.

Based on what I knew about the people I'd been living with, none of them would betray the Resistance—or Jag—by blabbing to Director Hightower.

The only picture left was mine. A sudden, terrible thought struck me.

Could Director Hightower have come to claim me?

And even more horrifying: *Do I want him to?*

Our detour added three hours to the trip to Cedar Hills, which sat just south of a dead border in the foothills of an unnamed mountain range. I'd always wondered what had happened to the country on the other side of the border, but I'd never asked.

They'd likely died in the Great War or the subsequent fires, or the years of darkness and sickness and starvation that followed. Three out of every four people had died then, allowing the Thinkers an almost too-easy road to domination.

"Zenn?" Saffediene asked from beside me. We'd both settled onto our boards for the long flight. I sat, my legs dangling over the edges of my board in an attempt to enhance circulation. She sat, her knees tucked to her chest.

"Yeah?"

"Why do you always call Van 'Director Hightower'?"

My brain buzzed. "Do I?"

"Yes," she said. "You do."

I scanned the horizon, as if it would hold the answer. "I don't know."

She hummed in her throat and didn't say anything more, but in my head I heard, *Maybe you hold him in higher regard than you thought.*

And maybe I did.

Cedar Hills sat in complete blackout. The only reason I saw it was because it sucked in the light from the surrounding land. It was a void. Or a whole city trying to hide. From who or what, I couldn't guess. The Association. Us. I had a hard time deciphering between the two at this point.

Saffediene led the way to the ground, and I touched down next to her in silence. I set about making a camp while she pulled blankets and extra clothes from the packs. I shivered and pulled on a second shirt and another sweater to ward off the chill.

We wrapped ourselves in blankets, and I asked her what she wanted to eat. After generating a bowl of steaming chicken chili for her, I ordered myself a stack of toast. The darkness and silence settled around us in thick layers.

"We'll try first thing in the morning," she said. "Maybe they've got the lights out to conserve energy."

"I don't believe that," I said.

"Me neither, but I'm too tired to think about the real reason why." She laid her head on my shoulder, and I gently lowered both of us to the ground. With her wrapped in her blanket and me in mine, sleep swallowed us whole.

When I woke up, the space beside me radiated a chill.

Saffediene was gone.

Both of our backpacks were gone.

Even my hoverboard was gone.

Jag

21.

I blamed the evacuation on Thane. That solved all my problems. I already disliked him. And then I wouldn't have to think about or deal with one of my own team betraying me.

We had enough hoverboards for everyone in the cavern except Indy and her team, who had arrived by transport. Our escape would not be fast or easy. The transport had been parked several miles to the southeast, hidden in a grove of trees. I sent Indy and her assistant, Lex, to retrieve it.

By the time they returned, the food was packed. Pace had the tech boxed up. Extra clothes and blankets had been bagged. Everything went through the emergency exit and into the transport.

I put Indy's people in with the supplies and sent them off. "Vi, anything?"

"Thane definitely got a comm from Van, but I don't sense the Director anywhere near here."

I turned to Thane. "Could it have been a repeat? Sent earlier and you're just now getting it?"

"You've asked me that four times. The answer is still no." Thane alone seemed undisturbed by the flashing blue light and the flurry of activity surrounding him.

"Gunn and Raine, you're on deck. Fly west. Meet up in Grande."

"You got it, boss," Gunn said, guiding Raine through the emergency exit first.

Five minutes later I sent Thane out into the wild with Indy and Pace with strict instructions for them to watch him closely. Pace saluted, but Indy glared. Vi and I were the only ones left in the cavern. I deactivated the alarm and stood in the shadows, waiting.

"I don't think he's here," Vi said. "Honestly, I don't."

"Do you think he knows where this place is?"

"Possibly." Her tension indicated that she had more to say, and that I wouldn't like it.

"Then we can't stay here," I said.

"Raine should be scanned again."

My arms felt heavy as I raised them to stretch. Exhaustion clung to me. Sleepless nights kept Vi from entering my nightmares, but I was paying the price. "Anyone who's been inside city limits should be scanned again," I said.

I motioned to her hoverboard. "After you. Use the solar portlet until the sun goes down."

She climbed out, and I followed. I unfolded my board and set our course more toward the west than the south. Vi brought her board close and took my hand in hers. This simple touch ignited a fire in my blood.

We flew side by side, hand in hand, until the sun went down.

With true night closing in, I needed to find somewhere safe to spend the night. I touched down near a couple of trees, thinking we could use them for shelter. This excursion reminded me of the morning Vi and I had found refuge in an old shack in the Fire Region of the Goodgrounds.

I wondered if she remembered. What had been taken from her? I knew her memories of me were limited at best.

"I remember," she said, landing behind me. "I remember everything now."

"Nice," I whispered, pulling her close. Her blue-green eyes were two bright spots against the reigning blackness.

She closed her eyes and kissed me. White noise filled my ears. I couldn't bring her close enough. She couldn't hold me tight enough, despite the twinges of pain from the healing skin on my back.

A low sound came from her throat, one I took to mean *I love you, Jag Barque*. I matched the moan, our mouths moving in sync. I would never tire of her lips, but I slid mine over her neck and toward her ear. She pressed closer in response.

The thin barrier of clothing between us was too thick. Vi's skin felt searing hot.

"Jag," she breathed, but it wasn't her usual *We have to stop*. It was more like *I want you to kiss me forever*.

I was more than happy to oblige. Her hands slid over my shoulders and tenderly down my healing back, along the waistband of my jeans. My fingers tangled in her hair, and then pushed the collar of her shirt to the side, revealing her milky white shoulder. I kissed her there, desperate to hear her approval.

She gave it in a single word. "Jag."

I wanted her to say my name again and again in that throaty, pleasure-filled voice. I didn't expect what came next.

"Stop."

I didn't. I couldn't. Or wouldn't. They were the same.

"Stop." This time her throatiness was replaced with urgency.

I stopped.

"We're not alone," she whispered, hastily adjusting her shirt with one hand as she clung to me, looking over my shoulder into utter blackness.

Zenn

22.

"I am alone," I said out loud, to myself, and the words disappeared into the endless sky, confirming their reality.

Jag

23.

We're not alone. Vi's voice sounded in my head this time, spiking the panic already welling in my gut.

Zenn

24.

I took three steps toward Cedar Hills and called Saffediene's name. I changed direction and repeated this procedure until I'd gone in a complete circle. I reached out with my mind, desperate to find her lurking just over the hill.

She wasn't. The closest person I could find was collecting water from a well outside the border.

A squeal pierced my ears and my left hand flew to my left ear to deactivate the cache. While it shut down and restarted, I recalled the basics of the mission to Cedar Hills.

Enter through the friendly northern border and proceed to

Greenhouse Eighty. Cedar Hills was in the business of preserving and classifying species of flowers, trees, shrubs, and herbs.

The flora was then transported to other cities for the repopulation of the country's greenery. Greenhouses covered the entire northern half of the city and nearly every Citizen of Cedar Hills worked in them.

According to Gunn's dad, Greenhouse Eighty was run by Insiders. Meetings were held there, beneath vines and aspens. The foliage and soil of the outgoing plants contained coded messages.

The sun beat down on me, but I clung to my thin blanket, the only thing I had to my name at this point. As my cache came online, a red band flickered across my vision-screen, indicating I had unread messages.

I blinked, pulling up my comms. I had two from Saffediene, both flagged as urgent.

The first read, *Zenn, I couldn't sleep and heard people talking. I went to investigate and got caught.*

Heard people talking? I thought. *Out here?*

The second message read, *Zenn, I'm inside Cedar Hills. The Greenhouse is secure. Make your way here as soon as you can. Sorry they took your hoverboard. You'll have to walk.*

I knew immediately that the second e-comm wasn't from Saffediene. Number one, she would never mention the

Greenhouse in something as traceable as an e-comm. Number two, she knew I didn't need a hoverboard to fly.

I dropped to a crouch, taking refuge in the tall grass while I thought. If the second message wasn't from Saffediene, maybe the first wasn't either. Sneaking off in the dead of night to eavesdrop sort of sounded like her, but at the same time it didn't. Why wouldn't she wake me to go with her?

On the other hand, if someone had taken her while we were asleep, why did they leave me? With a blanket and nothing else?

Nothing made sense. I stood up and walked straight toward the border—and the person still loitering at the well. As far as I was concerned, the plan had changed.

The boy lingered near the well, his job already done. A wet patch of dirt to his left showed where the well had been leaking. He'd likely been sent to repair the couplings or adjust the connections.

I couldn't tell his height, crouched as he was, drawing in the dirt with a stick—a behavior that alerted me to his heightened thinking skills. The brainwashed don't dawdle in their tasks, and they certainly don't create art.

He wore the traditional clothing for a Cedar Hills Citizen:

white long-sleeved shirt, brown cotton pants, a pair of rubber shoes, and a hat that blocked the morning sun.

His milky-colored fingers snuck out of the pool of shade created by his hat as he directed the stick this way and that. The boy seemed unconcerned that the gate lay a mere hundred yards away, and anyone could observe him breaking the rules.

I searched his mind and found his worries were few. That, or he'd learned to hide thoughts he didn't want anyone to read.

"Hello," I said in my most placating voice.

Instead of startling to a stand as I expected, the boy simply looked over his shoulder. "Hello." He continued to draw.

"I'm Zenn Bower," I said, advancing with deliberate steps. "I need to get inside your city." I quickly catalogued all sensitive information and filed it away in the furthermost parts of my mind. Half of me thought he could probably read my every thought, and the other half wondered if he was mentally slow.

The boy stood up, dropping the stick on the ground. He brushed his hands on his pants, obliterating the picture in the dirt as he shuffled his feet. At his full height, I could see he was no boy. In fact he was probably a fair bit older than me.

"Can I get through the gate with you?" I asked, willing him to say yes.

"Yes," he said in a hauntingly low tone. A brainwashed tone.

"Perfect," I said. "Tell me your name."

"Greene Leavitt."

My pulse jumped. Greene's name was listed in the journal. "How old are you?"

"Twenty." His answers came quick and sure. He stared at me—no, almost *through* me. I couldn't tell the color of his eyes because of the shade of his hat.

"Why are you out here alone?"

"I was waiting."

"For what?"

His shadowed eyes shifted, then found mine and held them. "For you."

I took an extra breath before continuing. "Well, you found me. Let's go."

Entering Cedar Hills turned out to be crazy-easy. With Greene by my side, I simply walked through the gate and into a world of glass houses. The very air seemed to be holding its breath. The streets were paved with packed dirt, barely wide enough for Greene and me to walk side by side between the Greenhouses.

Freedom had maintenance crews to clean every surface to a silver gleam, but here, a white film clung to the metal frames. A metallic square with a number hung from the top of each door. The Greenhouse in front of me bore the number thirty-nine. The soft sound of sprinkling water added to the peacefulness of the city.

"Are you ready, Zenn Bower?" Greene asked, tearing my attention from the decor. The way he spoke my name sent tremors down my spine.

"Yes," I said. "But first I need to find another friend of mine. Maybe you've seen her? Saffediene Brown?"

Greene suddenly turned down another narrow path between two Greenhouses. I followed him just as plodding footsteps approached from a direction I couldn't place. The sounds echoed between the metal and glass, making it impossible to pinpoint.

Greene strode away, his narrow shoulders brushing the glass of the flanking Greenhouses.

He ducked into Greenhouse Sixty-Four (how had we gone from Thirty-Nine to Sixty-Four?), casting a cursory glance at me as he did. Inside, the smell of soft roots and wet dirt hit me like a punch. I'd never seen so much disorder. Little shovels lay in a metal tray by the door. Muddy boots and coils of hose festered in heaps under the metal tables holding flower after bush after tree.

I'd only been in two Greenhouses, both of them on the roof of Rise Twelve. Neither of them looked like this. There, plants were laid in neat rows, organized by height. This seemed like someone had held a giant handful of seeds and simply dropped them. Wherever they landed, they grew.

Utter chaos, this gardening in Cedar Hills.

Greene stood a few feet down the first row, his back to me. The stillness of his body and the way he hardly spoke set my nerves on edge. And I was used to being the cool one.

"Eighty-Nine is one rung north," he said, turning to face me. "Then go west until you get to Eighty. It'll be on the left." He removed his hat and wiped his forehead. "I believe Saffediene is there."

I nodded, unable to look away from his face. Or his scalp, which was almost blindingly white and utterly hairless. His milky skin couldn't hold pigment if it tried. His eyes, a strange shade of pink, dared me to say something.

"Who are you?" I asked, wondering how his name had landed in the journal.

"I am a rescuer," he replied. "Your friend shouldn't have gone snooping."

Worry caused a sharp snag in my airway. "Is she okay?"

"Minds had to be tampered with," he said. "And that takes talent and energy, neither of which we have much of here in Cedar Hills."

"Is she okay?" I repeated, disturbed by his oh-so-white

eyebrows and color-of-cream complexion. And the way he held so deathly still.

"She is waiting for you in Eighty," he asserted, as if that answered my question. "I must get back to the city center, Zenn Bower." With that, he snapped his fingers and disappeared without a sound.

I hadn't seen a ring on his albino fingers, so either Greene Leavitt was tampering with my mind, causing me to think he'd turned invisible, or he had access to tech that didn't need to be contained in an object to be used.

I chose to go with the tech. Maybe he was like Vi and could control it somehow. I took a deep, cleansing breath and immediately regretted it. Dirt and rot and dung didn't exactly make breathing pleasant.

Outside Greenhouse Sixty-Four, all was quiet. A wind blew across my face, hot and lazy. I stroked it with two fingers, whispering for it bring me a cooler draft. Wind shouldn't be hot.

A moment later, the current dragging across my skin turned cold, almost icy. "Perfect," I murmured. "Now mask any sound I might make."

With the wind as my ally, I crept toward Greenhouse Eighty.

Jag

25.

I twisted to protect Vi by shielding her with my body and shoved her backward when the screaming started. My ears rang with the sound's depth of pain, even after it stopped.

A flare of light ignited behind me. I turned to find that Vi was on fire, literally. She'd somehow made her entire hand glow with unnatural flames. I stared at her fist, unable to tear my gaze from her pristine skin that wasn't really burning.

She marched away from me, leaving me in the dark, stunned. I scrambled to follow and immediately wished I hadn't when the scent of blood hit me. The terrible, cloying

smell told me there was a lot of blood. Vi's hand-torch illuminated a body, and I had to force myself to take the last few
steps to join her.

The body breathed, the chest rising and falling in ragged
gasps. The body wore jeans, but its shirt had been clawed to
ribbons. Blood seeped from its wounded flesh.

The body twitched, causing a wet squelching sound to
shatter the quiet.

I closed my eyes for fear of throwing up when I looked at
the face. Or what was left of it.

"Vi," I said weakly. I doubled over, pressing my eyes closed
to block out the sight of all that blood.

"A scout," she said in a distant tone. "There will be another
one. They travel in twos."

I opened my eyes and straightened as Vi searched the
darkness by the light of her freaky burning hand. I thought
for a second I might be hallucinating, because this situation
was too surreal. Vi didn't hurt people. She didn't make them
hurt themselves.

In the strange light Vi's face caught the shadows and
trapped them. She looked fierce. Dangerous.

Deadly.

"Violet," I said, a pleading note in my voice now.

She didn't spare me a glance, but strode over to our

hoverboards. I hadn't taken three steps when more screaming shattered the darkness.

Vi darted behind a tree, haloing the branches with her mind-induced light. She looked perfectly calm, pressed into the trunk, waiting for the shrieking to stop. I covered my ears until I couldn't hear anything, and then I approached Vi slowly, as if she were a vicious animal I might spook.

And she was.

She stood so straight it must've hurt. Her fist burned. Waves of energy practically poured from her body.

I maintained a healthy distance between us and didn't look at the body lying a few feet away. I felt certain that if I did, I'd never be able to close my eyes without seeing—

"Violet, please." I didn't want to believe that Vi had entered the minds of the scouts and made them kill themselves. But she had, and I knew she had. "Violet?" I asked now.

"He's already sent a preliminary report," she said coldly. "Four teams are on their way to this location. We need to leave. Now." She went to retrieve our boards and backpacks.

Then she tugged gently on my hand, which hung lifelessly at my side. I couldn't move.

"Come on." She spoke softly, like she was talking to a child.

I stepped onto my waiting hoverboard, unable to command it to operate.

Didn't matter. Vi could control the board. She could control anything.

The two dead men lying on the ground were a testament to that.

Nightmares looped through my alert mind. First the one where I was buried in the capsule. The sound of dirt pinging against metal: I would never forget that sound. I jerked to attention and listened.

Nothing.

No pebbles landing above me. No hiss as oxygen forced its way into the confined space.

I settled back into the lulling vibrations of my hoverboard and immediately saw Vi use her mind control to torture people. Suddenly I had a horrifying thought.

What if I hadn't been buried alive? What if the Thinkers had just made me *think* I was? The way Vi made those two scouts think their own flesh needed to be peeled from their bones?

I closed my eyes against the memories. I couldn't decide which was worse: being buried alive for real, or the mental violation if I hadn't.

For the longest time I felt nothing from Vi. She existed inside her own sphere of reality, and I managed to keep breathing in mine. Perhaps I was simply too wrapped up in my own troubles, because the next thing I knew, Vi was sobbing. I couldn't hear her, but I was aware of her pain as if it were my own. A wave of her grief/regret/guilt/horror flattened me, physically pushing me onto my back on my hoverboard.

I had no idea what to say to make this better. Instead I flew in close to her. She cried into my chest. "Tether," I whispered, and her board attached to mine. I wrapped my arms around Vi in an effort to protect her from herself.

We touched down when the night breathed out the last of its darkness and the sky held the first hint of day. Vi had used her technopathic abilities to keep the boards flying. She'd stopped crying hours ago, but she hadn't moved. Hadn't spoken.

Hadn't explained.

I drank half a bottle of water from my backpack and made Vi drink the rest. My eyelids felt impossibly heavy, my body still vibrating from riding the hoverboard all night. But I wouldn't sleep.

I couldn't. Every time I blinked, I saw that body. And every time I saw that body, I wondered what Vi had made them see to cause them to shred their own skin.

Vi and I lay beside one another, each covered in separate

blankets. I stared into the empty sky, wondering which star would have to explode to annihilate the earth. Maybe dying would be better than trying to fight this war, than watching Vi use her mind control in ways she despised. If I didn't keep my thoughts busy, they returned to the body haloed in light from my girlfriend's burning hand.

The problem was, every thought I had only added to the guilt I constantly carried. Blaze's disappearance. Zenn's defection. My parents' deaths. Leaving Vi. Getting buried alive.

Watching Vi torture—

I cut off the thought, only to repeat the circuit of damaging memories.

"Tell me something happy," I said to break the cycle. The heaviness of dawn hung over us, and I couldn't stand this silence for another second.

Vi emitted a tiny sigh of frustration. "I can't," she said. "I don't have many happy stories."

"Then tell me what you're thinking."

"I can't," she said again.

"Why are you so relieved?" I asked, hoping she'd punch me for reading her emotions. At least then I'd know she was back to her normal self.

"I'm relieved that you're still talking to me," she said.

"After . . . after I lost control." Her breath shuddered through her throat when she inhaled. "I'm so tired, and my emotions were all out of whack because of, you know, you kissing me like that. That scout, he would've killed us, no questions asked. He would've tased us both." She paused, but I didn't have a chance to say anything before she continued.

"I had to do something. So I just . . . let go. It was so easy, Jag. That's what scares me the most." She scooted closer and propped herself up so she could look at me properly. "It was so easy."

Tears traced paths down her face, leaving clean tracks through the grime.

"That's the hard part," I said, wanting to touch her but not daring. "It's not about doing what's easy. It's about doing what's right."

She nodded. "I know. I know I shouldn't have. . . . But he would've killed us."

"I know," I said. "Sometimes we have to do things we don't like." No one knew the truth of those words more than me.

She laid her head on my chest. I held her tight, trying to erase this new awkwardness between us with simple pressure.

"Do you hate me?" she asked, her voice close to cracking.

"Of course not, babe." It was the first time I'd called her

that since we'd been reunited. And as Vi radiated gratitude, I knew I'd said the exact right thing at the exact right time.

"Where to next?" she asked.

"I have no idea," I answered. I closed my eyes and wished for sleep. Thankfully, my wish came true.

Ants scurry across my face. I scream, but no sound comes out. I've been silenced. I feel the tech on my throat as I swipe at the insects on my face and neck.

My ears. My arms.

They're everywhere. And not just ants. Flies, with their multifaceted eyes. Spiders. I can feel their eight legs. Dry, cool snakes slither up my torso. Along my arms and legs, sharp pinches burn with heat and venom as the spiders and ants and snakes bite me.

I yell and yell and yell, but am greeted with only the hum of insects.

I jerked awake, brushing my hand across my—thankfully—insect-free face. The air around me was filled with light.

I am not in that capsule. Those insects are not torturing me.

"I don't think they ever did," Vi said from beside me. "I think that was a mind trick." Her skin looked gray, her eye sockets sunken.

"Did you sleep?" I asked.

"No."

Guilt and relief cascaded through me. "How long have I been out?"

"It's okay to feel relieved. I wouldn't want someone living inside my nightmares either."

I shoved the blanket in my backpack. "That's not what I meant," I said. "I just—I don't want you to have—"

"You don't have to explain," Vi said. From the detachment in her face to the position of her body to the violet fire blazing in her eyes, everything screamed, *Be afraid!* "But you don't have to protect me either, Jag. I'm more than capable of taking care of myself."

"I've seen that," I said before I could think.

Her eyes narrowed. "You've seen what I wanted you to see."

I stood up, anger battling the fear that swelled in me. "Are you threatening me?"

She stood too, her movement fluid and graceful. I held my ground as she advanced. Adrenaline surged, making my blood race through my body. I hadn't felt this alive in a long time.

Vi marched up to me and put her hands on my chest. I tingled at her touch. She stretched up to kiss me on the mouth. I grasped her too tightly. I returned her kiss too roughly.

She laughed as she pulled away. "There you are," she said. The fire in her eyes had been replaced with her usual Thinker edge.

"There I am?" I asked. "What kind of freaky game was that?"

"You've been wallowing," she said.

"I—wallowing? I have not."

She cocked her head to the side. "I think I would know."

I shouldn't argue with that, but I said, "You don't *have* to invade my mind."

"Right. Like you don't *have* to feel my emotions."

I threw my head back and laughed, which felt foreign and freeing. "You win."

She let me kiss her again before she set about packing up her blanket. "But I do believe the insects were all an illusion." She said it casually, as if we were talking about the humidity.

"Why do you think that?" I kept my gaze on the horizon, noticing a blur in the blue.

"I couldn't enter your mind," she said. "All of the other times, I was you in the dream. I lived it through you." She swung her backpack on and shouldered her hoverboard. "This time, I could only watch. I don't think it was real."

I nodded, again wondering which was worse. The mental

violation, or actually being covered in writhing snakes and hairy spiders.

"I think someone's coming," I said, looking into the midday sun but seeing only bright light.

"Indiarina," Vi said, a definite bite of jealousy in all five syllables.

The shock surely showed on my face. "How do you know?"

Vi cast her eyes to the ground and then quickly back to mine. "I can sort of find people I'm connected to."

"You're connected to Indy?"

"No." She practically spat the word at me. "But I am connected to Thane, and he's with Indy. They'll be here in a few minutes."

"Nice," I said, but not thinking it was nice at all. I didn't want to have a close encounter with her father when my emotions were still spiraling.

"They found a safe house in Grande." She smiled, but it clashed with the true emotion riding beneath her calm exterior.

"What aren't you telling me?" I asked. She opened her mouth to lie about her nerves, but I cut her off. "I can feel it, Vi. You're anxious. Why?"

"Indy—"

"This has nothing to do with Indy." I tipped my head to the side, trying to get a better read on her wavering emotions. She was getting better at concealing them. Still, I tasted uncertainty, some fear, but mostly anxiety. Anxiety over the unknown. Anxiety over her—

"My mother is at that safe house."

Zenn

26.

I loitered in the Greenhouse across from Eighty, peering through the soil-stained glass at the door. It didn't move, even when I sent a southern breeze to knock on it. The windows were black, covered by plastic on the inside.

With my limited mind capabilities, I couldn't find anyone. Yet Greene had said Saffediene was there. I took a deep breath and moved to exit my hideout and enter Greenhouse Eighty.

I halted when two men who were just as tall as Greene, but twice as wide, advanced down the path toward me. I melted into the shadows of a towering tree, grateful that the disorganization of the Greenhouses could conceal me.

They paused outside Eighty, casting furtive glances down the path before they each raised one fisted hand and together rapped four times on the metal door. The thuds echoed across the path, shaking my bones.

Not half a heartbeat later the door swung open, and the two men disappeared inside. I coerced the wind to jam the door, but it settled shut despite the force of the elements.

With little choice left, I squared my shoulders and marched across the path. Using both my fists, I pounded four times on the door.

It immediately opened, revealing a tangle of vines amid the darkness. I slipped in, allowing the door to latch behind me.

I hadn't thought past getting into Greenhouse Eighty, and before I could take one step, four hands grasped me, two on each of my arms. My first reaction was fear, but anger wasn't far behind.

A rough voice spoke in my ear. "Who are you?"

"How'd you get here, outsider?" another asked.

"He knew the knock," someone else said.

"It wasn't hard," I said, trying to rip my arms away. "I just watched the door for ten seconds."

Someone punched me in the stomach. My knees gave out. I gasped. The two men holding my arms didn't loosen their grip. I hung there, trying to breathe, anger flowing through me like techtricity.

"Release me," I managed, my voice weak. Still, the grip on my right arm slipped.

I regained my feet. I straightened. "Let me go." This time my voice came out properly. They let me go.

"Where's Saffediene?" I asked. I wished this place had some lights.

A moment of silence was punctuated only by the shuffling of feet. I blinked, and a flicker of a match brightened the room. I thought I'd imagined it, but on the next strike, the fire caught. It illuminated someone's hand and cast orange patterns on their soil-crusted T-shirt.

They held the flame to a candle and passed it around the room until two dozen candles were lit and the space came to life. I glanced from face to face. There were twenty-four men and women in the room, all of them glaring at me. Saffediene wasn't among them.

"Fire?" I asked. "Really?"

"Fire requires neither tech nor ability," someone said. The words reminded me of Greene. So did the way they all stood perfectly still, not so much as a blink or twitch.

They obviously knew *Insider Tip #8: Don't fidget. It's a sign of nerves, which can indicate a lie.*

"Where's Saffediene?" I asked, trying a different tactic. "She and I are from Freedom, and we were told Eighty was on the inside track."

The woman across from me blinked, which I took as a sign that something I'd said held power. "We just received a return shipment from Freedom," she said. "Last week, wasn't it?"

"Yes," the man next to her said. "Two trees that didn't take to the weather."

"We need to examine those trees," I said. "Where are they?"

"What's your name?" the woman asked.

"Zenn Bower. Yours?"

"Min Holyoak." She flicked her eyes to the man next to her. "And Shade Rodriguez." They took their candles and turned to leave.

I followed them into a long corridor that had so many potted plants and trees and shrubs that I hardly had room to walk. The candle cast flickering light onto leaves and branches, which transformed into clawing fingers and shadowy hands.

"Your friend has already examined the trees," Shade said. "She found nothing."

"Impossible," I said. "The Insiders in Freedom wouldn't have returned the trees without sending a message with them." I'd seen Trek at work with his gadgets. He could code a portlet to malfunction at exactly the right moment. He could falsify any type of communication. He could change what his voice sounded like, could replicate intonation and personality.

He had a piece of tech for everything, and what he didn't have, he invented. He'd have done something with the trees. He must have.

We turned a corner, and the corridor opened up into a larger room. Long, silver counters ran in rows with spilled dirt and rusted gardening tools. The black plastic only covered the windows; natural light streamed down from skylights. But the plants here all looked to be in various stages of dying.

Saffediene sat on a counter in the middle of the room, her legs swinging, staring up through the glass ceiling.

"Saffediene." I pushed past Min and hurried toward her. She looked at me, moving in what seemed like slow motion. Dried tears crusted her face. I gathered her into my arms, automatically stroking her unbraided hair and soothing her with my voice.

She gripped my shirt, her body tense tense tense. She didn't cry. The embrace only lasted a few seconds before she pulled back.

"What happened?" I asked. "Are you okay?"

She nodded, taking both my hands in hers. "I'm sorry I left you. I—" She stopped. "I felt something weird."

"Felt something weird?" This statement from Saffediene didn't fit with her *goes-for-specific* personality.

She shook her head. "I know it doesn't make sense. I woke up to voices, and the city was glowing with light."

"Why didn't you wake me?"

"The two men talking? They said your name, and I knew if they found you, it would be bad. So I let them find me instead."

"So the e-comms," I said. "The first was from you. The second—"

"They forced me to send it. I knew you'd figure out it was a fake. The Insiders sent Greene Leavitt to find you, and Min and Shade sent a body double to act for me at the jury."

"She searched the trees," Shade said. "And found nothing."

"Show me, Saffediene," I said, without power or control but with a gentleness that surprised me. She released my hands, hopped off the table, and lifted two potted trees onto the counter. They had very few leaves and bark the color of slate. The soil lay in uneven mounds, as if she had sifted through it meticulously. That was the Saffediene I knew.

I ran my hands from the soil up the tree trunk. It felt cool and smooth. When I met the first branch, my fingers followed it, trying to feel something invisible. A leaf snapped off with a spark.

I jerked my eyes to Saffediene's. "Did you see that?"

Saffediene picked up the leaf. A wisp of smoke trailed out of the stem. She turned it over, examining the back of it.

"It's nothing," she said, handing it to me.

I ran my finger over the delicate veins, desperate to find something. Nothing, despite the spark I'd seen. It really was a leaf.

What am I missing?

What? What? What?

Only a handful of leaves remained on the tree. Impulsively I pinched them all off, sparks flying with each one.

As the last one fluttered to the countertop, a p-screen fizzled to life, the tech leaping and arcing from the detached leaves to form a viewing area the size of my palm. Trek's face flickered on it. "Message from Freedom: All feeds are being checked and double-checked by Director Hightower himself. Please update to the following frequency. Alpha kappa one five gamma row three."

The transmission ended; the screen dissipated.

"I don't believe it," Min whispered.

"When did you get this?" I asked.

"Five, maybe six days ago," Shade said.

"Code all outgoing plants," I told Min. "Employ all your runners and have the message out by tonight so everyone will know in the next two days." She nodded, waving at Shade.

"Saffediene and I will leave messages in the cities from here to the Southern Region."

"I'll inform Greene," Shade added, already retreating back down the corridor. Min hurried after him.

I looked at Saffediene, who was watching me with wide eyes. "What?"

"You reminded me of Jag right then. So authoritative."

"Let's fly," I said, ignoring her comment. "We've got loads of work to do."

Saffediene and I separated, and I flew east while she went west. We would cover the corridor from Cedar Hills down to the Southern Region. *Six days*, I thought. Director Hightower could've learned so much about the Resistance efforts in six long days.

I left a message in the correspondence tube outside Cave Pointe, and then flew south to Freedom. Just after noon I touched down on the northern border and opened my cache to Trek. *The birds fly north in winter.*

I waited, hoping Trek had received the message, and that he could come right away.

Twenty minutes later Trek appeared from behind the wall. He strode toward the techtric barrier without a backward glance. His eyes were bloodshot, his hair a tangled mess.

He scanned me the same way I was analyzing him. "You look awful," he said, his voice semimuted through the barrier. "You must not sleep either."

"Not much," I said. "We were in Cedar Hills and just got your message."

He cursed and shoved his hands in his pockets. "I knew we should've sent a message to the safe house. But after you guys took Thane, we weren't sure who'd be watched. And Starr couldn't risk another meeting with Gunn."

"We lost six days."

"Yeah, and it's six days we don't have. The General is preparing to leave in the morning." He smoothed a hand over his unshaved jaw. "Hightower has been checking the feeds from every city, and he found several false vids. That's how he located your safe house. The false feeds either come from my hub or from Pace's, and since he didn't get the message, Hightower found his fake routing info."

"So Director Hightower found the cavern because of the

false feeds we've been sending?" That settled in my stomach so much easier than a spy living in the hideout.

"Right. And the General is leaving for Castledale in the morning, as those feeds account for the majority of the false vids."

"Pace was doctoring all those."

"Right. And since no one received our message, we weren't able to bury the coordinates before they were found."

I exhaled. "Damn. Well, I've got the code going out through Cedar Hills's plant network. Everyone should know by tomorrow night."

"That won't help Castledale." Trek pinned me with a meaningful look.

"I'll go. What am I telling them?"

"General Darke is leaving in the morning. Our people will make sure his board will only have enough charge to get him to Arrow Falls, where he'll be forced to stop to recharge. That will buy you about eight hours. He's going to Castledale for a full status report. If you leave now, and fly nonstop, you'll have approximately eighteen hours to evacuate all Insiders, and Director Pederson will need to make his completely noncompliant city absolutely compliant. Otherwise . . ." Trek let the words hang there, and I knew what followed them.

General Darke would take over. Director Pederson would die—and so would anyone who exhibited qualities of non-compliance.

"I'll get them out," I said, the determination in my voice covering my fear at having to return to Castledale and my doubts that I could really get an entire city compliant in under twenty-four hours. "We had to evacuate our hot spot. I'm sure we'll find a place in the Southern Region."

"You have. City of Grande. Cache Laurel Woods when you get there."

"Laurel Woods?" The name tickled my memory. I had Gunn's journal in my backpack; maybe her name was listed inside and I'd read it over and over.

"Yeah, she runs an underground communication loop for the Resistance. She'll direct you."

I nodded, anxious to leave for Castledale, yet never wanting to touch down there again.

"Tell Jag that I've been promoted to the Transportation Rise, technology specialist," Trek said.

"Is Starr still in Twelve?"

"Yes, and she has free reign of the city. She's in Hightower's back pocket."

"How's she coping?"

"As well as can be expected. She plays both sides flawlessly." He grinned a sly smile that reminded me that Trek and Starr were together. "One more thing."

"Go," I said.

"Starr was going to cache this to Gunn on their next meeting, but now that the hideout is lost, I might as well tell you. Hightower has called for school to close at the end of the month. All students on Levels Three and Four have been moved into the Rises and begun professional training. That's why I'm in Transportation." He glanced over his shoulder. "Something major is going on. When will you guys be ready to launch the attack?"

Anxiety thrummed through my system. I wasn't Jag. I couldn't answer that question. "I don't know."

"What was the plan?"

"Two weeks, I think," I said. "The travel team had four more objectives to complete."

True fear skated through Trek's eyes. "I don't think we have two weeks." He spoke so softly, I had to read his lips to understand.

"I'll see what I can do." I turned, ready to get out of there.

"Zenn," Trek said. "Be careful with the elements. Hightower has ordered the Directors in Arrow Falls and Allentown to make special note of anything unusual in the climate. There's a backpack of supplies at the usual spot outside Castledale. It has a generator cube for you."

"Great. Anything else?"

"We can relay additional instructions through Laurel. We're wasting time. You'll need every minute in Castledale."

"Right." But I knew he could've said more. "Thanks," I said, before stepping onto my half-charged hoverboard and setting my sights to the west.

Trek's information wouldn't settle into silence. Director Hightower had moved fourteens and fifteens into professions already. If he was closing school at the end of March, he'd have a damn good reason.

Besides a complete annihilation of the Resistance, what could he be planning? I thought briefly of the premier Rises— Medical, Technology, and Evolutionary. Could he have had a medical breakthrough? Manufactured some horrific disease that would kill us all?

Or maybe he'd created a piece of tech that could . . . I didn't even know. Had he managed to complete a successful batch of clones?

My heart thundered as I turned to watch the glow of Freedom fade. Part of me wanted to go back and take my place as Van Hightower's replacement. The other part longed to see that city burn to the ground.

The problem was, in my mind, both parts were equal.

Jag

27.

Thane touched down two seconds before Indy, whose expression said *I could kill you with my bare hands*. I may or may not have taken a step behind Vi.

"Status," I said.

Indy pressed her lips into a thin line. Vi slipped her hand into mine and squeezed. Thane catalogued the movement and mirrored his mouth to match Indy's.

"Oh, brother," I growled. "Vi and I are together. Deal or don't. But you better damn well report."

Indy folded her arms. "Our people are secure in Grande.

Laurel is organizing her moles. Everyone will be instructed to meet in Grande or Beachfront."

I nodded, switching my gaze to Thane. "What do you have?"

"Nothing. I didn't want to stay there without my daughter."

I almost laughed. "What a load of crap. I know you're hiding something." I squinted at him, wishing I could see inside his head. We still needed to discuss the microchip Starr had sent with Gunn, but I didn't want to do it in front of Vi.

"I am not hiding anything," Thane said. "I've been relaying everything I've done and everything I know to the appropriate contact."

Which wasn't me. It could never be me. I hated that, but Thane and I couldn't work together. In fact it was my rule, one of the very first I'd made.

But now everything had changed.

"I am your appropriate contact from now on," I said. "Neither one of us is in hiding anymore."

"Noted," he said, his tone cool and his hands fisted.

I turned my attention back to Indy. "What else? Why did you really fly all this way? You knew we'd show up at the safe house soon enough."

Indy held her ground, which I'll admit I admired about her. "Well, there's another tiny snag."

"Tiny snag?" I asked. "Define 'tiny snag.'"

"Grande is surrounded by Van Hightower's people. Thane and I were on watch, which is why we're not at the safe house."

"Hightower's people," Vi repeated. "What kind of people?"

"Clones," Indy said.

My blood ran cold. A high-pitched squealing started in my ears. The images of all that purple, of those fetuses, of Cash Whiting, filled my head.

They'd done it. They'd finally cloned a superhuman, even without Cash's notes. In my stupor, I wondered if the clones could control the elements, or if they could read minds, or command people with ultrapowerful voices, or all of the above.

My Resistance cannot survive against an army of super-humans, no matter how talented we are. I thought of Starr. Her last convo with Gunn had been a few days before, and she'd been so concerned with Raine draining Thane.

Starr said she'd warn us, but maybe she didn't know. Around me, the earth moved in slow motion. *Clones, purple, Cash, clones, can't win, Starr, purple.*

"Jag?" Vi's hand on mine jolted me out of my fear.

"What's their talent?" I asked.

"We don't know," Thane said. "Those clones were not made while I was in Freedom."

"Three weeks is awfully fast to manufacture an entire fleet of clones," I said, the feeling returning to my limbs. Cash had said thirty days. Starr's destroyed microchip wasn't even that old.

"Van's been on the brink for a long time," Thane said. "One of my Insiders destroyed a crop of successful embryos mid-February—and he paid for it with his life. This could have happened a month earlier."

I knew about the sabotage. I had cracking witnessed it. I began pacing, wild and unorganized thoughts running through my head. "Why didn't we burn that place to the ground? Destroy all their notes?"

"Things like that take time to plan," Thane said. His calm reply boiled my anger into fury.

"And you weren't available to plan them," Indy added.

I shot her a death glare. She'd had access to Thane's information. "You should've—"

"I was running your precious Resistance a thousand miles away. Don't you dare—"

"Enough," Vi said quietly, but with force. Indy and I didn't take our eyes off one another.

"Are our people secure inside the safe house?" Vi asked.

"Yes," Thane answered. "But Laurel won't be able to get out her moles, and we can't get in."

"So we need somewhere else," I said. "Beachfront? Who's there now?"

"Director Palmer, and he's friendly. But we don't have the manpower to organize our people, unless you plan on flying to the thirty-one cities in the Union yourself."

A sob hiked up my throat. I swallowed it down. "If I have to," I said.

"No," Vi said, putting her hand on my shoulder to stop my incessant pacing. "Let's go see what the situation is in Grande before you freak out and fly off."

"I have never freaked out and flown off."

"Have too," Indy and Vi said at the same time. They both smirked. A grin looked like it might break out on Thane's face.

I turned my back on them and stared into the sun as it bathed the plains. "Fine. Let's go see what the situation is in Grande."

Clones stood shoulder to shoulder along the perimeter of Grande. Beyond the clone barrier, nothing moved. No workers in the streets. No movement in the common areas. The public transit didn't stir.

After a preliminary check, I hovered with Indy, Thane, and Vi a great distance away from the city, out of sight of any enhancements a person could have, clone or not.

"Can we freak out and fly off now?" I asked.

"Quiet," Vi said. "I need to concentrate." She closed her eyes, reaching for me to keep her balance while she invaded the minds of the clones. Apparently their brains weren't that complex, because only a beat passed before she said, "Use your voice. Then my—" She swallowed hard. "My mom can get the moles out. We can relocate to Beachfront or wherever."

"There are at least five hundred of them," I said. "I'm supposed to tell them one by one to take a nap or something?"

"You're the one with the snappy voice," she said. "And he can help." She hooked her thumb toward Thane.

I looked at Thane. It was obvious that neither one of us wanted to work with the other.

I shelved my pride. "Voices?"

"Voices," he confirmed.

Zenn

28.

When my older brother found out I was involved in the Resistance, he punched me in the face. That was the first time I broke my nose. He stalked out of the house while I bled on my mother's pristine floor.

When he returned, my father was with him. The resulting discussion wasn't a discussion at all. More like a shouting match between my father and my brother. My father won. He always did.

And since my father favored me, I won too.

I had no idea my brother had wanted to join the Resistance

and my dad wouldn't let him. I didn't find that out until I'd been matched with Vi and quit. I didn't know he'd joined until after he'd left home—and we'd never talked about the Resistance after that.

The second time, my nose broke at the mercy of Vi's fist. We were fourteen, and she was livid I wouldn't tell her where I went at night without her. I was protecting her then, just like I do now.

But that didn't matter, because I quit the Resistance a few months later, and then Vi and I snuck out together at night.

I forced away the memories of my brother though I flew closer to him every second. I touched my nose, remembering the anger in his fist, the silence that had come between us ever since.

I rode a westerly until ten miles outside Arrow Falls. Then I thanked the current and asked it to go back the way it had come. I powered on my board, flying low to the ground to travel unseen.

The city of Arrow Falls was a tiny thing, with a fence surrounding the main buildings. Now, in mid-March, the radiating fields lay plowed and ready for planting. The first seeds would be sown in a month or two.

I stopped just outside the city and left a message for

Saffediene, detailing everything Trek had told me. She could alert Jag about General Director Darke. After that I zipped past the city without incident. The air felt stagnant, and landlocked as Arrow Falls was, I couldn't expect anything different. Ten miles past the city, the red light on my board flashed. I activated the solar portlet again so it would charge, and called on the wind.

I rode the breeze past Allentown, a city devoted to improving air quality. No walls, no barriers, and no Insider support. Not that Jag hadn't tried. He'd been in every city, met with every Director. Some of his escapes required more skill than others, and it was no wonder why everyone in the Association knew him on-sight.

He'd refused to alter his appearance for meetings. He'd refused to let anyone negotiate but him. He'd refused to let anyone shoulder what he called "his burdens." He couldn't seem to grasp that living a brainwashed life was a burden *everyone* bore.

The closer I flew to Castledale, the harder my heart pounded. I knew how to get into the city. I knew how to find Fret. Those things didn't worry me. I hadn't been to Castledale for over three years. Whenever it came up as an assignment, I made sure someone else took it. Castledale didn't hold anything but hateful words and angry silence, and I wasn't sure how to bridge the gap between my brother and me.

As the sun settled to sleep, I landed a few miles away from the border of Castledale and found the backpack Trek had mentioned. The tightening in my gut didn't have anything to do with hunger, though I ordered a stack of toast and a mug of hot chocolate.

My breath steamed out of my mouth, and my fingers ached with cold. I wanted to sleep. I wanted to cache Saffediene and make sure she'd made it to a safe house okay. I wanted to be anywhere but here.

Instead I zipped my jacket up to my throat and shoved my hands into my pockets. Then I powered on my freshly juiced board and entered Castledale just as the curfew alarm sounded.

I stuck to the shadows, avoiding the guards chatting with the noncompliant people still in the streets. The guards didn't have orders to arrest anyone, and the pair I watched accepted a drink from a man and settled on the steps, laughing.

I watched the totally noncompliant behavior, proud that I'd played a part in achieving it on such a grand scale. I swallowed the bitterness at having to eradicate such freedoms in the next twelve hours.

I darted across the street to the sound of the track system.

It should've shut down by now, yet people spilled from the train after it stopped. They laughed, they touched each other casually, they moved down the street in twos and threes, unconcerned about curfew or noise restrictions.

I used their ruckus as cover to sprint down the sidewalk, north into the City Center. The city wasn't quite as large as Freedom, but Castledale still housed towering high-rises and impeccably clean streets.

At curfew, Fret would be on the move, hopefully toward the only hideout I knew about. Fifteen minutes and many random turns later, I stood outside a shiny glass building. Under Director Hightower this door would've been locked. Here, in Castledale, it wasn't.

I marched through the lobby, my shoulders square and my adrenaline running on high.

Outside the last room on the left, I paused. The door required no special knock. There was no black plastic to keep prying eyes out. In Castledale there are no prying eyes.

I pushed open the door and entered. A long oval table was covered with tech gadgets and snacks and microchips. Several people, both men and women, clustered around a screen.

Director Pederson sat at the head of the table, engrossed in a conversation with my brother.

Fret Bower.

When he saw me, he stood slowly. The chatter died into silence. I must have looked haggard, because Director Pederson waved, and a girl brought me a glass of water and a wet cloth.

I ignored them both. I stared at my brother. He'd had some serious eye enhancements, and now his irises blazed a freaky green. His hair, still the color of murky water, fell to precisely protocol length. He played the Informant as well as I did, conforming during the day and planning a secret overthrow in the hours between dusk and dawn.

"Fret," I said. "Can I have a word?"

"Say it here," he said, his shoulders so stiff and his lips barely moving around the words.

I had so much more than just one. And I said them all, my voice sure and strong.

By the time I finished speaking, Director Pederson had sweat dripping into his eyes, and Fret had fallen back into his chair.

The people in the room seemed to breathe as one. Someone coughed, and the moment broke. Director Pederson stood and began issuing commands. Fret joined him, his voice the only one I heard in my head.

Fret ordered the immediate evacuation of the Insiders. He migrated toward me as he spoke. "We'll be out in six hours." Fret studied me, his expression softening. "Thank you for coming to warn us, Zenn."

I nodded, finding it crazy-hard to swallow. "Can you get the population compliant in time?"

"If anyone can do it, Director Pederson can." We both turned to watch the Director in action. When he spoke, people responded. The spark in his eyes danced, and when he motioned for us to follow him out of the room, Fret and I went.

Back in his personal quarters, Director Pederson continued to issue directives to his networks inside the city. Sirens wailed. Lights flashed. I stood at the window, watching the streets empty, listening to the public alert system announce General Director Darke's imminent arrival and the need for compliance.

I wasn't an empath, but I definitely felt a panic that hadn't existed when I'd arrived in the city.

That anxiety bled through my body too, when a dome of techtricity activated around the city sealing everyone—including me—inside.

Jag

29.

I didn't want Thane to fly out of my sight, but that couldn't be helped. So I assigned him the clones near Indy, where she could watch him. I was also worried about leaving Vi alone with Indy, but again, that couldn't be helped.

After I agreed to meet everyone back at the safe house, I shot straight into the sky and arced over the city toward the eastern border. I descended in front of two guards, not even bothering to get off my board. "Sleep."

They dropped to the ground, fast asleep. I flew south around the perimeter, repeating my command over and over.

The clones were no match for my voice. They didn't seem to have talent at all. They didn't even focus on me before they began snoring.

Halfway around the circle, I found where Thane had obviously started. I dismounted and examined the sleeping clones. I knelt next to one and commanded him to wake up. His eyes, a nondescript blue set against his white-as-snow skin, opened immediately. "What's your name?"

"Name?" he asked.

"What's your talent?"

"Name?" he repeated.

"Useless." I stood up, brushing my hands on my jeans. Vi touched down next to me. "They're not a threat," I said, thinking of the intense fear Cash had held in his voice when he'd said, *Subject 261 will be brought in for DNA donation.*

These were the standard clones Freedom had always produced. They were castoffs of experiments that didn't work. I looked around, expecting the real clones to emerge from the sky. It remained cold and clear, and utterly empty. "This is too easy."

"Let's get to the safe house," Vi said.

Vi had practically squeezed my hand off by the time we arrived at the hideout. "My mother, I mean, she—"

We waited for Vi to continue, but she just shook her head. I felt her desperation, her fear, and a longing so deep that I wondered at its source. Then I got it.

"You don't need Ty as a buffer anymore," I said gently. "You're your own person. And either your mother will like that or she won't." I eased my hand out of hers and brushed her hair out of her teary eyes. "*I* like you."

She tried to smile, but it came off wrong. "Okay. Yeah, okay."

When I turned toward the door, Thane was wiping his eyes dry. Something inside me shifted. I realized—for possibly the first time—that he'd lost a lot over the last decade as well. Just like Vi had. Just like I had.

Just like we all had.

Indy opened the door, and we were met with noise. Voices assaulted me on all sides. Some people argued in groups, some watched vids, some spoke in hushed tones, and some worked on tech at tables. The smell of sweat and blood and canned food filled the air. Garbage littered the floor. Standing in the middle of it all, and moving from group to group, was a tall brunette.

A long ponytail hung down her back, and she kept slicking her bangs off her sweaty forehead. She wore jeans and a tank top, despite the fact that the March weather called for long sleeves.

She turned when the winter air filtered into the room, but she didn't stop talking until she saw Thane. Then she walked away from her conversation and wove her way to us.

"Violet Schoenfeld," she said, her voice full of emotion. I felt it infect me with love, with sadness, with fury.

The woman drew Vi into a tight hug. "You're alive," she kept saying. "My baby girl is alive."

Vi cried—that's right, she cried. I knew from experience that it took a helluva lot to make Vi cry. She was either really, really angry or really, really scared, or—I didn't know what else.

"Ty," she choked out, and then it became the Schoenfeld family reunion. Thane hugged both Vi and her mom, and they were all crying, while Indy and I stood there gaping at each other like we weren't sure if this was real or not.

Vi gathered herself together first and shook off Thane. Then she stepped away from her mom and cleared her throat. "Mom, uh, this is my boyfriend—this is Jag Barque." She sidled next to me and gripped my hand. "Jag. My mother, Laurel."

"Hello," I said, extending my free hand and wondering if I should be afraid to meet Vi's mother. "Thanks for taking in my people. I hear you've got a system to get messages out to cities across the Union."

"Jag Barque." Laurel shook my hand and stepped back to appraise me. "I knew you were young, but I had no idea you were this young."

I bristled, but held my tongue.

"He's the leader of the Resistance," Indy said. "Has been for years. He knows more—"

"I know what he knows," Laurel interrupted. "I know all about him. Jag Barque is a legend."

I was very aware of Vi's pythonic grip on my fingers. I wished her mom hadn't used the word "legend." That wouldn't help Vi's insecurity issues about which of us was more important. I glanced at the dozens of people who were staring at us. They elbowed each other and whispered my name.

"If we all already know each other, let's move right on to business, shall we? We need to gather our Insiders here as soon as possible," I said. "Word is you're the leader of an underground communication loop. True?"

"True," Laurel said. "Thorne, Ace, activate the moles." She gestured to me as two men approached us. "Message, Mr. Barque?"

"All Insiders need to relocate to the Southern Region, city of Grande. We launch an attack on Freedom in fourteen days."

"Seven days," a voice corrected.

Saffediene stood in the doorway, her hair wild, her face lined with exhaustion.

"Seven days? Where's Zenn?"

"It's a long story." She strode toward me. "But yes, seven days. If we wait much longer, we won't succeed."

"Why not? What do you know?"

"Zenn left me a message at Arrow Falls. He met with Trek, then left for Castledale. The General is leaving Freedom tomorrow morning, which makes Freedom an easier target. Hightower is canceling school and has moved all upper-level students into the professional Rises. Trek and Starr are worried that if we don't strike in the next week, we'll be too late."

I felt like I was preparing for a war I couldn't win— especially not in seven cracking days. I needed a dark room to lie down in and think. Maybe reason it all out with someone who could shed more light on the subject.

Everyone stared at me, waiting for my next direction. I felt like the weight of the world rested on me. *I don't think I'm strong enough to do this,* I thought, knowing only Vi could hear.

Her eyes softened. She nodded. *Yes, you can. You can, Jag.*

"Is that even enough time for our people to get here?" I asked.

"Our people can get here in a week if you tell them to get here in a week," Laurel said.

And she was right.

"We can use the teleporter rings to bring them in," I said. "We can evacuate a city in hours, and move to the next."

I looked at Thorne and Ace. "Message: All Insiders must relocate to the Southern Region, city of Grande, by March twenty-seventh. Six days. We enter Freedom on the twenty-eighth." I turned to Laurel. "Is my brother here? He'll have the teleporter rings for your runners."

"He's in the weapons room," she said, motioning for Thorne and Ace to get a move on already. They disappeared down a hallway. I watched them go, numb. Laurel said something about breakfast, and Vi led me through the still-staring crowd. We made it into the safety of the dark hallway before I drew her into a desperate embrace.

"Tell me I'm doing the right thing," I whispered into her neck. "Please, tell me we can win this."

She just held me, her silence saying more than her words ever could.

Zenn

30.

Fret handed me a micro-chip. "Help us out with a few things, okay?"

"Sure," I said, trying to mask the worry in my voice. If the tech barrier was up, how were we going to get out? I managed to keep my feelings submerged, and Fret went back to his communication port. He issued directions from Director Pederson.

I put the chip in my wrist-port and brought up the info. I scanned the evacuation to-do list and knew I needed to clear the tunnels and activate the emergency teleporters.

I suppressed a shudder. I couldn't think of anything I hated more than being trapped underground. I could practically smell the confining stench of the cavern I'd been hiding in for the past few weeks. Surely the tunnels here in Castledale would be just as stale. Just as airless.

Especially if they haven't been cleared in a while. Or ever.

I contacted Brynn Fowler—the girl listed at the top of the Evacuation Emergency Plan. We cached back and forth a few times, and she sent me the coordinates to the underground entrance. I left without saying good-bye to Fret, because he was crazy-busy. I did catch Director Pederson's eye, and he waved at me as he continued to speak to someone over a handheld communicator.

Outside, the cold air sliced like techtricity through my lungs. It should be warming up, but in the dead of night the chill overrode any thought of spring. As I flew, I thought of Saffediene. Surely she'd check the message center in Arrow Falls. Hopefully Jag would be able to mobilize the Insiders.

When I arrived on the outskirts of the city, about ten yards from the barrier, a group of people had already gathered.

"You must be Zenn," a girl said as she approached. "I'm Brynn."

"Where do we need to clear?" I asked.

"I tried caching you," she said as we joined the group. "These guys just arrived from Grande. Jag Barque has authorized the evacuation Union-wide. He sent teleporter rings, so we don't need to use the tunnels."

Relief flooded my body. Saffediene had gotten the message—and she'd made it back to the safe house. And surprise, surprise, Jag had listened.

I was supremely glad Vi wasn't here. I could already hear her voice in my head, chastising me. *Come on*, she'd say. *Jag listens*.

I needed to listen to the real conversation in front of me, not the one in my head with a girl who could hardly stand to look at me.

". . . only two rings," one of the runners from Grande was saying. "But if we start now, we can have your people out in a couple of hours. Then we need to get to Baybridge, which Van also knows has been sending false feeds."

"Is Director Hightower en route to Baybridge?" I asked. Trek hadn't said anything about the Director leaving Freedom.

"We don't think so," a runner said. "Jag doesn't think he'll leave his city unprotected. We believe he sent someone else."

"Who?" Brynn asked.

The runners shrugged. "Don't know. Our job is to evacuate Castledale and Baybridge by morning. We need to get started."

Brynn looked at me. "I'm going to send you the list of Insiders here in Castledale. Can you message them the coordinates? I'll start at the top, you start at the bottom."

"Sure thing." A moment later, a list appeared in my cache. I started sending message after message. Ten minutes later, people started appearing in the field.

Wearing one ring, a runner could take two Insiders to the safe house by linking arms and holding on tight. I watched the evacuation, a sense of rightness settling in my system.

By three a.m., only Brynn, Fret, and I remained in the field with the two runners from Grande.

"That's everyone," Fret said. "Director Pederson will have the city and the general population in full compliance for General Darke."

"All right," Brynn said. "Let's get out of here. Thanks, guys. Good luck in Baybridge." She linked arms with one runner, and Fret did the same with the other.

They disappeared, leaving me alone. Thirty seconds later, Vi appeared.

I cried out in surprise. I glanced over my shoulder as if Director Hightower or General Darke would descend and snatch her away from me. "What are you doing here?"

"Bringing you in," she said. "I wanted a minute to talk to you. Alone."

It still amazed me how easily she could break down my barriers. How quickly I turned from someone who knew what he was doing into someone who didn't.

"Okay, talk."

But she didn't. She watched me for a moment, and I got the distinct impression she was rooting around inside my head. "What do you see in there?"

"I'm sorry, Zenn," she said. "For—"

"We've been through all this," I said. "You don't need to apologize. It actually makes this whole situation with us worse." I held out my hand.

"What?"

"The ring. I just want to sleep."

Hurt passed through her eyes, but I didn't care. She'd chosen. During the summer she'd chosen Jag. All throughout the fall and winter she'd chosen not to remember—until Raine had started talking about Jag. When the transport picked us up three weeks ago, she'd chosen again.

Always Jag.

I knew now that she'd always choose him over me. Over her parents. Over Ty. Over everyone.

"I didn't pick him over Ty." Barely contained fury accompanied her words.

"You did," I said, still holding out my hand for the teleporter ring. "She died, and he didn't."

"You'd be happy then, wouldn't you, Zenn? If Jag died."

I threw my hands up in frustration. "What do you want me to say? That I wish he were dead? Of course I don't. Do I wish that I meant more to you than him? Damn right I do. But I'm sick of wishing for something that won't come true."

"My mother is at the safe house," Vi said, her voice strained and filled with pain. I knew what it cost her to talk to me about her mom. She's the reason Vi left her house in the middle of the night and came to my bedroom. But I wouldn't be the one to help her—not this time.

"Another reason for you to run to Jag for comfort." Bitterness permeated my words.

"You're a jerk."

"Me?" I asked. "Who did you come to when your mother treated you badly? Who made you birthday cakes when she wouldn't? Fixed your broken heart when Ty left? Dried your tears and told you he loved you? Took you to the Abandoned Area just so you wouldn't have to sleep in that house alone with your memories and your mother? Was it Jag? No. Does he even know about all that stuff?"

She opened her mouth, then shut it again.

"Does he?" I challenged.

She shook her head, her jaw clenched tight tight tight.

It hurt me to open her wounds, but it seemed like she'd forgotten everything between us as soon as she'd met Jag. And she hadn't even tried to remember in the months since. I'd thought she'd seen me—really seen me—down that dark alley in Freedom. Why couldn't she see everything I'd done for her? Couldn't she feel the love I reserved only for her?

"I remember," she said, shifting her feet back and forth. "I remember everything about us."

"Yet you still choose him."

"Zenn—" She shook her head, as if saying my name said it all.

I stepped closer. "I want you to choose me." I released everything I'd boxed up so she could see. Every emotion. Every dream. My frustration with Vi faded, replaced with only the love I felt.

She refused to look at me. I put my arms around her and she melted into my embrace. I breathed in the scent of her hair. My brain felt fuzzy, and my legs ached. I hadn't slept in forever.

But with Violet, none of that mattered.

"I will always choose you," I whispered. "And I want

you to choose me." When she looked up at me, I seized my opportunity.

I kissed her.

My desperation transformed into euphoria—at least until my head snapped back. Blood spurted from my nose.

Vi rubbed her knuckles. "Don't ever do that again," she growled. She tossed the teleporter ring at me and blinked into oblivion.

Jag

31.

Something shifted in the bed where I slept. Darkness blanketed everything, but I knew a warm body had joined me. A body that vibrated with life, with energy, with anger.

I started to ask Vi what was wrong.

"Go back to sleep," she whispered. So I slid my arms around Vi, and slept.

I woke when Zenn snapped, "Get up, Jag. We need you out here." He didn't linger to see if I got up.

The space next to me was empty and cold. I stumbled out of bed and into the hallway. Emergency lights set into the floor illuminated the path toward the conference room. I entered, still rubbing the sleep out of my eyes. Only one chair at the head of the table remained vacant.

"Report, Laurel." I sat down and leafed through the stack of papers in front of me. Saffediene's writing adorned the top sheet. Zenn's decorated the second.

Laurel recapped the night's events, beginning with the evacuations in Castledale and Baybridge. "The Goodgrounds, the Badlands, Cedar Hills, Arrow Falls, White Cliffs, and Oceania have also been completely emptied of Insiders. Those Directors have their cities and remaining Citizens in full compliance."

"On today's docket for evac are Harvest, Lakehead, Northepointe, and Fort Houston. Our small contingencies in Buffalo Ridge, South Gulf, Lobster Bay, and Highland Ranch are relocating to the nearby cities of Lava Springs, Rockwelle, New Boston, and Tri-Rivers."

"Fantastic," I murmured, still studying the report Saffediene had submitted from Harvest. "Pace, tech update, please."

"Our rings are holding their power pretty well. The evacuations should continue without a problem. The falsified feeds have been rerouted through Trek's hub inside Freedom."

I half listened as I flipped the page in Saffediene's report.

She'd scrubbed something out several times and written over it.

I glanced up at Zenn, who was watching Pace. My brother smiled when I looked at him. "Everything is set. We can completely wipe our caches, make them untraceable by the Association. I'll set a new frequency, one only we can use to communicate with each other."

Gunn frowned. "What does that do to my ability to chat with Starr?"

"It makes it impossible. If she has intel, we'll need to get it before we reset your cache," Pace said.

Gunn looked at me. "Go," I said. "Find out all you can. Tell her we'll be invading on March twenty-eighth."

"I'll go with him," Raine said quickly. I understood, really. He was the only one she knew. Gunn had been working with her to get her memories back. My reports said she'd made great progress.

"No, you won't," I said. "No way you're getting anywhere close to Freedom."

She stiffened. "I've been checked for trackers. I'm not carrying anything."

"I realize that," I said. "You're simply too valuable to the Association. Which means we can't lose you. Gunn can go with Thane or Indy." I could tell Gunn wasn't happy about that—and I didn't blame him.

Indy glared. "I'd love to get out of this hellhole," she said. "Count me in."

"Super," Gunn said. "We'll leave after the meeting."

"Find out everything you can about where Hightower is, what his schedule is like, what's going on in the major Rises," I said. "We probably won't talk with Starr again before we launch."

I flipped another page in Saffediene's report before setting it down and starting Zenn's. I skimmed the details on Cedar Hills and found his Harvest notes.

I glanced up, knowing we needed to begin planning the invasion of Freedom. "Thane, Raine, do we have a detailed map of Freedom?"

"Let me bring it up," Thane said. The tabletop shimmered and turned into a p-screen. Snaking lines cut across the surface, drawing green areas and streets and buildings.

I kept reading Zenn's report. My breath came quicker as I realized his report didn't match Saffediene's. She'd said Director Benes met them in the air, overlooking the city; Zenn said he met them on the roof of a building.

I stole a glance at Saffediene. She had her finger pinned to a building on the map, and she was talking with Vi. Raine traced a path where the tech barrier lay, and Gunner put X's on possible locations to hunker down and hide.

Zenn circled the Confinement Rise, the Evolutionary Rise, the Medical Rise, and Rise One, and then they glowed red. He turned Rises Twelve, Nine, and Six blue, claiming these were safe spots where Insiders had coded flats and scrambling devices.

Neither Zenn nor Saffediene seemed the least bit worried that I was reading their reports. I shuffled them to the bottom of the pile. The next several sheets of paper held information I already knew. Lists of talents from the incoming Insiders, Hightower's plans to shut down school, a compilation of Darke's hideouts across the Association.

I slid that one to Zenn. "Let's try to ruin as many of these as we can during the attack."

He studied the list. "Our people have been pulled from these cities already."

"Friendly Directors?"

"Mostly. But Jag, if we start blowing up General Darke's refuges, he'll know we're coming after him."

"He's going to know anyway," I said.

Zenn folded the paper and put it in his pocket. "Consider it done."

I almost allowed myself to smile. I imagined Ian Darke, traveling from one of his precious cities to the next, only to find that those cities didn't belong to him anymore. That the people who lived in them had taken control of their own lives. And when he just wanted to go home and have a drink, he'd find his flat a smoldering heap of cement. Just like so many Citizens in his Union had.

Was I evil for thinking that way? Probably. But Vi didn't chastise me, or even look my way.

I listened while the group discussed Freedom and the best way to get as many people as possible into the city and positioned in key areas. While I hated Freedom, I knew every intricacy of it. I'd been there a few times, and I didn't always stay in the Confinement Rise.

"Let's lay low," I said, tapping the map to erase it. "Laurel, have we got enough food for those coming in?"

"Yes, sir."

"Don't call me sir," I said. "I'm sixteen years old."

"Yes, sir," she said again, and Vi actually started laughing.

"Nice," I said, rolling my eyes. "Meeting's over." As everyone stood to leave, I called, "Zenn, Saffediene. I'd like a word."

"A riot?" I asked for the third time.

Zenn rubbed his face and winced when he touched his nose. There was another story there, another secret he was keeping from me. "A labor dispute. Something with the Transportation Director. We didn't think it mattered, and it doesn't. Benes—"

"Sent his Insiders," Saffediene finished for him. "And the report they brought with them says that the riot was worked out. The elected official is Director of Transportation. The people chose—"

"And their decision was upheld," Zenn finished.

I would've thought their little finish-each-other's-sentences thing was cute, if they hadn't lied to me. If Zenn wasn't tenderly touching his nose. If Saffediene didn't keep stealing glances at him. If they didn't have caches they could use to make their story line up.

"What else do I need to know?" I asked them.

"Nothing," Saffediene said. Zenn remained silent—the first indication of a lie.

"You're my prime traveling team. I trust you to tell me everything," I said, infusing a heavy dose of guilt into my voice.

Saffediene cast her eyes down. She nodded. "Yes, sir."

"Do not call me sir."

Zenn held my gaze, his jaw clenched. His nose was a little off-center, and definitely swollen. "You can start by telling me what happened to your face."

"Nothing happened to my face."

He was brilliant at playing both sides. At acting cool and collected. Had he fooled me in the past? Undoubtedly. But he wasn't tricking me now.

"Who hit you?"

Saffediene swallowed as she scooted away from Zenn. "I think I'll try to catch Gunner," she said, standing up. I waved her away without comment. She was innocent, a new recruit. Anything she'd done was because of the guy sitting next to me.

"She follows your lead," I said. "And you're teaching her to lie to me."

"I am not."

"Then what do you talk about when she's lying in your arms at night?"

Defiance and fury emanated from him. I'd struck something sensitive. "You think I don't know?" I asked.

"What do you know, Jag?" His question sounded like a threat.

"She's in love with you. If you asked her right now to leave here and fly north across that dead border and start a new life with you, she would."

He drew a sharp breath. "Saffediene is not in love with me."

"She is."

"Well, I am not in love with her."

258

"So, you're using her, then. Getting her to doctor reports and say what you think I need to hear. Is that it?"

"Absolutely not," he said, but some shame leaked from him.

"Did she punch you when you tried to kiss her?"

Zenn sat very still. "No."

"Then who did?"

Zenn pushed his chair away from the table, stood, and left. I watched him go, thinking, *I can't trust him.*

I gathered my papers, remembering the one Zenn had given me that read *Should I say yes?* He'd been asking me if he should let Hightower recruit him, mold him into a Director.

As I went to find breakfast, I wondered if Zenn wouldn't be better off on the other side. He could lead his own city, without having to report every detail of his life.

"I guess it doesn't matter," I said to myself. "No matter what, he'll have to deal with me."

32.

The next six days passed slowly, having to watch Jag holding Violet's hand while they whispered preparations for the invasion of Freedom, and not having any chance to escape and be alone.

Gunn was awful company, as he'd learned that Starr had been sent to Baybridge as Hightower's representative. He and Raine spent most of their time huddled together in a corner somewhere, talking.

I felt terribly alone. Before, I'd had Vi, and together we'd blended with other couples. Now, I felt abandoned by the friends I'd had in Freedom, simply because I didn't have a partner.

I avoided Saffediene. I didn't want to be the guy Jag had accused me of being. I would not use Saffediene's crush on me to influence her behavior. I knew what rejection felt like, and I couldn't do that to her.

Vi hadn't told Jag about our kiss. If she had, I would've been punched again. And Jag is considerably stronger than Vi.

I spent most of my time following Jag's exact orders and lying on my cot, wondering if I wanted to return to Freedom as Director Hightower's protégé.

Finally, March twenty-eighth arrived.

Jag found me in the weapons room, getting my cache reset and the Resistance frequency uploaded. Pace scurried around, activating belts and vests and making sure we had all the equipment we needed for the attack.

"Zenn, you and I will stick with Vi." Jag stood just out of the fray, dressed in black from head to toe, not a stitch of tech anywhere. Typical Jag. He wasn't exactly anti-technology, just cocky.

"Did you hear me?" he asked.

"Yeah, stick with Vi. Got it."

"Between the two of us, she'll be safe." He stepped toward the door.

"Did it ever occur to you she might not want me around?" I called.

"More than once," he said. "Vi doesn't hold much back, you know." He looked straight through me. "But I know you're the one person who'd rather die than allow her to get hurt." Then he left before I could respond.

I didn't have a defense anyway. He was right. Over the past few days I'd tried to imagine a situation where I'd leave Vi in danger. Where I'd fly away while she bled, or where I'd turn her over to Director Hightower to save myself.

I hadn't succeeded. Vi didn't want me—she didn't even like me—but I couldn't stop loving her. I was pathetic.

Pathetic and alone.

While Pace plugged a line into my transmission portal, I thought about what life could be like north of the dead border just beyond Cedar Hills. I could build a house. I could scavenge for food. I could live a simple life, full of nothing but breathing and chopping wood and purifying water. I wouldn't have to worry about girls or Thinkers or Jag Barque.

I could simply take the backpack Pace had given me, get on my hoverboard, and fly away. Far, far away.

It sounded like the best idea I'd had in a long time.

I also knew I'd never do it.

I worry too much about what people think of me. And I want my life to mean something. I want to be important.

Armed with my backpack and my hoverboard, I joined the others in the open field behind the safe house. Stars twinkled overhead, partially eclipsed by clouds. Close to two hundred Insiders had arrived over the course of the last week, and everyone was restless for the invasion of Freedom to begin. Tense whispers filled my ears, but I didn't join the groups of people surrounding me.

I stood behind Jag—forever behind Jag—and Vi, waiting for who-knows-what. Part of me died a little when he turned and kissed her. The rest of me wanted to howl in pain.

Finally, everything was in place, and Jag gave the signal to lift off. He'd assigned everyone a specific spot in the advance party, and everyone had a task in the city too. Voices were flying up front, so I nosed my board between Gunn and Thane while keeping an eye on Vi.

Jag flew in the lead position, with Vi just behind him.

Where's Raine? I chatted to Gunn.

She's staying here.

Bet she's happy about that.

Actually, she is, he said. *She doesn't want to run into her father.*

I nodded in response. All I wanted to do was run into my father. I wondered where he was right now. Did he still work in the Transportation Department in the Goodgrounds? Did he still have clearance to the best tech?

I could've sent someone to find out. I hadn't. If I didn't know for sure, then I could imagine the best possible scenario.

Hey, you okay? Gunn's question sliced through my thoughts.

Yeah, I chatted. *Just great.*

It's going to go fine, Gunn said.

We only have four voices, I said. Me, him, Jag, and Thane.

That's all we need. He sounded so confident. I allowed his enthusiasm to infect me as we flew around the tech barrier.

The ocean below me felt dark and sinister. The water chopped toward the shore. The lights emanating from the Rises gave the city a false sparkle, making it almost seem inviting.

I caught bits of conversation from the others around me, but I didn't join in. Speculation just isn't my thing. I didn't want to stew about what I might or might not encounter in the city.

I'd find out when I arrived.

About ten minutes from shore, Jag motioned with his hand, and I sent the chat out to everyone. *Maintenance teams veer north-northwest toward Rise Twelve. Rescue teams stall and hover. Tech teams veer southwest toward the orchards. Circle the barrier and rendezvous at the Tech Rise.*

As the group split into four, thirteen people remained in the lead group. Me, Jag, Vi, Gunn, Thane, Saffediene, Indy, two technopaths from Baybridge, an empath from Northepointe, and three people to run communication between our group and the others.

Our target: Rise One. Our goal: capture and detain Director Hightower. It sounded easy in my head. I knew it wouldn't be.

Water met land, and I nudged my board north, following Jag. Just when I thought we'd successfully executed the element of surprise, bright white tech lights blinded me.

I automatically slowed my board to a stop. Next to me, Gunn did the same. To my left, the Confinement Rise strobed from ground to roof. The door gaped open, and out marched two men, shoulder to shoulder.

They split as soon as they left the building, creating a space for the two men who followed them. And the two who followed them. And the two who followed them.

I hovered, stunned, as clone after clone after clone filled the street in front of the Confinement Rise.

"Thane," Jag said. "I think you can handle them by yourself.

Let's continue, guys." He maneuvered his hoverboard away as Thane descended toward the Confinement Rise. I paused, waiting to see just how many clones there were.

They kept coming and coming and coming. "Ja-ag," I said, but he was too far away, and the hoser didn't wear an implant. Saffediene heard me, and she settled by my side to observe.

Thane had reached the clones. Nothing happened. I waited, expecting him to put them to sleep, the same way he had in Grande. Saffediene had cached me the report, and while I knew she'd wanted to talk about the clones, I hadn't engaged her because I didn't want to "use her" the way Jag had accused.

What's he doing? Saffediene asked over my cache.

Thane gestured wildly at us. Without another chat, Saffediene and I took off to help him. The frontward clones pulled out tasers. The motion rippled back through the crowd until *every single one* was armed.

"Whoa," I said out loud, forgetting completely about being stealthy. They obviously already knew we were here.

Thane shot straight up as at least twelve tasers fired in his direction.

Evasive maneuvers, I chatted to Saffediene. *Thane! What did you say to them?*

My heart beat double time, my body vibrated with crazy-adrenaline as I flew in close to the clones who had already discharged their tasers. I had a three-second window before their weapons would be ready to fire again.

"Sleep," I said in my most powerful voice. The clones didn't move. They didn't so much as blink.

I ducked as taser barbs arced toward me. Saffediene cried out behind me. She didn't have a voice; she couldn't do anything but get killed. *Retreat*, I commanded her.

Thane! I called again. I couldn't find him in the night sky. The lights surrounding the Confinement Rise were too bright.

I twisted back and flew in front of the clones who'd just fired at me. "Deactivate your weapons," I said. I'd never achieved this level of control in my voice. It should have worked. They should have pocketed their tasers.

They didn't.

Another wave of taser fire caught my board. The hover-craft lurched under my feet and went right while I continued left. I couldn't help it. I screamed.

I was falling, falling into an army of clones that wouldn't respond to my voice. I hit the ground hard. Four clones stood over me. I reached for the taser at my belt. If my voice wouldn't work, maybe I could at least fight my way into the orchards.

Zenn! Thane's voice over my cache could barely be heard over the pounding of my heart.

I fell! I chatted, sprinting down the line of clones. If I could just make it to through the fray . . .

I'll pick you up on the beach, Saffediene said. *Can you make it there?*

I dodged a clone as he stepped out of line. I plowed into another clone, and we both fell to the ground. My legs and arms tangled with his, but I scrambled to my feet just as a taser discharged. Techtricity struck where I had stood a moment ago.

I ran. *I don't think so.*

"Stop! Stand down! Drop your weapons!" I shouted as I ran.

They don't respond to voice control, Thane said.

What gives? I asked. *They're just clones.*

They're deaf, he said.

Horror struck me, and I tripped over my own feet. I slapped away the reaching hands of a clone even as the whine of a taser filled my world. I pulled myself to my knees, desperate to get away and reach the safety of the orchards.

We're screwed, I thought just before the techtricity entered my body.

Jag

33. A jolt of fear struck me as Vi's voice sounded in my head. I didn't wear an implant, but when she screamed, *Jag!* I heard it reverberate in every cell.

I twisted to find her several yards behind me, hovering in the air, pointing back the way we'd come. Below me, where the ground was once black and forbidding, it was now streaked with light.

Curses flew through my mind. I zoomed toward Vi, but I didn't need her to tell me the problem. Zillions of tech lights chased every shadow into the orchards.

Thane hovered near the roof of the Confinement Rise,

but I couldn't see anyone else. Anyone besides the hundreds and hundreds of clones.

Deaf, Vi said inside my head. Her voice rattled around in there, as if it didn't quite know where to settle.

I cocked my eyebrow at her. *Deaf?*

Meaning they can't hear, she said. *Your voice won't work.* A tremor shook her body. *Zenn fell.*

Should I have been worried? Yes. Was I? Absolutely. I'd seen the naked fear in Zenn's eyes when he'd spoken about Hightower. I'd heard him say, *You don't know what he's like.* I could not abandon Zenn here.

Where? I asked.

I don't know. I can't find his mind, either. It's like he's . . . She didn't finish the thought, but she didn't need to.

A rocking *boom!* shook my attention from Vi's escalating worry about Zenn. We faced the direction of the noise. Rise One wasn't hard to spot, what with it being the tallest building in the city. Smoke wafted from it, illuminated by a pulsing blue light.

Can you communicate with Thane? I asked Vi.

Yeah.

Tell him to stick with Saffediene and try to find Zenn. We have to get to Rise One.

She looked at me, and her accusation didn't need to be

said—or thought. I could read it in the way she stiffened.

Are you coming? I asked, unwilling to apologize for what needed to be done. Did she think Zenn didn't know the risks? That he wouldn't leave us all behind to finish the job? He knew this was bigger than one person—even bigger than him.

"It's Zenn," she said out loud, which was somehow worse than her infiltrating my mind.

I couldn't leave her there, but I couldn't waste any more time stalled in the sky. "I know, babe," I said, and that would have to be enough.

I swung my board around and held my hand out to Vi. She took it, and our group advanced toward the smoking Rise One.

Because of the other Rises, I didn't see the swarm of Enforcement Officers until we crested the last building. The square mile of green area surrounding Rise One was completely filled with Officers. Armed and dangerous Officers.

They wore standard-issue uniforms and held tasers at the ready. They didn't move, not even a twitch. Normal people couldn't stand that still. My breath stuck in my throat.

The Enforcement Officers were either clones or—

"Jag Barque." The voice belonged to Van Hightower, and it echoed through the empty streets, rattling off the tech buildings and coating my nerves in fear.

What was I supposed to say in return? *Hello? I'm here to burn your city to the ground?* That didn't seem quite right. So I said nothing. I nodded to Gunner, who flew in closer to the Officer-clones. He spoke, and nothing happened.

"Deaf," I said. Despite all my careful planning, I honestly hadn't anticipated that my greatest weapon—my voice—would be useless.

"Vi," I said. "Can you read their minds?"

A strangled cry escaped her throat. "I've been trying. I can't find their minds."

"Maybe . . ." I didn't finish, because I couldn't think of a single reason why Vi wouldn't be able to find and read their minds.

I watched Gunner fly along the perimeter, still attempting to use his voice to coerce the Officers. The seconds ticked by, but a battle raged in my head. Deep inside, I knew I'd never get another chance at this. I'd been working toward this takedown of Freedom for years.

In all my planning, I'd never imagined I'd be fighting clones. It was always Hightower, and he always fell.

Suddenly every Officer-clone stretched out his left arm as if they were one unit. Three of them hit Gunner's hoverboard. One of them grabbed Gunner. A yell surged from my mouth. Anger pounded through my head.

"He's controlling them," I said to no one, really. "Indy, get everyone out of the city. Alert the rescue team that we've got two down here. Runners, go warn our tech team. Vi and I will get the maintenance crew." That would put me at Rise Twelve, and maybe I could get my Insiders out. Maybe this mission wouldn't be a complete loss.

"Nothing?" I asked Vi, just to make sure.

"I think he programmed them," she said. "And he's the only one who can get in their heads. Like he's got the frequency, and we can't communicate with them without it."

In the crowd, each clone completed the same movement. I watched, helpless, as Gunn was shunted toward the entrance of Rise One. His body was limp; his eyes were closed.

"I'm going to try something," Vi said.

I felt the triumph emitting from Vi. I didn't know exactly what she might do, but I had a feeling that whatever it was, it would be successful.

And extremely dangerous.

"Don't," I said, far too quietly for her to hear with her ears.

She flew in close and stepped onto my board. "Tether my board to yours," she said, wrapping her arms around my waist. "Don't drop me."

She looked right into my face, her teal-turquoise eyes swirling with fear and power and a million other emotions I couldn't read before she said, "Don't let me die."

Her body became deadweight as she closed her eyes. I stumbled to my knees on the hoverboard; Vi's head lolled to the side.

"Vi?"

She looked dead.

"Vi!" I shook her. Adrenaline rushed through my veins, and I looked around for help. But I'd sent everyone away.

Taser fire erupted on the ground. I ducked, shielding Vi with my body. But none of the techtricity swept by us.

Instead the cries came from the ground. I straightened and watched the scene below me unfold into utter revolution as one of the frontal guards unleashed blast after blast on his unit.

In a matter of seconds the clones became a smoldering heap of bodies. Rancid smoke rose up to meet us.

"Stop!" I cried. "Violet, stop." I volleyed my gaze back and forth between Vi's still-limp form, and the very angry guard on the ground. She was inside him, controlling him. And as soon as Hightower found out, the guard Vi possessed would become the target.

When one taser ran out of charge, she simply pried

another from the grip of a fallen clone and kept firing. And firing. And firing.

My stomach clenched in a knot of pride and horror. She was winning. But at what cost? Worry seethed through me as she continued tasing clones. *Will she be able to find her way back to her own mind?*

Before, when she'd coerced the scouts into killing themselves, she'd maintained consciousness, probably because she could find their minds. Probably? Who was I kidding? I had no idea about the extent of Vi's abilities.

Violet Schoenfeld was more than dangerous. More than powerful. More than deadly.

She was a deity.

As the taser fire continued, I stroked Vi's hair off her forehead, whispering, "Please wake up."

34.

Somewhere far away a taser buzzed. The high-pitched whine made my head ache and set my teeth on edge.

It shouldn't be this dark, I thought. I hate the dark. It makes me examine things I'd rather not see. It reminds me that I'll never hold Violet again. Never kiss her or have her look at me like I'm the most wonderful person in the world.

In the dark, I can't outrun the pain.

And this time the agony existed in my body as well as my mind. My back felt broken. My fingertips tingled with tech-tricity. I couldn't move my arms or legs.

Something cool and wet swept over my face. At last the blackness lightened to charcoal, and then gray. And then blue, and finally white.

I opened my eyes, crazy-surprised to find they still functioned. I was even more shocked to find myself staring at a sterling silver ceiling. A fan whirred behind the duct, and voices floated nearby.

I couldn't understand their meaning. I still couldn't feel my arms or legs. Blinking seemed to be the only movement in my repertoire.

For the longest time I lay staring at the ceiling. No one came to check on me.

The light faded again, and Director Hightower came into view. "Ah, there you are, Mr. Bower." He smiled, and his scarred cheeks stretched into wicked curves.

"You're recovering from a nasty burn," he said pleasantly, as if we were discussing my homework.

I struggled to move my mouth, but couldn't.

Director Hightower waved a needle across my line of sight, but I didn't feel him inject me. "This will help."

I wasn't so sure of that, but I wasn't in a position to argue.

"Now, Zenn, let's chat, shall we?" The Director pressed a button and the bed brought me to a seated position. I found myself in a small room, a p-screen broadcasting my prognosis on the wall. A narrow window in the door showed a much larger lab outside my room.

Director Hightower sat across from me, his legs crossed and one hand stroking his beard.

I didn't remember him having a beard. For some reason it struck me as funny. I laughed, though no sound came out. I didn't see how I could "chat" while silenced. Director Hightower didn't seem concerned. In fact, he smiled again. "Here's how this is going to go," he said.

I flew toward the beach, because that's where Saffediene had said she'd wait. I didn't know how long I'd been unconscious, or how long the "chat" with Director Hightower had lasted. I did know the sun was halfway through the sky, and I did see three jagged lines had been carved into the sand on the beach. If connected, they'd make a Z. I believed Saffediene had drawn them. Sure enough, within seconds of landing, she launched herself at me, crying and talking and hugging.

I held on to her, afraid I might collapse if I didn't. My throat hurt from the silencer. My brain hurt from the talk with Director Hightower.

But nothing hurt when Saffediene formed her mouth to

mine. Nothing at all. For once I didn't think. I just let my body do what it wanted.

And it wanted to kiss Saffediene Brown.

We arrived at the safe house in Grande to find it empty. It appeared the hideout had been evacuated in a hurry.

"How long was I gone?" I asked.

"A day and a half," Saffediene said. "I told Thane I'd wait for you. He didn't say they'd be going anywhere else." She frowned as she released my hand and moved into the abandoned room. "Why would they leave us behind?"

"Jag doesn't operate that way. He's forever forging ahead." I followed her into the hideout, closing the door behind me. We made our way to the war room, where Saffediene trailed her fingers over the table.

"We lost a lot of people," she said. "Thane said our rescue teams were annihilated. The maintenance crew met resistance, but Jag managed to get some of the Insiders out of Twelve. The tech team didn't even make it out of the orchards."

"Pace?" I asked.

She shook her head, tears falling. "Indy," she said, her voice shaking. "They didn't make it out of the city. We don't know where they are."

My chest tightened. I swallowed back the emotion, wondering if I had the strength to carry on. To do what needed to be done. Director Hightower's words rang in my ears: *You have two choices, Zenn.*

Pace didn't have two choices. Not anymore.

"Gunner?" I asked.

Again, Saffediene shook her head. "Not sure."

"Thane?"

"He made it out. He waited with me the longest. Said he'd do what he could for us."

Which was nothing. Director Hightower had been clear on his feelings for Thane. *Don't let him trick you, Zenn. The man hasn't spoken the truth in a decade.*

But I hadn't either.

"Vi?" I asked next, scared of the answer but needing to know.

"She took control of someone's body and brought down an entire army before Hightower could retaliate."

My mouth went dry. "Is she—?"

"She was unconscious last time I saw her, but she was breathing."

I sighed with relief, even though taking control of someone else's body was crazy-talented in a crazy-creepy way.

I crashed into a chair and hung my head in my hands.

With my eyes closed, the world felt heavier. Director High-tower's words looped through my head. *You could be Director, Zenn. Big things are happening here. Are you sure you're on the right side?*

The right side, the right side, the right side.

"Saffediene, what's the right side?" I asked.

The chair next to me squeaked as she sat down. She didn't answer immediately, and I didn't move my head from my hands, but somehow, being with her relaxed me.

"I think the right side is the one that feels like home," she said. "Like you'd be welcomed back no matter what you've done, no matter when you show up."

I scrubbed my hands through my hair. "Should I let Director Hightower recruit me?"

"I don't know, Zenn. You said you couldn't go undercover again." She sighed. "Besides, what will you do? Live it up in Rise One, eating stacks of toast and waiting for the end?"

I pressed my palms to the tabletop. "It's better than waiting for the end in a cave, eating rations from a pouch."

"Is it?" She stood up and paced over to the window. I watched her unbraid her hair and cross her arms. Tension knotted her muscles, and I wanted nothing more than to erase it.

I joined her at the window. "I don't know what to do," I whispered.

She turned toward me, her mouth set into an angry line. "That's not what you told me when you recruited me."

"Remind me what I said."

"You said we could win. You said that a functioning government wasn't necessarily better than living freely. That there was a better way to live than being brainwashed. You said I could choose. Everyone could choose. You said—" Her voice cracked.

I stood there, not sure what to do.

"Saffediene, don't cry," I finally said. I reached for her and drew her close. She buried her face in my chest and sobbed.

I did the same thing I'd done when Vi had had her mini-breakdowns. I simply held her and stroked her hair. Words weren't needed. Only the physical presence of someone who cared.

Saffediene finally composed herself, wrapping her arms around me and holding on tight. Just as I started thinking about kissing her again, a crackling sound emanated behind me. Saffediene and I turned to find the table wavering with light.

Static confused the words coming over the transmission. The entire surface blazed with an image of a man. A fire burned behind him on the right, and smoke obscured everything on the left.

I tapped the table to open the communication portal. "Repeat, please."

The man in the destroyed city threw a panicked look over his shoulder. He leaned closer and his mouth moved. All that came through the feed was, ". . . demolished . . . Baybridge is in . . . evacuate to . . . Darke."

"Baybridge," Saffediene whispered.

"One of our strongest cities," I said. "Starr was there." Had I lost another friend?

"I'm checking Castledale," she said, pressing her fingers to the table. Another of our major cities, with an ultra-sympathetic Director. Had General Darke destroyed it too?

The feed switched from the smoky, chaotic city of Baybridge to the absolute stillness of Castledale. Not a soul moved in the street. No one flew in the skies; the train sat dormant. The buildings were various shades of blue and gray that didn't seem natural.

"Weird," Saffediene said. "It's midafternoon. Where is everyone?"

"Can you rotate the feed? The buildings don't look right."

She flipped the image, and we both sucked in a breath.

The shadows on the buildings spelled "RESIST AND DIE."

35.

I didn't leave Vi's side until she woke up. Even then, she only said three words, "Did we win?" before falling back into unconsciousness.

"Win" was such a relative term. She'd taken out an entire army, but not before they'd hauled Gunn into Rise One. We'd gotten Trek out of Rise Twelve, but our tech team didn't even make it to the Technology Rise. I'd sent Pace on that route and hadn't heard from him since.

I didn't know for sure that Indy was gone, but she hadn't escaped with us. Over half my people hadn't made it out of Freedom.

My head hurt. Just thinking that Freedom had claimed another one of my brothers drove me to fury. My throat narrowed, and those cracking tears filled my eyes again.

"Jag," Starr said from the doorway. She'd flown in from Baybridge last night. She put one hand on my shoulder. "How's she holding up?"

I didn't know, so I shrugged. Starr dropped her hand. "I can feel her mind. She's a fighter. She'll be awake before you know it."

I turned and looked at Starr. "Thank you," I said. "That means—" I cleared my throat. "Thanks."

Starr waved away my gratitude. "They need you out there. Incoming transmission from Grande. It's Zenn and Saffediene."

"Will you get Laurel?" I stroked two fingers over Vi's cheek, relieved I wouldn't have to tell her that Zenn was dead. I never wanted to be the one to tell her that, even if I didn't like the thought of them together. "I don't want her to wake up alone."

"Sure." Starr left, and I felt that familiar itch under my skin. I wasn't doing enough. I needed to find a hoverboard and visit every Director within three hundred miles.

"I have to go talk to Zenn," I whispered to Vi. "Your mom is going to sit with you. I love you." I pressed a kiss to her forehead as Laurel entered the room.

"Thanks." I stood up. "Where's Thane?"

She put her hand on my shoulder, and a strange understanding passed between us. "They're all waiting on you."

The bunker where we'd crashed had twisty-turny halls that radiated from one large, circular room. We'd converted the smaller rooms into a dining hall, a kitchen, food storage, and sleeping quarters. Any tech we had here we'd taken from our safe house in Grande.

After Vi had incapacitated the Officer-clones, we'd taken as many tasers as we could carry. We had three food-generating cubes, a handful of scramblers, a half dozen tele-porter rings, and enough tech to broadcast a transmission over a specific frequency.

Gunner had given his father's journal to Zenn, and then Zenn had been tased and taken. I'd had to make another hard decision and evacuate the safe house before he'd returned. I hated that Resistance information could've fallen into High-tower's hands, but I couldn't do anything about it. And now Zenn had returned.

I entered the room to whispered conversations and the sight of Zenn and Saffediene broadcasting onto the wall. Thane stood at the front of the group, talking about Vi and her expected recovery. Zenn visibly relaxed, and some of the tension seeped from his shoulders. Next to Thane, Trek manned the gadgets to keep the transmission open. My chest tightened. Pace should be doing that. Pace was my tech—

"Jag," Zenn said. He seemed beyond relieved to see me alive. Was I thrilled to see him alive? I'll admit that I was.

"Hey, bro," I said. "You look rested."

He gave a mirthless laugh. "Director Hightower detained me for a little speech."

"Oh yeah? Did he have anything good to say?"

Zenn's eyes flickered to Thane and back to me. "He said Thane's a liar."

The room erupted in laughter, and I allowed myself a chuckle. "Yeah, well, who isn't?"

Zenn cracked a rare smile. "Saffediene and I intercepted a transmission from Baybridge. The city's been destroyed. Sounded like they were evacuating, but we didn't catch where." He swallowed and exchanged a glance with Saffediene. I watched his body language, the way he shifted toward her, how she put her hand on his forearm.

Zenn had himself a new girlfriend—and his feelings seemed genuine. Nice.

"Have you heard from Starr?" Zenn asked.

"She's here," I said. "Everything in Baybridge was fine when she left. Our people got out." I saw her hurrying out of the room, probably to check with her contacts about what had gone down in Baybridge.

"We checked Castledale," Saffediene said. "We found a message there."

"Well?" I pushed.

"Resist and die," Zenn said.

"Was the city dormant?" Thane asked from the front of the room. "The people sequestered?"

"Yes," Saffediene said.

"Let me guess," Thane said. "The message was in a funky location or as a puzzle. Am I right?"

"As these weird painted 'shadows' on the buildings. We only found the message after we rotated the image," Zenn confirmed.

"Okay, so what?" I asked. "We've known for years that Darke wasn't going to just roll over. Why does this matter now?"

"Did you say Baybridge was burning?" Thane asked. "Or it was already burnt?"

"Burning," Saffediene said. "Lots of smoke in the projection, and a fire in the building behind the guy."

"What guy?" I asked. The Insiders in Baybridge had been evacuated with everyone else.

"Probably not an Insider," Thane said. "Probably just someone trying to get a feed out, searching for help."

"Where are you guys?" Zenn asked. "Can we fly in?"

"Arrow Falls," Thane said. "We should be able to get you in tonight."

Zenn and Saffediene nodded, but I wanted to go back to the burning versus burnt question. "Why does it matter if the city was burning or already burnt?"

Thane angled his body so he was looking at me and at the p-screen. "It lets us know Darke's timeline. He's not in Castledale right now; he left the message there and flew to Baybridge, which was *burning.* So he must have just launched the attack there."

"So we can launch an attack on him when he returns to Castledale," I said, seeing where Thane was going with his reasoning.

"Exactly. From Baybridge to Castledale, you're talking a two-day flight. If the feed Zenn saw was in real time, then we've got a short window to prepare a second wave."

I nodded, proud of myself for having a conversation with Thane without wanting to tase him. "Let's pack up," I said. "We're heading to Castledale. Zenn, can you guys meet us there?"

"By morning," he said.

"Can you check Freedom first?" Raine's childlike voice piped up. "See if there's any word on Gunner?"

Trek put his arm around Raine. "See if you can cache Ivory Bills. She'll be in charge of communication now that I'm gone."

Zenn nodded, his jaw set. "I'll find out, Raine. I promise."

I'd heard Zenn say those words before, but this time was different. This time I believed him.

Zenn

36.

Ivory Bills met Saffediene and me on the north side of Freedom, near where I'd met Trek a week earlier. She stood just beyond the wall, her eyes narrowed in our direction. I'd activated my cache, but I wasn't sure I had a frequency she could hear. Pace had reset them all before the invasion.

I heard whispers of thought only from Saffediene, but Ivory had obviously received something. She strode forward, her reddish-brown hair barely brushing her chin. Her slate-gray eyes scanned me, then Saffediene, stalling on our joined hands for a moment longer than necessary.

"Hey," she said, her voice wavering as it passed through the barrier.

I squeezed Saffediene's hand to signal that I thought Ivory would deal better with her than with me.

"Hey," Saffediene said. "News?"

Though I didn't expect anything different from Saffediene, I almost smiled at her all-business attitude. I tamed the urge when Ivory folded her arms and remained silent.

The loudest sound became the sighing of the breeze as it mixed with the crackle of the techtric barrier.

She squinted at us again, as if that might allow her access inside our heads. My skin crawled; I felt exposed, like that's exactly what she was doing.

"Your caches have been altered," she finally said.

"Yes," Saffediene immediately responded. "Trek Whiting said you were his second and would be able to fill us in on any developments inside the city." She took a deep breath as Ivory visibly relaxed.

"Trek sent you?" she asked. "You're part of the Resistance?"

"Yes," Saffediene said. "We're most concerned about a talented Citizen, Gunner Jameson, and our tech developer, Pace Barque."

I cleared my throat. "And the second-in-command, Indiarina Blightingdale."

If any of those names meant anything to Ivory, she didn't show it. Talk about one cool cat. With every passing second, my chest felt tighter and tighter. Maybe she was sending an e-comm to the Enforcement Officers with our location.

Ivory blinked, then focused on us again. She'd been checking something on her vision-screen. "Pace Barque and Gunner Jameson were logged into the Evolutionary Rise yesterday." My heart skipped a beat at the mention of the Evolutionary Rise. Pace and Gunner wouldn't come out of there alive, and their DNA was probably under fifty scopes right now.

"That's not good," Saffediene said. "What for?"

"Experimentation," Ivory said, her delivery smooth and unemotional. She was the perfect Insider. She'd probably get along real well with Jag.

"Are they dead?" Saffediene's tone pitched a little higher.

"Their status is 'experimentation,'" Ivory said. "And Indiarina Blightingdale has been slated for Modification."

I closed my eyes and felt my body slump. Modification. A new life. A new name. Like Raine, who still struggled to introduce herself properly. After the procedure was done, Indy wouldn't remember Jag or me or the Resistance. Nothing.

"When?" Saffediene asked.

"Friday."

What day is it today? I cached Saffediene.

Tuesday, she said.

"Can your team get them out?" I asked.

Ivory squinted at me again. "I think I know you."

I raised my eyebrows. "Yeah? How?"

"Couple of years ago, someone needed an emergency teleporter in an alley outside Eleven. I was sent."

My blood ran cold. My heart raced double time. I'd tried to forget that night. The strobing lights. The barking dogs. That empty alley where I'd left the memory of Blaze and made Jag hate me forever.

I shook my head to disagree, but Ivory forged on. "It was you. You look older, but it's you. I threw the capsule. You left without even saying thank you."

Zenn, you're hurting me. Saffediene's voice stopped my downward spiral.

I released her hand, unaware I'd been squeezing so hard. I swallowed. "Someone died that night. Jag Barque's brother."

Ivory shifted her weight onto one leg, waiting for more of an explanation.

"Blaze Barque was an Assistant Director. He couldn't get caught evacuating Insiders. I could do the job without him, but he wouldn't stay. I voice-controlled him. Forced him to remain in the alley. I thought he'd be fine. I was in and out.

He wasn't there when I returned, and I had to leave so fast."
My words sounded like excuses.

"You could've said two words," Ivory said.

"I wasn't thinking clearly," I replied. "But I am now. Thank
you. We're flying to Castledale to launch a second wave on
General Darke. We desperately need Pace, Gunner, and Indy,
though." Ivory scowled, and I quickly added, "And anyone
who wants to come fight for freedom."

I had a feeling that's what she wanted. She hated this
city, this controlled life, and she hated me for not taking her
away from it years ago. I waited while she stared at us, but not
really. She was vision-screening again.

"When are you leaving?" she asked.

"As soon as possible," Saffediene said. "We told Jag we'd
be there by morning."

Ivory focused on Saffediene. "We can't get your people
out by morning. But we can launch a breach when you throw
your second wave at Darke. When is that?"

"We'll arrive in Castledale in the morning," Saffediene
said. "The second wave goes out when Darke arrives back in
the city." She glanced at me. "We're not exactly sure—"

"Day after tomorrow," I said. "Full dark."

Ivory scrutinized me again. Her lips pursed, and she
brushed her hair out of her eyes. "Day after tomorrow. Full

dark. That should give us enough time. We won't launch too early so as to draw Darke here instead of back to Castledale."

"It's a deal," I said.

After Ivory had walked away, and after Saffediene and I had climbed on our hoverboards and set a course for Castledale, my body buzzed with adrenaline. It felt good to be working in the Resistance again. Really working.

If only I could quell that nagging voice in the back of my head. The one that spoke in Director Hightower's timbre. The one that asked: *Are you sure you're on the right side?*

I can't outfly Director Hightower's words, just like I can't hide in the dark.

"Here's how this is going to go," the Director says, still stroking his protocol-breaking beard. "You're going to lead me directly to Jag Barque, and once we've annihilated his Insiders, you're going to come back to Freedom with me."

I can't move, and I can't speak. But the horror inside me must show on my face—or maybe the Director is inside my head. It doesn't matter, he knows what I'm thinking.

"I know it's Jag's group, Jag's objectives, Jag's everything. None of this has anything to do with you, Zenn."

I wish it were my Resistance. My cause. But I know it's not, and Director Hightower knows it too. "You simply got caught up in the Resistance before you were old enough to know better."

I want to tell him I do know better, but he smiles in that patronizing way that makes me both angry and afraid. "You didn't know better then, Zenn. You do now. And you know what we're fighting to maintain. Clean water. Jobs and food for everyone. A life without sickness, without suffering."

He nods. "Yes, I know what you've seen in Harvest."

He knows nothing of what I've seen. I try to look away, to break the connection between us, but I'm too weak. I've felt defeated before. Like I don't matter. Like I'll never be good enough. But I've never felt this level of anguish before.

I search for the root of this pain and find it hidden deep within myself. I hate the truth that I've been trying to hide from, but Director Hightower speaks it, makes it alive and real.

And deep in my soul, I know he's right when the Director says, "You could be Freedom's Director, Zenn. Big things are happening here. Are you sure you're on the right side?"

The streets coming into Castledale were just as Saffediene and I had seen them on the feed: lifeless. Part of me wondered why, and the other part already knew.

Even though Thane had said sequestered, I knew the city had been abandoned. I'd learned about ghost towns in my ancient civilizations classes; they usually died because the water dried up or legend claimed a spirit haunted the area.

In this case, General Director Darke drove away the people with threats and mind control. Already the buildings seemed older, the sidewalks cracked. I imagined what this city might look like in fifty years. In one hundred years.

Would it look like Seaside? Or the Badlands? The Citizens there had survived wars and fires and brainwashing. People had survived. Built new buildings. Cultivated trees. Castledale could be repopulated, no matter what General Darke had done.

With my resolve to defy Director Hightower firm, I squared my shoulders and entered the only building in use in Castledale: the safe house where the Resistance would make its final stand.

I steered clear of Jag. He was stormy and dangerous, what with Vi unconscious and over half his crew dead or missing. Saffediene filled him in on our convo with Ivory. I'd asked her to keep any mention of what had happened with Blaze out of the report.

She'd do it, even if she didn't like it. During the eight-hour flight here, I'd told her about the mission to Freedom when he'd died. She'd listened—something Jag had never done.

Blaze's death wasn't my fault. He was the Assistant Director of Seaside; he should not have been assigned a mission that could have compromised his position in the Association.

His death was Jag's fault.

Of course we'd both spent the last two years blaming ourselves inwardly and each other outwardly. But I'd learned that blaming someone doesn't help. It only colors your view of them, and I'd been watching Jag through a red haze for a long time.

Everything he did angered me. Everything he said, I questioned. And when he took Vi from me, my blame and fury and guilt were easily dumped on Jag. I didn't know how to overcome it, so I waited on the fringes for Saffediene to report, and then I took her hand and led her down a posh hallway. "Did we get room assignments?"

"We need to see Laurel for that."

So we did. Laurel had organized the building into wings, with our tech facilities and infirmary in one, the dining hall and common areas in another, bedrooms in a third, and the war room in the last.

Everyone seemed to be in the war room with Jag, so that's exactly where I didn't want to be.

The lodging wing was dimly lit and crazy-quiet. Four hallways branched off the main corridor, with girls down two of them, and boys down the other two. Half of me wanted nothing more than to rush to Vi's bedside and urge her to wake up. The other half wanted to slip into the privacy of Saffediene's room and forget I'd ever loved another girl.

Neither half won. Saffediene kissed me quickly on the mouth before disappearing down one of the girls' halls. I listened to her retreating footsteps mingle with the dull chatter from the war room.

Then I escaped to my room, which consisted of a narrow cot shoved against a wall and a single shelf above it. Sitting on the bed, I seriously considered leaving. What would happen if I did? Would anyone care? How long would it take for them to notice?

"There you are, Zenn," Vi's mom said from the doorway. The light haloed her, and she looked younger than I remembered. "I need you in the tech department. Have you got a minute?"

"Sure." I followed her down the hall, through the war room, and into the opposite wing. Immediately the stench of burnt metal and hot smoke filled my nose. My dad used to smell like that when he came home from work. My stomach twisted, and I felt a profound sadness. I hadn't seen my father in so long.

I forced away those thoughts when Laurel turned into a

brightly lit room and gestured me inside. Counters ran the length of the room, some covered with bits of tech and others overflowing with bare filaments.

"It's all raw," I said with a sinking feeling.

"See why I need you?" Laurel introduced me to a couple of guys whose names I forgot as soon as she said them. I nodded at Trek, who instructed the two guys in words that sounded like English but held no meaning for me.

Laurel and I moved down the counter to a station stacked with bins of what looked like scrap metal with wires sticking out of one end. "I need you to weave these filaments into receivers."

I took a step back. "I know next to nothing about tech," I protested. "I don't even know what a receiver looks like."

Laurel pointed to a spherical silver ball the size of my pinkie nail. "That's a receiver. We need about fifty more to complete the teleporter rings."

"We have fifty rings?" I asked, incredulous.

Laurel glanced at the two guys in the front of the room. "We will when you get those receivers made," she said. She left, and I knew those of us working in the tech department had been tasked with the impossible.

Jag

37.

Vi woke up twelve hours before Ian Darke was scheduled to arrive in Castledale. I'd just finished my disgusting breakfast of a fruit-and-nut TravelTreat. I'd been going crazy, waiting for her to wake up, half believing she never would. When her eyes fluttered open, I drew a sharp intake of breath. Vi blinked a couple of times, her pupils too large. "Mom?" she said, her voice little more than breath.

"Vi, babe," I whispered. "I'm here."

Her head turned toward me, almost robotically. Fear flashed through me. What if she couldn't remember me?

A slow smile spread across her face. "Jag."

I hugged her and cried into her neck. Just as quickly as the relief filled me, anger took over. I pulled away. "Don't you ever do anything like that again," I said.

"Okay," she agreed, probably a little too fast. I didn't care if I'd influenced her with my voice.

"Where's my mom? I swear I heard her singing earlier."

"Raine was singing," I said. "Some of us have been sitting with you in shifts."

"Zenn?"

I stiffened, though I tried not to show it. "He's been really busy in the lab." Translation: *He's alive, but he didn't want to see you.*

"He completed the receivers we needed for the teleporter rings. He's never worked with tech, but your mom said he's brilliant at it."

Vi's eyes grew wistful. "He's brilliant at a lot of things. Most everything he does, actually."

"I know."

"We hurt him," she said simply.

"I know," I said again, wishing it could be different, but accepting that it wasn't. That was something Vi hadn't quite done yet: accept us.

Choose me over him.

elana johnson

"I have," she said, her voice whisper quiet. "And he knows it, which is why he hasn't been to see me."

Did this surprise me? I'd be lying if I said it didn't. Vi wasn't super great at making choices, and I didn't know she'd gone so far as to decide between Zenn and me, and communicate such a thing to Zenn.

"I punched him after he tried to kiss me. Well, I mean, he kissed me, and I punched him."

I laughed, the sound echoing through the infirmary. "No wonder his nose was all swollen a few days ago. He wouldn't say why."

Vi pushed herself into a sitting position. "Tell me what's going on."

Against my many protests, Vi suited up for flight after a late dinner. T-minus fifty-eight minutes until we would launch the second wave against the Association. We'd received word that Darke had indeed arrived in Castledale. He'd flown into the Security Department with a contingent of guards, and my report said he would depart at five the next morning.

Seven hours.

I paced, the anxiety a living, breathing thing inside my chest, pumping right along with my heart. Everything was set; everyone had been prepped. Now we just waited for the moment to strike.

I gripped the teleporter ring in my pocket. Zenn stood nearby, talking quietly with Saffediene. Besides checking with him about the receivers, I'd only seen him for five minutes during the past two days. We'd spoken maybe ten words.

I suspected he was hiding something from me, but I couldn't feel any deceit from him. Just sadness and loneliness and indecision. Maybe he'd really moved on and didn't need to spend his energy being angry with me anymore. I remembered when we used to play cards and laugh, and as he leaned closer to Saffediene with a small smile on his lips, I missed my friendship with him.

Zenn would be flying with Saffediene and a handful of others, leaving the city from the south and circling around to the Security Department on the fourth leg of the attack. Laurel had her team clustered together, their faces identical images of determination. They were flying out east and coming in hot on the second shift.

Thane stood with his back to me, Starr Messenger at his side. Since our earlier conversation, we hadn't spoken. He'd taken a few shifts with Vi, but when I relieved him, he simply left and I sat down in his place.

He'd been assigned the third leg, which would attack

from the west. Raine and Trek and a handful of others were staying behind, monitoring our tech and checking the feeds. I couldn't afford to lose another technician, especially one as capable as Trek. And Raine, though she was improving greatly, still forgot her real name on occasion.

I was leading the first wave, and we were due to fly directly into the Security Department. I'd assigned Vi to my team because she refused to stay behind, and I hated to admit that her newfound ability might be useful in this fight.

As the hour drew near, the mood in the room shifted from eager anticipation to a dull fear. The talking gradually quieted, and finally I raised my hand. "Let's move out."

I led my team to the roof, where we stepped onto our hoverboards, and flew.

The night tasted bitter, like leftover smoke. Darke had forced everyone out, either with fire or mind control. Rumor had it that Harvest had taken in thousands of refugees. So had Arrow Falls, and I'd heard reports from cities as far north as Lakehead.

It didn't matter. We had Darke's agenda, and he was due to visit Harvest the day after tomorrow. After he changed their transmissions, the people would be forced to flee again.

I set my jaw. No, they wouldn't. We'd stop him tonight.

We have to, I thought. *If we don't* . . . I didn't finish, because I was afraid of what might follow.

Zenn

38.

Jag marched out with his team of twenty, his chin tilted up and his hand clutched in Vi's. Seeing them together didn't hurt as much as it used to. Certainly not as much as her fist connecting with my nose.

Ten minutes later Laurel's team exited the building, leaving me with Thane and Starr. I hadn't talked much with them. I hadn't talked much with anyone since arriving in Grande, besides Saffediene. She was the only one who didn't kindle old arguments and strained memories. I'd enjoyed being with her without a mission objective.

She'd come to the tech lab and sat next to me while I

assembled the receivers. Turned out I wasn't half bad at it. One of the rings Trek had fashioned, with the receiver I'd constructed inside to make it work, now sat in my pocket. Almost everyone had one; fifty hadn't been quite enough for all of us, but close. The Insiders in Grande had done a great job of collecting tech materials.

Worry seethed just beneath my skin. I tugged on the sleeve of my jacket to release some of the anxiety. Didn't work.

A flicker of light crossed the p-screen near Thane, but flatlined into nothingness. I didn't realize how much I wanted to see Jag on that screen, though he'd only been gone a half hour and couldn't have achieved victory so quickly. I needed to hear him say he'd completed the objective. Craved the sight of his triumphant smile.

Because I didn't want to leave the safety of this building. In here I knew what to expect. Out there anything could happen. Anything at all.

When Thane departed with his squad, I started pacing. Besides Saffediene, my team consisted of three guys from Baybridge, and two guys from Harvest who'd learned to fly hoverboards yesterday.

They weren't my top picks. Jag had assigned those people to his contingency. It didn't matter. If the other teams weren't successful, my pathetic team of seven wasn't going to tip the balance.

I glared at the p-screen as if it were to blame for not broadcasting the images I wanted to see. All too soon the buzzer on my belt went off. "Time to go." I strode toward the door with what I hoped looked like confidence.

The chilly air outside felt dense, thick as water, inside my lungs. When I cleared the roof and turned south, I caught a glimpse of fire to the north. The Security Department.

The top half of the building danced with flames. I hovered there, staring. Jag had done it. I didn't know why, but I honestly thought we might never succeed. He'd been trying for so long. Trying—and failing.

"Zenn?" Saffediene asked.

I pulled my attention from the orange glow. She hovered with the others, waiting for my directions. "South," I said. "Stick to the plan. We haven't been alerted of any changes."

I ignored the smoke curling into the sky. I ignored the emptiness in the streets and the buzz of techtricity hanging in the air.

All of it unsettled me. Something about this felt too easy.

As we circled in from the north, the unease grew. My breath came fast. I crouched low, scanning scanning scanning the horizon. I expected a flood of lights to illuminate the downtown area and an army of clones to make their appearance.

When they didn't, I wondered why.

And then I saw someone that erased all my thoughts.

A low moan escaped my mouth.

My hands clenched into fists.

I braced myself—

    just—

        before—

            ramming into—

My father.

After that, everything happened so, so fast. Next to me, Saffediene cried out. I spun wildly out of control from the collision with my dad. When I regained equilibrium, I found Saffediene a few feet away, shaking tech-sparks from her coat.

My father hovered with his back to me, regaining his balance on his board. When he spoke, his voice sounded off, but I hadn't seen or heard from him in over a year.

"Come with me, Zenn."

"Dad?" I asked, so many questions buried in that single word. I swung my attention back to Saffediene. "Saffediene?" I whispered.

She closed the gap between us and slipped her hand into mine. "You should go with him."

"Come with me," I said, squeezing her hand.

She shook her head. "Go work things out with him. I'll carry out our directive and meet you back at the safe house."

I kissed her quickly, just as my dad called my name again. I'd longed to hear his voice for so long. My father held out his hand to me.

The ache that had grown inside withered and died. "Dad." I flew over to him. "What's going on?" I had so much more to ask him (*Where have you been? Why didn't you message? Did you know Fret used to live here?*), but in the middle of a mission didn't seem like a good time.

"Come with me," he said. He curved his board expertly away from the burning Security Department.

I glanced at Saffediene and saw techtricity arc out of the flames and hit her board. She seized as the energy lightninged through her body, and then she plummeted toward the ground, her mouth open in a silent scream, before being caught by an electro-net. She hovered in empty space, her blond hair splayed, her eyes filled with pain, her left leg bent at a weird angle.

"Saffediene!" I shouted as my father yelled, "Zenn!"

I shot toward the electro-net, toward that girl I'd recently started falling for. I'd abandoned my father for another girl, years ago. But I couldn't leave Saffediene.

My board sliced the ashy air, but before I could reach Saffediene, it lost power. I began to move backward. I spun around. My dad had tethered my board to his and was flying us away from the Security Department.

"Stop!" I cried. "Dad, please."

He ignored me as he zoomed downward, undisturbed by the spark of a taser over there, or the shout of someone behind us. I couldn't take everything in fast enough.

Beyond the Security Department, my dad had little difficulty navigating the city, which added more questions to the queue. He flew us into a portal, and we disappeared inside a building.

The tunnel grew lighter and lighter until I entered a tech-lit room filled with hover technology. Boards, balls, cars, the works. Jag would kill to get in this room. Maybe he already had.

We were alone, but I didn't trust myself to speak first. My dad stepped off his board, but—

It wasn't my father at all.

It was General Director Darke.

My vision blurred, but the image of the General didn't waver. I should've immediately backed up and retreated through the tunnel. I should've said something in my most powerful voice. Something like *Leave me the hell alone* or

How dare you impersonate my father? I should've done something more than stand there and stare.

"Zenn Bower," the General said, his eyes deep pools of intrigue. "We finally meet under appropriate circumstances."

If he thought morphing himself into my father—or getting inside my mind to make me think I was seeing my father—and then forcing me to follow him constituted "appropriate circumstances," the man was delusional. He slicked one hand over his graying hair and smiled.

"What do you want?" I asked. I didn't know what I expected from the General. He hadn't made it to the crown of the Association by playing nice. I imagined my friends out in the sky, fighting to find the very man that stood before me. Dying, maybe. I saw Saffediene in that net. My hands clenched and unclenched as I worked to control my escalating anger.

"I believe you've already spoken with Van." General Darke's eerily calm smile never wavered as he spoke.

My throat turned dry. "I don't like his offer."

"I didn't say you had to like it, but you do have to accept it." The General casually sat down and plucked something from his jacket pocket.

"I don't think—"

"Ah, now there's the problem," the General said. "You think too much."

I shook my head. "No, I don't." I plan. I calculate. It's one of my best qualities.

"Oh, but it's not, Zenn," the General said, revealing his ability to read my thoughts. "Why don't you try being a little spontaneous for once?"

"I'm spontaneous," I argued, remembering how Gunner had said I didn't argue when I was right.

General Darke stood up. "Prove it." He took several steps toward me. "Come with me. Escape this oppression. Live how you want, wherever you want. I'll give you any city in the Association."

I swallowed as he stopped directly in front of me. "I've been working against people like you for years."

"I know." The General smiled. "And it's not doing you any good. Why not give the other side a try? You might just find that we're right."

Time stretched itself into seconds that became minutes. I wanted to argue with the General. Sure, his government functioned. And I had seen the effects of free choice. Riots. Death. Inequality. But that society was *free*. Which was better?

I felt like I was arguing a losing debate. That deep, buried part of me that had responded when Director Hightower had said, *You know I'm right*, surged upward.

"Any city?" I asked, hating the weakness in my voice.

"Any city."

"My friends go free." I forced some measure of control into my voice.

General Darke put his hand on my shoulder. "Oh, Zenn. They're not your friends."

I opened my mouth to protest, to tell him I'd go with him if Vi could go free, if he'd let Saffediene out of that net. He cut me off. "And they will die. Sadly, war has casualties."

"But—"

He squeezed my shoulder a little too hard. "But nothing, Zenn. Either you're all in—or all out." He stepped back. "Your choice."

I replayed my convo with Saffediene about enacting change from within. I thought about the riot in Harvest, the fires in Baybridge, the relative ease with which General Darke had emptied a city of millions in only a day.

I felt a tear ripping down the middle of my body.

I saw myself helping Jag. I saw him win. I saw myself helping General Director Darke. I saw him win.

I remembered the things I'd said to Vi to keep her out of trouble with the Association. I remembered doing nothing to get Vi out of her brainwashed state in Freedom.

I'd recruited Saffediene. I'd escaped Freedom. I'd flown

to city after city, implementing the changes from Gunn's journal.

And for what? For the opportunity to wear rags and eat expired cans of stew? To watch an Insider-friendly city burn?

How much had I contributed to that? I gave intel to both sides; my reports inspired action on both sides.

I'd played the Informant-Insider for far too long. It was time to choose.

I took a deep breath as Saffediene's words sounded in my mind. *You could always go back undercover. You could make the necessary changes we need—from within.*

"I want Freedom."

39.

No one stood guard outside the Security Department, but that didn't make me feel any less nervous. My reports said General Darke had a dozen bodyguards, and who knew what equipment or which talents.

We met no resistance. Vi's tension infiltrated my senses. I turned toward her, only to find determination etched on her face.

"We're here," Vi said, and it sounded so loud in the sleeping city. We touched down in the street and entered the Security Department through a glass door.

I wondered if the monitoring systems in Castledale were

still functioning, and if my picture had just been taken, or if our entrance had been logged.

It didn't matter. Darke was in this building, and I didn't wait to see who followed me or where they went afterward. I strode forward, my boots making heavy thuds against the metal floor.

I ascended to the top floor with Vi, and we placed our charges down the hall and around the only door. After descending to the lobby, I pressed the button on my belt and my world exploded.

When I woke up, I smelled wet cement and smoke. I wasn't in the building anymore, and someone crouched nearby, backlit by a flickering orange glow.

I moaned, and the figure turned, scrambling back to me. "Stay down, Jag," he said. "You took a piece of metal right to the head."

Jag? I thought. *Is that really my name?*

The man turned, looking back down the alley. "Vi! He's awake."

I didn't know who Vi was, so I asked, "Who are you?"

40.

When General Darke and I left the tunnel, the Security Department still burned brightly against the midnight sky. He didn't spare it a glance, but I flew backward and watched until I couldn't see it anymore.

I never saw anyone else flying nearby. I never heard anyone call my name. I'd never felt so alone, not even when I'd left Vi to begin training with the Special Forces or when my father stopped responding to my messages.

We flew all night, using two spare packs to keep the

boards going. We arrived in Freedom just as the sun crested the ocean waves.

The city lay in silence, broken and smoldering, the tech-tric barrier ruined.

Jag

41.

The girl kneeling in front of me stared, her eyes flashing with blue and turquoise and purple. The color purple really freaked me out for some reason, like I'd seen it recently and it meant something bad was about to happen.

She'd come running when the man had called her name. When she spoke, her mouth didn't move, but her voice echoed in my head.

I'm Violet Schoenfeld, she said. *And you're Jag Barque. Don't you dare forget.*

Easy enough for her to say. Before I could respond, *Look, I have forgotten*, she whipped around.

"No," she said, dashing to the corner of the building again. The still-nameless man joined her. "No, no, no." She watched the sky. Somewhere around that corner, a fire burned. The flames reflected off the tears flowing down Violet Schoenfeld's face.

When she turned, the look in her eye scared me, scared me, scared me. I flinched away and bumped into a soft body lying next to me.

The girl slept peacefully. Her chest rose and fell in an even rhythm, and her bright yellow hair fell in jagged lines to the dark ground. I felt something for her. Friendship?

I recognized this girl. I'd seen her sleep before. I'd seen another guy keep his hand possessively on her back, showing everyone that they were together.

I took a deep breath, trying to reason through these weird feelings, and trying to place this beautiful Violet girl who seemed to want to punch me and kiss me at the same time.

"Vi?" I said, testing the name the man had called her just after I'd woken up.

She left the corner and strode toward me. "Don't 'Vi' me." With her words, another vision barged into my mind. One in which this girl shoved me backward. Told me I shouldn't have left her to cross the border alone. After she forgave me for leaving her in the Goodgrounds, we watched the sunset together, content in the silence that followed.

I loved this girl. "I think I love you," I said out loud, trying those words in my mouth. They seemed to fit.

Vi sighed, awakening more memories within me. She reached out and pulled me to a standing position. "Come look at this."

She led me to the corner. I hobbled from the shooting pain in my ankle and the dull pain in my head. Sure enough, a building burned beyond the alley. "The Security Department," I said, more and more pieces of my life coming to my remembrance. I looked at Vi. My Vi. "We did it."

"Zenn left with Darke," Vi said. "I saw them."

Something inside me roared, blocking out the worried look on Vi's face, the choking smell of singed metal and melting plastic, and the memory of her father—who was watching me.

A flood of memories crashed down upon me. I remembered everything, especially how Zenn had betrayed me once before.

"We're depleted," Thane said back in the war room. He handed me a hemal-recycler, and I held it to my head wound to absorb the blood. Meds flowed into my bloodstream, and I felt the pain recede instantly. "We lost half our members. We need time to regroup." He lifted his mug of steaming coffee and drank.

We had to evacuate this city—fast. Who knew how long it would be before Darke sent a cleanup crew? I'd tasked the surviving Resistance members to pack up our remaining tech and food. Vi sat next to me, holding my hand, while Thane mused through possible locations for our retreat.

Retreat. The word sang through my body the same way the meds did, forcing me to admit defeat. We hadn't killed Darke. We hadn't destroyed Freedom. Had I been dreaming an impossible dream for the past four years? Imagining a future that would never be?

I pushed away from the table. I limped away from Vi, away from Thane, away from their questions and feelings. I didn't really want to be alone, but I didn't want to be with them either.

I left the building and stood in the shadows of a doorway across the street to wait for the impending sunrise. I'd first kissed Vi in a doorway almost exactly like this. I'd never felt anything so magical as her lips against mine.

Tears burned behind my eyes, and I let them fall. I was glad I could remember kissing Vi. For a few minutes after I'd woken up, I couldn't even recall my own name. Then everything had come back, and I'd been told a few things I wished I didn't know.

Namely that Thane had saved me. We hadn't heard from

Laurel or anyone on her team since before the launch. We didn't know if they'd made it into the Security Department or not. Those twenty people had just disappeared. Gone. Zenn's crew was unaccounted for as well—even Saffediene, who I never suspected would abandon the Resistance, despite her feelings for Zenn. It made sense that if he'd flown away with Darke, she had too.

I considered my remaining personnel. I couldn't afford to lose Trek. With Pace gone—my throat squeezed—Trek was the only one qualified to run our advanced tech operations. Starr could probably manage in a pinch, but she lay unconscious in the infirmary.

My charges had compromised the Security Department, but Darke's people had thrown a few last-ditch tech grenades. Starr had been hit by one soon after she and Thane entered the building. That's where they'd found Vi and me passed out under a solid metal beam.

Thane had dragged out Vi first. After he'd passed her off to his team, he'd re-entered the burning, collapsing building to get me. And then Starr.

I'd never trusted Thane, not completely. But now? Now I did.

He wasn't the one who'd abandoned his team and flown east with Darke. I felt the rage building inside. The first time

Zenn had abandoned me and the Resistance, I was hurt. It was as if his girlfriend meant more to him than freedom— more than me, his best friend.

I thought he'd changed. I thought he understood our situation. I'd forgiven him for abandoning me once, but twice? Now I felt nothing but fury. At Zenn. At his weakness. But also at myself, for allowing him to be so intricately involved in the Resistance. For trusting him, even a little bit. I wished he didn't know so much about our plans to take down Hightower. I wished he didn't have the journal, which listed all of the Resistance codes and Insider safe houses.

Vi stepped in front of me, settling next to me to watch the sun rise. "But he does. So Zenn knows our plans. So what? Hightower knows everything anyway, right?"

Glad she had come to find me, I gathered her into my arms and held her close, relishing the fact that Zenn never would. Violet Schoenfeld was mine.

"And you're mine," she whispered, tilting her head up to kiss me.

"I wish you'd stop reading my mind," I said, sliding my hands under the hem of her shirt.

"I can stop—if you want."

"No, no, it's fine," I said, repeating what she'd said to me last summer as we crossed the desert. That felt like so long ago, when we were just getting to know one another.

She slugged me. "Come on. My dad wants to discuss looking for my mom's team."

For thirty seconds it was just me and Vi, and the weight of the world had lifted. As soon as Vi pulled away, that pressure returned. At least the darkness was giving way to a new day.

But I'd only taken two steps back toward the hideout when an unmistakable sound carved fear down my spine.

Hoverboards.

Zenn

42.

Bodies littered the orchards. The camps. The green area surrounding Rise One. All clones. The men near Rise One were dead, and had been for a while if their smell was any indication. "Vi killed these men a few days ago," I said, lifting the collar of my jacket to shield my nose from the offensive odor.

General Darke was silent. He flew away from the carnage and toward the Evolutionary Rise. Smoke billowed from the building, adding to the stench in the city.

The Medical Rise tilted dangerously to one side, and the Technology Rise still had coals glowing at its base. Rise One seemed untouched, but I knew better. The metal and glass simply hid the damage we'd find on the inside.

I followed the General, unsure of how I was supposed to feel. Happy the Resistance had debilitated Freedom? Furious? Neutral, the way General Darke seemed to be? Better to let the General lead—he'd been doing it for decades. He slowly circled the Evolutionary Rise.

"We'll rebuild," he finally announced. "Citizens cannot leave their houses without authorization." His voice sounded detached, as if it didn't matter that people had died. A lot of people.

"I'll get to work on the barrier and do a damage assessment," he said. "You get rid of all these bodies."

And that's how I went from Director to grave digger.

Jag

43.

"Vi-i," I drawled. "Who are they?"

She cocked her head to the side before she spun and gripped my shoulders. "Refugees from Freedom."

Hope leapt inside me. Could Pace be with them?

"How many?"

Vi shook her head, meaning she couldn't tell. Four seconds later, the whine of hoverboards became a deafening growl. River Isaacs, her father, and a few others landed in front of us. Their hair and clothing were matted with ash.

River wiped her hair out of her eyes. I'd never seen someone look so tired.

"Hey," she said easily, as if she'd shown up for a party.

"Hey." I scanned the group of seven. No Pace. A figure lay prostrate on a hoverboard. Hope surged again. "Who's that?"

A girl switched her gaze between me and the figure. "Gunner Jameson. We evacuated him from the Evolutionary Rise."

I swallowed hard and nodded. "Anyone else?"

Vi put her hand on my arm, and I knew. No one said anything, and the people from Freedom shifted nervously. I turned away, angry that Pace wasn't among them. Neither was Indy. I leaned against the doorway for support.

I felt like dying. Maybe then this pain wouldn't hurt so much. Like somehow death would release me from this anguish. I couldn't even cry. I just felt like someone was ripping my stomach out through my throat.

"Lighten up, Ivory. I know how he feels," River said, and it sounded far away. "You guys got anything to eat?"

Such a normal question. Before I could stop myself, I started laughing. Vi glanced at me like I'd lost it. Maybe I had. But hey, it was either laugh or cry.

After I'd led the new arrivals from Freedom across the street and into the hideout, I found Raine sitting at the table. Starr's awake. She searched my face, looking for an answer about

Gunn. I nodded toward the infirmary before I announced, "Breakfast."

The twenty people remaining in the Resistance introduced themselves as we used the food-generating cube to produce breakfast. We ate waffles and sausage, and drank milk (always Vi's first request) and soda, and finished the meal with cake and ice cream.

Nobody spoke about the attack here in Castledale. No one reported on what had happened in Freedom.

For that one hour, we were friends. Not rebels.

All too soon someone bustled the dishes off to the kitchen. Trek took Starr by the hand and disappeared into the tech wing. Vi delivered breakfast to the infirmary, where Raine refused to leave Gunner's side.

Thane talked quietly with the new arrivals from Freedom, then he assigned them bedrooms and returned to the table while most of them went to catch up on sleep. I wanted to rest too, but first I needed to hear Mason Isaacs's report.

They'd taken down Freedom. Set the Technology Rise on fire. Reduced Rise One to a skeleton of rafters. The Evolutionary Rise had toppled, and while the Medical Rise hadn't, enough damage had been done to deem it structurally unsound.

"Ivory's a genius," Isaacs said. "She had this patch that dissolved walls. The whole wall! That's how we gutted Rise One."

"Nice," I said.

"We should get her set up with Trek after she's rested," Thane said.

I nodded. "Continue." Vi had returned from the infirmary, and I rubbed slow circles on her back as a way to distract myself from thoughts of Pace and what might have happened to him during the attack on Freedom.

Hightower hadn't expected a second wave in Freedom. Elsewhere, yes. But not in his city. And certainly not with his clones guarding every major Rise and forming a humanoid perimeter of the city.

Hightower also hadn't anticipated anyone else being able to control the clones, especially with Vi out of the picture. Isaacs had activated his team in Rise Twelve but hadn't been able to gain access to the Technology Rise. Good thing his daughter was a genius with creating fake identification credentials.

They'd simply walked into the Evolutionary Rise with fake badges and wide-brimmed hats. There, Ivory had modified a piece of tech that would make the deaf clones hear.

They found Gunner in the Evolutionary Rise and busted him out. Since he was the only one with a voice, Gunner took out the clones, despite his weakened condition.

I shivered at the voice power and mental fortitude that must've required. People without voice talent didn't understand the gravity of using it. Or the responsibility— and the guilt—that accompanied extreme verbal persuasion.

I made a mental note to talk to Gunner privately when he woke up. He'd need the emotional support, and he'd need it from me.

"Did you see my brother?" I couldn't bring myself to say his name.

Isaacs studied me for a moment, his mouth turned down. "I'm sorry, Jag. Pace did not survive the experimentation. I think the only reason Gunner did is because of his adaptability to tech. That, or Van was keeping him alive because of his multiple talents." He cleared this throat. "I'm sorry," he repeated.

"And Indy?" Vi asked.

"No sign of her," Isaacs reported. "The records show that Modification had not occurred before our attack, so . . ."

I would not give voice to my hope, though my mind screamed, *She could still be alive!*

"Once the clones were gone, the rest was easy," Isaacs continued. "Van had no defense. We took out his Technology Rise, which forced the techtric barrier to fail, and then we hightailed it out of there." He sat back in his chair, finished.

"Where's Van?" Thane asked, as if he was the leader. Annoyance bolted through me, but I held my tongue.

"Dead," Isaacs said. "He did not survive the collapse of Rise One."

I wasn't glad for anyone's death—not even Van Hightower's, as his daughter sat just down the hall, and someone would have to tell her. That someone would most likely be me.

"Our team had considerably less success," I said.

"We lost Zenn," Vi added from beside me, her eyes closed.

"We didn't *lose* Zenn," I argued. "He abandoned us." The words made me ill. The four waffles I'd eaten and the half gallon of milk I'd drunk swam in my stomach. "He's a traitor. He *chose* to go with Darke. He's—"

"We lost Zenn," Vi repeated. She put her hand on my leg under the table, and some of my anger drained out through her touch.

But I didn't apologize. Zenn *was* a traitor.

Thane shot me a glance. I nodded for him to continue. Without Indy or Zenn, Thane might as well act as my second-in-command.

"Okay, so there are twenty-five of us," Thane said. "We

have two tasks: find Laurel and her team—and anyone else who might be out there in the city—and evacuate. I think our window of opportunity for both is shrinking. We need to be in the sky by nightfall."

As much as I didn't want to, I agreed. I said so, and then assigned everyone four hours of sleep—Thane included.

We'd face the city at noon.

Zenn

44. It took thirty men three days to rid Freedom of the bodies. At my directive, they dug shallow graves in between the wall and the barrier. In the rubble of Rise One, I found Van Hightower's body.

For some reason, I couldn't look away from his face. Director Hightower looked peaceful, but for the gash across his neck. A strange sensation filled me from the toes up. Grief.

"So much death," I murmured. The crew collected the body and took it to the gravesite along with the others. We filled the shallow troughs, covered them with dirt, and began the process of restoring the techtric barrier.

General Darke still hadn't figured out how to do that. Little more than ash, the Technology Rise and all its capabilities were history. Rise One had been gutted. All medical records and scientific evidence had been lost. Runners had been sent to Grande and Arrow Falls to ask their Directors for any tech they could spare, but they hadn't returned yet.

All transmissions had been silenced for the past three nights. I wondered when the people would shake off their brainwashed haze. How long before they'd realize they could leave their houses without an alarm going off or even receiving so much as a citation?

Even the cache system had failed. General Darke and I had to speak aloud to communicate. He'd found a pair of empty town houses with minimal damage, and we'd moved in next door to each other. Today the city's remaining Thinkers were gathering for a meeting of the minds.

We sat in General Darke's kitchen-converted-into-warroom, waiting for him to arrive. When he did, we stood as one, each of us lowering our chin slightly to acknowledge his superiority.

I used to dislike these little acts of subservience. Now they allowed me to breathe without worrying about who I was to report to and what I'd need to lie about. Now I didn't live a lie. I simply lived.

The light coming in the skylight flickered. Lightning. A few minutes later, as General Darke spoke in his steady, controlling voice, rain pelted the glass.

I couldn't help thinking of Saffediene caught out in the thunderstorm. My mind wandered, imagining her wet clothes clinging to her chilly skin. Her hair slicked off her forehead as she frantically searched for somewhere to ride out the storm.

Briefly, that somewhere had been my arms. My breath shuddered on the way in, and General Darke cast me a knowing look. I buried my emotions deep, deep.

I hadn't been able to save Saffediene in Castledale, and I certainly couldn't now. I didn't know if she'd been rescued from the electro-net, or if she'd been captured. She had told me to work things out with my father, when really she meant I needed to figure out if functionality overrode freedom. Too bad this city—and this government—was no longer functioning.

I fingered the single-use teleporter ring in my pocket, part of me desperate to put it on.

Where I would go, I didn't know. It didn't matter.

Anywhere away from this conflict and dilemma would suffice.

Instead I made eye contact with General Darke. I wanted him to know that I was paying attention.

"We're a bit crippled without technology," he said. "We can't get our cache system to work, and the barrier is still down. None of the runners have returned." He turned to the Transportation Director, a Thinker I knew little about. "Marco, have you heard anything?"

"No, sir," Marco said. "The runners are trained to be fast. They have ways of communicating with the Directors without dealing with barriers and rules."

Three days had passed. They definitely should've been back by now, especially since both Grande and Arrow Falls are within a half-day's ride of Freedom. If General Darke was worried about their tardiness, he didn't show it. But Marco did. His hands twisted over and around each other; he glanced from one face to the next.

I caught his eye and made the slightest motion with my right hand. *Calm down.*

Insider Tip #9: Never show your agitation. Agitation is usually a sign that you have something to hide.

Which made me think Marco totally had something to hide. I'd need to position myself next to him before he left. Find out everything I could. That's what Directors do. They know everything that's happening in their city, and I needed to know what Marco was hiding.

General Darke spoke of the cleanup, reading verbatim

from my report. No one else knew that, but I did. He went through the list of people we'd lost during the Resistance attack. New Thinkers were needed in the Medical, Evolutionary, Confinement, and Technology Rises. Freedom needed a new Director, and that person would also become the new Regional Director in the eastern city belt.

He assigned new Directors, some of whom were in the room and others who would be promoted from their current jobs. New weight settled on the shoulders of those assigned to crumbled Rises, as they'd be responsible for getting them rebuilt and functioning.

"With the loss of Van Hightower," General Darke said, "Freedom needs a new Director. I won't be able to stay here forever." He surveyed the group, and I felt like he was judging each of us. I wasn't sure I met his expectations. Scratch that. As a seventeen-year-old who had very recently played for the other side, I didn't come close to the General's expectations.

The experience and talent—and loyalty—of the other Thinkers in the room outweighed mine, despite the General's recruitment speech in Castledale. I knew I had talents he wanted, I just didn't know if they were enough.

"Zenn Bower," he said finally. I don't know what he saw when he looked at me, but I saw a calculating old man when I looked at him.

I was the most surprised by the announcement, but definitely not the angriest. But no one argued with the General. They'd accept me as their Director, because if they didn't, they'd die. General Darke would make sure of that. For now, I appreciated his protection. My fists clenched as I wondered what would happen when the General left Freedom and I had to Direct by myself.

Once the General concluded his business, I edged my way over to Marco. I met cold glances and near-silent scoffs every step of the way, but I didn't care. I'd been on the fringes of the Insiders for weeks. The girl I loved disliked me so much, she'd punched me. Nothing here was as agonizing as being in the same room with Vi yet not being with her.

I sipped my bottled water as Marco chatted with the new Medical Director. He finally stepped away, and I seized my opportunity. "Tense in there, yeah?"

Marco looked at me, but said nothing. He zipped his jacket as if he might leave before General Darke dismissed us. He wouldn't. So I said, "The runners are probably just caught in the storm."

"Hopefully." He turned away from General Darke, who lingered near the head of the table, speaking with the new Evolutionary Director.

"You used to run, Zenn. What's it like out there?"

"Dangerous," I said, bringing my bottled water to my lips to disguise their movement.

"Hmm." Marco fisted his hands and shoved them in his pockets to mask his agitation. It was a classic Insider move. *When nervous, hide your hands*. I practically wrote the manual on Insider behavior, and I recognized all the signs.

"Who'd you send?" I asked. "Maybe I know them and can tell you of their flying abilities." I was lying, of course. Why would a former junior assistant from Rise Nine know any of the city's runners? Employing my voice power, I asked again, "So who'd you send?"

Marco bounced on the balls of his feet. "No one. I didn't send anyone."

I couldn't help it; I stared openly. Was he confiding in me, or had I coerced him with my voice? Was he playing me, the new Director of Freedom, hoping I wouldn't discipline him for his daring act of rebellion? Now, when the General would punish anyone who so much as sneezed before asking permission?

"What are you going to do about it, Director?" he asked, sneering out the last word. That's when I knew: He knew what I would have to do, and he was pushing me to see if I'd do it.

I made it to the bathroom before throwing up.

* * *

Three days later, Marco was buried in a shallow grave alongside the clones. General Director Darke stood next to me, his hand on my shoulder in a fatherly gesture of support.

I didn't cry. I'd done that at home. At night. In private. Well, mostly. General Darke had witnessed one episode when I couldn't call back the tears fast enough. He hadn't chastised me. He'd simply said, "Hard times call for hard decisions, Zenn. You wanted to run this city, you have to run this city."

Then he'd left me alone in my townhome to cry, cry until I didn't feel anything anymore.

Afterward, I'd ordered Marco's execution, and I'd sent runners to Arrow Falls and Grande.

They were due to return within the hour. With their intel, maybe I'd be able to get security back up in Freedom. Maybe I'd figure out a way to get the brainwashing messages out again.

Maybe I'd find a way to regain control of my Citizens. Six days had gone by without a single transmission. My voice wasn't strong enough to make recordings, even if I had the proper equipment.

And the people of Freedom were waking up. Yesterday Citizens began to venture outside their homes. I'd used the remaining Enforcement Officers to herd them to the green area outside Rise Two, and I'd asked the people to bring any tech they had stored in their homes.

So far only four people had brought items, and they ranged from a sleeve of microchips to the family food dispenser. I couldn't refuse them their only way of eating—I wasn't that heartless—and I'd sent them home again.

The only reason I hadn't been run out of town, or buried in the shallow graves I'd helped dig, was because of Marco's execution. The people were afraid.

I was running my city on fear.

When my runners didn't return at the appointed time, I retreated to my town house. I couldn't cry anymore. I'd made my choice when I signed Marco's death sentence, and I'd live with it.

If General Darke didn't kill me first.

45.

The heat is so strong, I can taste it. Fire rages all around me. I'm trapped in the middle of an inferno.

I jam a teleporter ring on my finger, but don't have time to say anything before I blitz into particles.

It doesn't matter where I end up. Anywhere is better than being burned alive.

When I land, it's much too quiet. I turn in a slow circle, seeing only desolate land. Nothing grows here, and I'm reminded of the projections I'd seen in school. The images of ash, of decaying bodies, of death.

This place smells like death. It's almost as horrible as being in fire, this being-out-in-the-middle-of-nowhere thing. I have a feeling no one's been here in centuries. It feels that decayed.

The sun shines weakly, and the ground is covered with a thin layer of frost. There's no wind here. It's as if even the elements stay away from this place. I start walking in what I hope is a southerly direction, because I think I'm in the country north of the Association—the country where everyone died.

You're lost, *I tell myself for the hundredth time. I've been walking for hours. The sun will set soon, and I'll be left in the dark, where no one will ever find me.*

At least there are no Thinkers, *but the thought doesn't ease my desperation.*

Suddenly Vi strolls next to me. She whispers that it's noon and I need to wake up. I try to find her, but the sun has gone out.

It can't be noon if the sun is down. Can it? Nothing makes sense.

And then it doesn't matter, because I'm in the capsule again, and the dirt is raining down, and there is no escape from that tomb.

I woke when I hit the floor. I thrashed, my injured foot making contact with something hard. I'd kicked a person, and they cursed.

"Jag, wake up."

I pushed into a sitting position to find Starr rubbing her kneecap. "Sorry," I said. "I don't wake up well."

"Vi said as much."

"Sorry," I said again. I looked at Starr and found her bright yellow hair appeared freshly washed. "You're looking good, Starr."

Her eyes reminded me of my mother's. Sharp and full of life. She didn't miss anything.

"Thanks to Trek," Starr said. "Thane's been nursing me back to health too."

"Is there anything that guy can't do?" I asked.

A smile seeped across her mouth. "He's got quite the temper."

"Is that a problem?" I asked, folding my arms behind my head. "All the best guys have tempers."

Starr laughed and turned to leave. "I'll go get Vi."

"Don't bother," I said. I could feel Vi's pity coming through the walls. "She's lurking in the hall." Annoyance flashed through me. Vi got someone else to wake me up?

"You have freaky dreams," Vi said, still out of sight.

I didn't answer. I hated subjecting her to my nightmares, but surely she realized what she was, what she could do. She'd need to figure out a way to block my thoughts, my dreams, everything.

"I'm trying," she said. "I've talked to Thane about it."

"Nice," I said in my most sarcastic tone. I didn't want her

talking to Thane about anything except maybe the weather or what to have for breakfast. Certainly not anything having to do with me.

"I'm not giving him specifics." Vi finally appeared in the doorway. Starr hurried out of the room, skating her fingers along Vi's shoulder as she went.

"It's after noon," Vi continued. "We're leaving."

"Northepointe?"

"That's where you chose," she said drily.

I stood up and brushed my hands on my dirty jeans. "Are we packed?"

She smirked. "We're just waiting for our fearless leader."

"Oh, shut up," I said, threading my fingers through hers. "And kiss me."

We left our headquarters in Castledale and flew west to Laurel's last known location. Thane had instructed us to watch for markings on the ground, on buildings, anywhere. "Knowing her," he'd said, "she'll have taken her team somewhere secure and left us a message as to where."

Starr spotted the black writing on the ground first. It looked like Laurel had burned the message in the field, and while I could read the letters, it made no sense to me.

E-D-N-A-R-G.

"Grande," Thane said immediately.

She'd spelled it backward. "Grande is dangerously close to Freedom," I said.

"She's smart," Thane said. "She'll have her moles back up and running in no time."

I consented and turned my board north. Director Kingston held no soft spot for the Resistance—in fact he was as ruthless as they came. Darke would never expect me to find refuge in Northepointe—which was exactly why I'd chosen it as our lay-low city.

That, and because of its location. See, Northepointe was way across the country from Freedom, and the flight would take two days. I needed time to sort through what steps to take next, and if Laurel could really get her underground message system running as fast as Thane claimed, I could operate the Resistance from Northepointe.

I'd just passed the last building in Castledale when Vi screamed. "Saffediene!"

I spun around as Vi streaked away from the group and disappeared.

I swore, Thane swore, and we both took off in the direction she'd gone.

I used Vi's high emotion to track her. She was crouched next to Saffediene's still form. Vi's hands fluttered over Saffediene's chest. When I landed next to her, she looked at me with wild eyes. "She needs help," Vi said.

Saffediene wasn't bleeding. No, her wounds were worse than that: techtricity burns. The flesh on her ankles oozed blood, and black patterns ran the length of her arms, legs, and torso. Her muscles twitched, her eyes blinked, but she didn't move. I wasn't sure how she'd survived.

Thane rummaged through his pack, producing meds and bandages. I did as he instructed, and we had Saffediene tethered to Thane's board in under five minutes. He rode on Vi's, and she stepped onto mine. We made a slow return to the group.

Finding Saffediene cast a somber mood on us, and we flew toward Northepointe in twos and threes, speaking only when necessary.

Mercifully, the sun stayed out all day, and we used the solar charge in our hoverboards. I hooked into a charge pack at night, and used the sunshine to recharge my board and the spare pack on the second day. By the time we saw the city limits of Northepointe, we were all slouched on our boards.

I flew sitting down, with Vi in front of me, her back pressed against my chest. We hadn't spoken much, instead allowing a measure of peace to exist between us during the brief respite from Resistance efforts.

"We're here," I said, so everyone could hear me. Then I repeated it softly so only Vi could.

Darkness—and the early April chill of the far north—would blanket the land in only an hour. We touched down, taking cover in a shallow ravine two miles outside of Northepointe. I sat on the shore keeping watch while everyone else used the food-generating cube to order dinner.

Vi brought me a bowl of steaming soup and settled next to me. I'd swallowed the last mouthful of broth when a light on the outskirts of Northepointe flashed three times.

Three lights asked a question: Are you there?

Two flashes in response meant yes. And of course if I wasn't here, I wouldn't be able to signal, would I?

Shrimp, my contact in Northepointe, flashed every night on the hour from nine to midnight.

"Two flashes will let them know we're here," I instructed Vi. "Can you produce them? Two seconds apart, please."

She fired off the appropriate response, and we settled in to wait for our escort into the city. Ten minutes later a squad of officers landed in front of us.

"You must be Jag Barque," one of them said. "So Shrimp was telling the truth." He glanced at his companions. "Guess we shouldn't have killed him."

Zenn

46.

"I sent them," I said for the fourth time. General Darke sat in his office, his hands folded neatly in front of him on the desk. "You were with me when I sent them."

He nodded. "I was. I'm wondering why they haven't returned."

"I don't know."

"Maybe the Resistance is not as dead as we'd like to believe."

"Clearly," I said. "Four of our Rises are in ruins, and we have no way to repair them. If we let our people out of their homes they'll know we have no idea what we're doing. And they'll think they can do a better job than we can."

General Darke frowned, the only indication that he knew my statement was true.

"Harvest is Insider friendly," I continued, "so I can't go there. Arrow Falls doesn't have much in the way of tech. Grande—"

"They'll have recording equipment," General Darke said. "Perhaps you should take today to travel and get some transmissions made."

"I don't have any more time to waste," I agreed.

"I am going back to Castledale," the General said. "I will take a task force of Enforcement Officers with me. We'll return with the tech required to restore the barrier."

His condescending tone grated on my nerves. I nodded because I didn't trust myself to speak.

"It's settled, then," he said.

"We'll meet again tomorrow morning."

"Evening," General Darke clarified. "My flight is twice as long as yours."

"Until tomorrow evening." I left his office and went directly to my hoverboard.

The flight to Arrow Falls felt twice as lonely as it once

had. Before, I'd always had a companion, someone to talk to, even if I didn't want to talk. Before, I'd had Saffediene.

It hurt to think about her, a lot like it pained me to think about Vi. I wondered how long it would take before I became as cold and heartless as the General.

As I flew over the mass graves, I thought of Marco. Maybe I didn't need to be more emotionally detached.

Maybe I was already more like Jag Barque than I'd thought.

The Director of Arrow Falls, a tall, thin man with gray hair, met me on the roof of their tallest building. He wore his traditional robes the color of deep, rich coffee. I wore what I'd been wearing for the past six days—a pair of jeans and a jacket over a long-sleeved, standard-issue T-shirt.

"Director Bower," the Director said, and his words carried a weight I had not been expecting. I was a Director now. Director Bower.

"The tech the General requested is being prepared for you now," he continued. "Won't you have lunch before you begin your recordings?" He swept his hand toward an open door that I did not feel like entering. I wondered what repercussions I might suffer if I declined. I didn't know, and I didn't want to lose any of my newfound authority.

"Thank you, Director Underson." I ducked into the darkness and took my first steps down a stairwell leading into the depths of the building.

After many flights downward, we emerged into a brightly lit room where technicians scurried from task to task. Some cast nervous glances at me, while others focused on their work as if their lives depended on it. It did, because I had asked them to produce the technology I needed, and I could take their lives if they did not deliver. A balloon grew inside my chest, filled with importance and pride. I tried to stop the swelling inside, feeling simultaneously ashamed and arrogant.

Director Underson glided through the room, and the technicians parted for him. Their counters seemed overfilled and underpolished, but I didn't say anything. While tech wasn't the crux of Arrow Falls's worth, they clearly had a lot of supplies. I had thought their focus was improving soil quality.

"We also provide help when needed," Director Underson said, clearly reading my thoughts. "Van Hightower and I were close, personal friends. His death saddens me."

In a world where emotions are rarely shown, the Director's words surprised me. He didn't appear sad, and I didn't have an empathic talent to tell if he genuinely felt sad or not.

Emotion belies weakness, I thought, but didn't vocalize anything to Director Underson.

He led me to a bank of traveling rings. "Blue for ascent, green for descent," he explained. "We're going to the second floor, where I've prepared my private dining room for lunch. You can use my study to complete your recordings."

"Thank you," I said, suddenly wary to record new transmissions for the Citizens of Freedom. I knew if I didn't, the consequences would be dire. I felt caged in my new position as Director, when I should've been enjoying my freedom.

I waited while Director Underson stepped into a green ring and disintegrated before my eyes. After a moment, I then stepped into the same ring.

My particles reassembled in a faux-wood-paneled room where a glass table had been set for five. The drapes were drawn; the only light emanated from yellow tech fixtures along the far wall. The room felt narrow and closed off, which added to my *I'm-trapped* feelings.

Director Underson selected a seat at the head of the table. I sat on his immediate right, wondering if it was proper to ask who would be joining us.

Before I could, one of the doors opened at the opposite end of the room. Three stern men at least twice my age entered. Each of them wore their Thinker robes, and the dark brown seemed to suck more light from the room.

I stood to greet them, lowering my chin before I realized that I held the same rank now.

"Director Bower, do sit down. It'll take some getting used to, won't it?" Director Underson asked, not unkindly and with a small smile. That smile vanished as he nodded to our lunch companions.

"Directors Marsh, Hideawae, and Long," he said, indicating each man with a wave of his hand. The men took the remaining chairs, with Director Marsh next to me. "They are my board of advisers here in Arrow Falls. I'm sure Freedom has a similar council of Thinkers."

Before I could answer, Director Underson continued. "Directors, this is Zenn Bower, the new Director of Freedom."

Director Long crossed his arms while the other Directors welcomed me.

"Doesn't Freedom employ a plethora of Thinkers?" Director Long leaned back in his chair.

"Oh, yes." I kept my eyes locked onto his. Looking to Underson for guidance would only make me appear weak. Not a trait I wanted to exhibit. "One for each of our Rises, and there are about twenty of those."

Director Long looked at the Director next to him, but it looked like he was rolling his eyes at me.

"Have you lived in Freedom, Director Long?" I asked.

Director Underson dropped his fork and someone gasped. No one was more shocked than me. I didn't even know where the question had come from.

Director Long narrowed his eyes at me. "Stay out of my head."

"I didn't—I mean—I can't read minds." Tension buzzed along the surface of my skin, making my hair stand on end. Clarity of thought accompanied the sensation, and I leaned forward. "But I think you lived there. Maybe got passed over for a promotion. That's why you dislike me."

A stretch of silence punctuated my statement. I thought about mentioning General Darke and how he'd appointed me as Freedom's Director, but I stayed quiet.

"There, there." Director Underson chuckled, finally breaking the moment. "Director Long is exactly where he needs to be."

Before either of us could argue, servants entered the dining room laden with platters of food.

After lunch I settled in Director Underson's study, alone. I'd asked him who recorded the transmissions for Arrow Falls, and he'd said, "Director Long is the only voice talent we have here."

I'd smiled tightly and entered his study. No way was I asking Director Long for help.

My biggest challenge remained: My voice wasn't exactly the strongest one out there. It might be enough to keep a few people brainwashed for a few days, but it was nowhere near powerful enough to keep millions from realizing that their government had fallen.

Not only that, many were already awake. I certainly didn't have the level of voice power I needed to regain control and keep them compliant.

My hands shook as I linked the last wire to the transmitter. The green light came on, indicating that my equipment was recording.

I cleared my throat, took a deep breath, and began. "Your Director, Mr. Zenn Bower, is a trusted leader. He will guide you through the dark and difficult days ahead. . . ."

Jag

47.

I thought to Vi, *Get Thane!*

"Stand down. Deactivate any weapons you have," I said out loud. My voice came out coated with pure authority. I knew I had enough control to talk down these six officers, but I needed Thane for backup. I wished Gunner was awake and healthy. His voice would be invaluable right about now.

Vi stumbled away, and when none of the officers made to stop her, I smiled.

When none of them deactivated their weapons, the smile slid off my face. "Toss those tasers over here," I said.

The lead officer grinned. I ducked and scrambled backward

as taser fire arced over my head. I yelled something unintelligible, hoping my people would scatter.

I'd taken two steps when someone grabbed a fistful of my hair. "You can't get away so easily, Jag Barque," the officer said. "We know all your tricks."

I thrashed and kicked and managed to free myself. I sucked at the air as I ran toward my team, not bothering to look behind me to see what the officers would do next.

"Jag!" Thane called and I veered toward his voice. Good thing, too, because a tethering strand landed where I had been a moment before. I would've been caught, shocked, and stuffed back into a hole.

My tension doubled at the thought of the capsule. I ducked behind an outcropping of bushes where I found Thane and the rest of our team. "Officers from Northepointe," I gasped. "My voice didn't work."

Thane responded by tossing a tech grenade over the bushy barrier. It sparked, then exploded, causing us to cover our heads with our hands. When the techenergy subsided, I peered around the bush.

Three guards had taken a direct hit. The other three advanced slowly, their weapons drawn. "Vi, can you get inside their heads?" I asked.

"No, Jag," she said. "I can't."

She could, but I knew what she meant. She wouldn't control people again, because she didn't know how far she'd go.

"Thane?"

He stared right at me, unblinking, for what felt like a long time. Finally he said, "I've deactivated their sound cancelers. Our voices will work now."

I leapt from behind the bush. "Deactivate your weapons. Kick those tasers over here." Almost as one person, three feet kicked over three now-deactivated tasers.

"Take off your clothes," I commanded them. The officers wore black pants over black books. Black vests over black jackets. I voice-ordered the guards until their boots were on our feet, and their jackets were warming our shoulders. I made them deposit their backpacks and their hoverboards at my feet before sending them back to Northepointe in their underwear.

Their feet might need medical attention, but my idea was to be many miles away before anyone in Northepointe knew why.

"Watch them," I instructed Thane. I called to my Resistance members. "Northepointe is out. We fly in five." I shouldered one of the officers' packs and tucked a fully charged taser into my back pocket.

Thane got a new weapon and his hoverboard back. He

carefully loaded a still-unconscious Saffediene onto one of the confiscated boards and tethered it to his. With all the supplies taken and rationed among us, I surveyed my team.

Sure, we were skinny. No, we did not know where or when we'd be able to sleep again. But dammit, we were still alive.

The Resistance is still alive.

I ran through a list of Insider-friendly cities, dismissing them all. Cedar Hills, Lakehead, Harvest—Darke would be monitoring each of them.

Laurel had gone to Grande; maybe we should too. Or maybe farther south, maybe down to Rancho Port, the southernmost city in the Union.

I hadn't been to Rancho Port since my capture. Could I face going back?

Yes.

Starr's voice in my head didn't surprise me. Her confidence in my ability to overcome my haunted history with Rancho Port did.

"Where to, boss?" Starr wasn't really asking, because she already knew.

"Rancho Port."

We flew straight south, combing back through the abandoned city of Castledale. From there, I sent Trek, Starr, and Saffediene to Grande to coordinate with Laurel. Trek could find out what had been going on in Freedom, and Saffediene could get the medical attention she needed. The rest of us would go farther south and send word when we arrived in Rancho Port.

I flew with the twenty members of the Resistance until I thought I'd never want to ride a hoverboard again. We finally reached the wide waters that lapped at the edge of our country. The Thinkers routinely cited the shrinking land masses as one of the reasons They needed to maintain control. Even I'd seen the maps showing how far out the land used to jut into the ocean. I knew we needed to preserve our natural resources, I just didn't think mind control was the way to do it.

We stopped at the water's edge, the heat of the day at full height. We'd been on hoverboards for two whole nights and two whole days, and I knew I'd have a mutiny on my hands if we didn't rest.

"We'll be here until morning," I said. "Make camp, generate something to eat, relax." I waited until everyone had set to work, then I stripped to my underwear and ran into the dark waves.

Water crashed over me, dragging me first one way and then carrying me another. I broke the surface, gasping and smiling. I swam out to sea, until the muscles in my arms and legs burned and I didn't think I could kick one more time.

I flipped over on my back and let the ocean waves return me to shore. In the water, I couldn't hear anyone talking. I didn't have to listen to Raine squabble with River over when to use the food-generating cube. I didn't have to listen to Thane whisper to Vi or see them look at me as if I might crack.

I let the dull roar of the water fill my ears, my soul, with music. I gave up my anxiety about going back to Rancho Port.

I hadn't told anyone about my last moments in Rancho Port, and I hadn't dreamt about them, so even Vi didn't know. As I drifted with the ocean breeze, I allowed myself to relive how I escaped.

I'd existed in that pod for what felt like lifetimes. I was sure that if I ever got out, the world as I knew it would've died. A new society would've emerged, and Vi would have been long gone.

But I'd still be sixteen, my body frozen in time while my mind advanced through decades of endless darkness and excruciating heat.

I imagined myself with hair down to my waist, and a beard to match, when I finally took my first step outside the capsule. Of course, I wouldn't even be able to walk, because the muscles in my legs would have atrophied from disuse.

Oh, the dreams I dreamed.

In each one, Vi was long dead. It was merciful, really. I didn't want to think of her struggling along in a crap world. Without me.

An Insider in Rancho Port rescued me from the capsule. He brought me up from the depths of hell and told me to run until I met the ocean. He said a boat would be waiting to take me to Fort Houston, and I'd be able to recover there under the protection of Director Ramirez. I knew Ramirez, and I knew how to run fast.

The way the man spoke stirred a memory inside my muddy mind. "Who are you?" I asked, though my voice was still silenced. But the man understood.

He shook his head. "It doesn't matter who I am."

"Were you part of my Resistance in the Badlands?" I asked.

"You don't have much time." He paled as several voices shouted. "Go!"

I went. I ran as hard as I could. My legs were weak from disuse, and I stumbled over patches of grass on the uneven ground. I fell with the first round of taser fire, but I wasn't hit.

"Xander Bower," a voice boomed. "I should've known you'd be the one to deceive me."

I stayed down, incredulous that Zenn's father had released me from the capsule. That, and I recognized the fury-lined voice chastising him.

Thane Myers had found me again. My heart pumped double time with fear, and I couldn't stop myself from leaping up. Across the distance, my eyes met Thane's. He looked toward me as guards flowed around him. I saw a guard pick up Xander Bower, his bright, blue eyes open and staring into nothingness.

I spun and ran, but not fast enough. There is no escape from the haunting blue eyes that belong to both Zenn and his father.

"Hey, you alive?" Raine asked, nudging me with her booted toe.

I made an indistinguishable noise. The ocean rocked me, and I didn't want to open my eyes and release that comfort yet.

"Dinner's on," she added. "And Vi's looking for you." She started to move away, her boots making sucking sounds in the surf.

"Raine," I said.

"Yeah?"

I pushed myself up on my elbows. "How well did you know Zenn?" Raine froze with her back to me, her shoulders very, very still. She remembered almost everything about her life now. Surely she could tell me what Zenn had been like in Freedom.

"Not that well," she said, her voice guarded.

"Did he ever talk about his father?"

Raine turned toward me. "No, never." She sat just out of reach of the waves. "I lived with Vi for months."

I wasn't sure what she really was trying to say. "I heard you were the one who woke her up." But when I studied her, I found the true meaning behind her words. She'd lived with Vi, and that's how Raine knew about me. "Thank you for not draining me." My voice barely left my throat, but it was loud enough.

"Thank you for coming to get me before I could drain Thane."

I stood up and waded to shore. "How's Gunn?"

"He woke up about an hour ago," Raine said. "He'll survive."

"He's tough," I said. "I need to talk to him."

"I think you better find Vi first," Raine said, pulling herself to her feet.

"I'm sorry about your dad," I said, and I meant it.

Raine paused. "Thank you," she said simply, and left.

I returned to my troubling thoughts about Xander Bower. Why was Zenn's dad in Rancho Port? He'd worked with Blaze before he became Assistant Director of Seaside. I'd heard of Xander Bower's fame, mostly from Zenn before he quit the Resistance the first time.

After Zenn defected, Xander kept our transportation hub alive in the Goodgrounds. Then his older son joined the Resistance, and they both requested new assignments out east. I'd let Indy take care of it, as I'd just started training with Ty in Seaside. My chest filled with bitter pain as my mind flashed with memories.

Ty and Pace and how they used to smile and hold hands. Both now gone.

Zenn, defected again.

Indy, lost before I had a real chance to say good-bye.

Everyone in the Resistance had a list of people they'd lost. Mine was particularly long, and I didn't know how many more names would be added before this war ended.

Terror edged out excitement when I saw Vi walking toward me. Walking didn't adequately describe her movement. Stomping was a more accurate word.

"I hate it when you disappear," she said. "Would it have killed you to say, 'Hey Vi, I'm going to swim out fifty miles into the water, then float back to shore. Don't freak out, okay?'" She cocked her hip and crossed her arms.

I couldn't help it—I laughed. This didn't help her anger, and she threw her hands into the air and stormed back down the beach.

I gathered my clothes and rejoined the group, who had set up camp where the land met the sand. And by camp, I mean a huddled heap of backpacks. I wiggled in between Vi and Raine, ignoring my girlfriend's heavy sigh of annoyance.

"For the record," I said to her, my voice low, "I'm going to swim out fifty miles in the water, then float back to shore again in the morning. Don't freak out, okay?"

She slammed her fist into my thigh. A strangled grunt tore through my throat on impact. "That's nice," I said.

"For the record," she said, not bothering to keep her voice down. "You infuriate—"

I didn't let her finish that sentence. She'd regret it later, and besides, I liked kissing her when she was mad. It always made her less-mad.

Except for this time. She actually bit my lip.

"Dammit," I said, putting my fingers to my mouth and tasting the stickiness of blood on my tongue. I leaned closer. "Are you really that mad?"

"Yes, Jag, I'm really that mad." Vi got up and stormed away, leaving me gaping at Raine.

"What the hell happened while I was swimming?"

Raine edged closer to Gunner, and I wanted to voice-control them both to sleep. "You went swimming," she said.

"We've established that."

Raine glanced at River, and I almost commanded them to tell me the truth. Girls had this thing about protecting each other. This girl rule had frustrated me in the Resistance, just as it did now. "Someone tell me."

"She was left here alone, and she didn't know where you were," Raine said. "She doesn't like being alone."

I wanted to argue that Vi had just left the group to be alone, but I didn't. "Thanks," I said, standing and following Vi into the darkness.

She'd tried to hide from me, but her feelings were too strong. I found her leaning against a rock, staring out over the moonlit water.

"I'm sorry," I said right up front, hoping to avoid getting punched and/or bit again.

She didn't respond, so I continued. "See, we—my brothers and I—have a tradition when we're at the ocean. We always dive in, swim out, then float back."

She kept her lips pressed into a thin line. Vi could be absolutely stubborn when she wanted to be.

"I should've told you," I tried again. "You could've come with me."

"I can't swim," she said, sullen.

"Yes, you can." I bumped her shoulder with mine as I sat

beside her. Her anger deflated until it was wisped away in the breeze coming off the water.

"You leave me a lot," she said. "At the border, in Seaside." She took a deep breath. "I don't like being left behind."

"Noted," I said. "And I'm sorry."

We sat in silence. After a minute I reached for her hand, and she let me hold it.

"I'm scared," she said.

"Me too," I admitted. "Rancho Port doesn't exactly hold fond memories for me."

"Sorry I bit you."

I released her hand so I could put my arm around her. "You bit me?" I asked, playing the game we'd started in the Badlands, where I had indeed left her to cross the border by herself. I'd explained the reasoning behind that act, but it was clear that all Vi saw was me leaving her.

She laughed, but it quieted quickly. "You can conquer anything in Rancho Port," she said.

I heard her words, but I wasn't sure I believed her.

Zenn

48.

Freedom felt foreign, almost like I hadn't spent the better part of the last year inside the city. The silence permeated the Blocks, pressed on the budding orange trees with stillness.

The faint sound of my hoverboard roared like a jet engine. I sped through the streets toward the skeleton of Rise One, gripping the sleeve of transmission microchips in my jacket pocket.

I stood in the once-magnificent foyer of Rise One, looking up through dozens of empty floors to the blue sky above. A strange sadness filled me, but not because the Rise had been gutted.

I was sad because I hadn't been here to see it. And most of all, that I wasn't strong enough to get back on my hoverboard and find the Resistance. Beg every one of them for forgiveness. Spend the rest of my life proving that I was on their side, that I believed in their cause.

I thought of what Vi would say to me should I ever see her again. I wondered what I could say to Saffediene to make things right between us. I touched my fingers to my lips, remembering what it felt like to kiss Vi. Then Saffediene. The feel of their mouths on mine was different, yet each wonderful. I pressed my eyes shut.

Sure, Jag's way of doing things was different from mine. *Different* shouted in my mind. I'd never truly taken the time to see things from his point of view. To be fair, he'd never offered me the same courtesy. We'd spent years as rivals, long before Vi entered the picture.

"I can't help loving her," I said aloud, my voice reverberating through the cavernous space.

Maybe he can't either, a voice responded, sounding very much like my own, as if it came from the bones of the building.

I fingered the transmission microchips in my pocket as I thought of Tyson, Vi's sister. I'd met her at the border of the City of Water, deep in the night. She'd breathlessly given me the Resistance password before she recognized me.

Then she cried, the same way Vi had that night she'd climbed through my window, claiming her mother loved Ty more than her. I'd taken Ty to Jag, both of us silent during the trip across the desert to the Badlands.

Jag spoke eleven words—*Thank you, Zenn. I don't know where we'd be without you*—before I turned around and made the lonely trek home. I'd gone straight to Vi's, though she was at school—where I should've been. My father had provided an excuse, citing he'd needed me for an on-site Transportation Department meeting.

I'd entered Vi's house using the passcode she'd given me and basked in the silence I found within. It was nothing like the quiet stillness I now endured in Freedom. No, Vi's house felt like home to me.

Her presence was there, calming me. I sat on her front steps that day until she arrived home from school.

"Run away with me," I'd said.

She'd half laughed, half snorted as she joined me on the porch. "Right." She peered toward the lake. "Where would we go? The Southern Rim? The forest?" She laid her hand on mine for half a second, but it was long enough to say *I'd go with you. Anywhere. I'd go.*

And she had. She'd broken rule after rule for me. She'd

sent me multiple illegal e-comms. Crossed borders to see me. She'd believed the best of me, always.

She still did.

And I'd repaid her with hidden trackers and half truths and stolen kisses with another girl because I was hurt. And lonely. And so, so jealous.

I bent my head and let the shame pour over me. I fell to my knees, my bones cracking against the hard concrete. I welcomed the physical pain, though it only added to my torment.

"I'm sorry," I whispered to myself. "I will—" I didn't know what I could do. Abandon Freedom?

If only I could. General Darke would hunt me to the ends of the earth if I did. He had more than one way to find me, and none of them were pleasant.

I fisted the microchips, feeling them give just a little. Could I break them? What would that accomplish, exactly? The General—*Ian*, I corrected myself—would know what I'd done. He was expecting my transmissions.

I wouldn't be able to lie to him.

"Not until evening," I said. "He doesn't expect me to have the transmissions until this evening."

I still had time. I could return to Arrow Falls, record new messages. General Darke—*Ian*—wouldn't listen to them. Thinkers never did. I could perpetuate the unbrainwashing in Freedom.

Hope flared inside me. I could do this, right under Ian's nose. Then I remembered the sneer on the Harvest man's face as he'd asked me who I'd voted for. I heard the cries of those whose Transportation Director didn't get elected. I heard that little boy's voice say, *They woke up.*

Again I felt myself break in two. Complete compliance and brainwashing on one side, with freedom and chaos on the other.

Could some semblance of order stem from that chaos? Could people govern themselves?

Instantly I heard my father's voice: *Give them correct principles, and they'll govern themselves.* He'd said this over and over during my childhood. I'd forgotten his words during these many months away from him.

How I missed him. How I needed his wisdom. I didn't know what to do, or who to follow.

Once again my father's voice resonated in my head. *Don't follow, Zenn. Lead.*

I got to my feet, the edges of the microchips biting into the flesh of my palm. I opened my hand and looked at them, and then threw them to the ground. With the thick heel of my boot, I ground the chips into the cement, feeling nothing but satisfaction.

I left the Rise and headed west on my hoverboard. I was

going to make new transmissions, transmissions that would teach the people in Freedom to govern themselves.

I'd just entered the outer Blocks in Freedom when I heard the buzz of approaching hover tech behind me.

I almost didn't turn to look. I didn't care. Let them have Freedom.

I glanced over my shoulder. A trio was coming in off the ocean. I recognized Trek Whiting immediately.

He shifted to the side, and there was Starr Messenger. My stomach twisted, but one thought kept me from heaving: *At least it isn't Jag.*

Jag

49. That night, after everyone fell asleep, I slipped away from the group. Even with Vi curled in my arms, I couldn't settle my nerves. I kept hearing falling dirt, burying me farther and farther underground.

I returned to the rock where Vi and I had sat earlier that evening. The gentle lapping of water against sand sang to me, and I watched the waves in an attempt to purge my mind of more troubling thoughts.

I felt Gunner approaching before I saw him. Exhaustion poured from him, with a little bit of shame.

"Hey," I said as he sat next to me. "Good to see you awake."

He grunted in response, and I knew that I'd be doing most of the talking. Another side effect non-Voices don't understand: Once you do something truly horrific with your voice power, you want to stop speaking. Maybe then you won't say something you'll regret.

"You did what you needed to do," I said. "You enabled the Resistance to wipe out Freedom."

He scoffed, and I heard what he meant. *I killed a whole lotta people. Including Raine's father.*

"You didn't kill him," I said. "And she knows that."

Gunner wouldn't look at me. "I'm not going to lie to you," I said. "It's hard. Remember that day you tased Thane? That was hard too. Holding someone's life in the grip of your voice never gets easier." I paused, remembering some of the more negative ways I'd used my voice.

"The fact is, you have a voice that people will obey. You need to use it for the right things. I believe using your voice to escape and help the Resistance was the right thing to do. Our lives should be our own, and I'm using my voice to accomplish that goal." I touched his arm. "So are you."

He finally faced me, and his eyes looked shiny, almost as if he was crying. "Thanks," he said.

"Yeah," I said. "Dealing with the voice sucks sometimes. I know how it is."

"You ever kill someone?" he asked, his words quiet and strong—the way he's always spoken. That's Gunn. He's got some real resolve.

"Yeah," I said. "Yeah."

Rancho Port perches right on the ocean. The wind blows constantly, and it's hot as hell most of the year. Even now, in early April, as I led our small band of Insiders to the swampy areas on the eastern border, the heat oppressed me.

Dread settled in my stomach. As if Vi sensed it, she nudged her hoverboard closer to mine. I didn't look at her. I wouldn't like what I found reflected in her eyes. My fear. Her reassurance.

Sometimes I really hated that my girlfriend could see inside my head.

Vi moved away, leaving behind a wake of her wounded pride. I let her go, needing to be alone. I flew over miles of swampland, breathing shallowly at the stench of warm earth, stagnant water, and dead fish. I found myself flying slower and slower. Everyone had pulled ahead of me by the time the first buildings came into view.

I drifted closer to the open water. I imagined the path I'd used to escape just several short weeks ago. That tree, had I paused behind it? That stretch of beach, had I run as hard as

I could, my feet sinking into the wet sand even as the next wave obliterated my footsteps?

And that stretch of open swamp, was that where the taser fire had hit me in the back? Where the silencers were applied? Where Thane stood over me, his eyes broadcasting hatred and his voice dripping with disdain?

Now Thane rode in the front of the pack—where I used to ride.

He spoke to Vi with a genuine smile on his face—like I used to do.

Before he saved me from the burning building in Castledale, I would've felt anger and hatred and distrust. Now I only felt sadness that could not be explained.

Sure, I'd cried many times. But that was usually from pure helplessness. Never sadness. I hadn't felt sad since my parents died. I'd closed off that part of myself, determined not to let myself get hurt.

I watched Vi's shoulders tense. Her sadness matched my own. She wanted me to let her in.

Could I do it? I'd established a boundary in all my previous relationships. Indy had not crossed it, though she'd tried—and she knew it. Other girls had been nothing to me. Vi had broken me within days, and yet I continued to push her away. I was constantly trying to re-establish the boundary she had breached.

Why? Her voice in my head felt so intimate. Anyone else, and I'd have barked at them to get the hell out of my mind.

Not her.

Never her. I asked instead of commanded, and I thought snippy things to hurt her, to drive her away, so I could blame her for my weaknesses.

I don't know, I thought. *I'm sorry*. I didn't have any other words that seemed adequate. I was sick of apologizing to her, but I would from now until forever.

She dropped back, letting the others flow around her, until we flew side by side. I reached for her, and she let me hold her hand. The act was simple, yet it spoke volumes.

"You mess me up," I said.

"Why, Jag Barque . . . is that a compliment?"

I smiled, looking at her. "I don't let anyone in." Naked fear flowed in my voice.

She heard it, loud and clear. "I won't hurt you," she promised. "I love you."

It was the first time she'd ever said it before I did. The words rang with truth, with power, and I knew she loved me.

"You have to find a way to let me in," she said. "I won't hurt you, but you're hurting me. I refuse to live like my parents."

"They love each other," I said, surprised by her statement.

"They love what they can do for each other," she corrected. "I love you for you. Not for your voice, or because you're the leader of the Resistance, or anything else. I love you because you're Jag Barque, and because that's good enough for me."

I felt something hiding between her words. "You're good enough for me."

"I didn't say I wasn't."

"You feel like you aren't."

She pinned me with a pointed look. "Because you act like I'm not."

I couldn't argue. When I wouldn't let her in, she heard *I'm not good enough for him. He doesn't trust me. He doesn't love me.*

"This is very difficult for me." I squeezed her hand. "You know that, yeah?"

She gripped my hand in return. "Yeah, I know that."

Vi and I caught up to the group just as we entered the city proper. My guard went up. Something felt wrong. It was silent. Still. No steam rose from the factories; no movement flowed through the streets; no life stirred in the buildings.

Just over a month ago this city had bustled with workers. Thane had been here; Zenn's father had been murdered. What had happened after I'd been taken to Freedom?

Thane swung around to fly beside me. "No transmissions."

"Vi?" I asked. "What can you sense?"

"No Thinkers," she responded. We all swept our eyes from side to side, expecting a threat to materialize out of thin air. "There are people here, but they're all . . . asleep."

"Asleep, asleep?" I asked. "Or brainwashed?"

"Asleep," she said. "It's one o'clock in the afternoon, and they're in bed."

"Insiders?" Gunner guessed. "Like Rise Twelve. They work at night and sleep during the day."

"The whole city?" Raine asked, giving sound to my question.

"What happened to their Director?" I aimed my inquiry at Thane. He had been here, after all.

"Director Jeffries was promoted after your capture," Thane said, squinting into the horizon. "Van made him Thinker over Confinement in Freedom. I don't know who was positioned here."

"They're not here now," Vi said. "I feel—" She squeezed her eyes shut. "A lot of strong will, but nothing like a Director."

"The Insider movement was well received here," Thane said. "Xander Bower had a lot of charisma, and he treated everyone like an equal. The people joined because of Xander's excellent leadership."

"Zenn's dad?" Vi asked, her voice pitching up an octave. "Is he still here?"

"He's dead," I whispered.

She jerked her head toward me. *Dead?*

"I'll tell you the story later."

Does Zenn know? she asked.

I shrugged, but not in a callous way. More like *I don't know, but I doubt it, and I don't want to be the one to tell him.* In fact I wasn't sure what I'd do if/when I ever saw Zenn again. Punching him seemed like a good idea though. Then apologizing, and then telling him about his dad.

Vi didn't remark about me wanting to hit her ex-boyfriend, so I knew she was seriously disturbed that Zenn's dad had died here. We landed, my team standing in the middle of the empty street, unsure where to go.

"This way," I said, striding toward a building where I could feel the slightest hint of emotion. "Gunner?"

He joined me, casting his eyes around, up, and down. "What is that?" he asked.

"Someone is unsettled," I said. "But not afraid. Not uncomfortable. Worried?"

He shook his head. "Worry feels almost right. But it's a warm kind of worrying."

"Yeah," I said absently. I'd felt this emotion before. From

a very good friend. My heart skipped with hope. "Vi? There's a man inside. Is his name Irvine?"

We'd reached the door. The panel on the top flashed with red lights—locked.

"He's keeping all personal information buried," she said.

I thought about Indy and what she'd do if she were here. She'd pound that door to the ground, yelling for her brother to cracking open up already. She'd look at me wildly, her pulse bouncing in her throat. She'd say my name in the most desperate way. I wanted the person in the building to be Irvine so bad. If not for myself, for Indy and her parents.

I looked up at the twenty-story building, imagining Irvine standing at the window looking down on us. "Irvine!" I yelled. "It's Jag Barque!"

Behind me, Thane hissed his displeasure at my announcement. I ignored him as adrenaline coursed through my body. Before I was caught in the Goodgrounds, Irv had been assigned to come south and infiltrate the government. He could've done exactly that. He could've taken over after Jeffries was promoted.

A nasty thought struck me. *Maybe he's not on our side anymore.*

"No Thinkers here," Vi murmured. "He has talent?"

"Yeah," I said. "He's a—"

"Technopath," Vi finished. "I can feel that now."

"Vi, can you get us in there? Gunn?" Desperation over-rode every other impulse.

Whether Vi did it, or Gunn did, or Irvine did, the door switched to unlocked. Green lights decorated the top panel. I charged inside.

The lobby of the building streamed with tech. P-screens adorned every wall. Gadgets blinked in each corner; seeker-spiders scuttled into hidden places.

Before I could smile—this place screamed *Irvine!*—a man materialized in front of us, solidifying into a tall, hulking shape with dark skin.

Irvine Blightingdale.

I exhaled for what felt like the first time since watching him disappear into the crowd in the Goodgrounds market. Irvine stepped forward and gathered me into a hug. I couldn't stop smiling and slapping him on the back. Near the end of the reunion, Irv said, "The time is now."

"The time for what?" I asked. Vi immediately took my hand, claiming me as hers. Irv noted the movement and raised his eyebrows. He knew me as Jag Barque, the *don't-give-a-damn, don't-try-to-get-close-to-me* leader of the Resistance.

"Irvine, this is my girlfriend, Violet Schoenfeld. Vi, this is Irv, Indy's brother and one of my best friends."

As they shook hands, Irvine leaned in and whispered something to Vi that I couldn't quite catch. She blushed.

After all the introductions, I pressed Irv again, "The time for what?"

"Freedom fell and is ready to be reborn," he said. "We're leaving for the capital in five days."

"We're coming," I said automatically.

"I imagine you've been traveling. Let's get you up to speed," he said,. turning toward his teched-out wall. "Anyone opposed to particle acceleration?"

As it turned out, we were all opposed to particle acceleration. Vi leaned against the wall, her eyes closed, moaning. My stomach lurched, upset it had been taken apart and put back together in under two seconds.

Irvine shook his head to reorient himself, then strode down the hallway and into a sunlit room. Gunn recovered faster than me but stayed with Raine, whose face was the color of white-crested waves.

Thane tended to Vi, which seemed ironic, all things considering. She motioned for me to go ahead, and my curiosity won. I stumbled down the hall and into Irvine's techno lair. Blinking, flashing, pulsing lights bounced along every surface. If the particle accelerator hadn't given me a stroke, this room would have.

The counters, shelves, walls, and ceiling were all silver, polished and reflective. Irv sat hunkered down in the corner behind a chest-high counter. The winking gadgets shone on his bald head, and he wore dark sunglasses as he worked with white-hot techtricity.

With his bare hands.

"Is it safe to come in?" I asked from the doorway.

"Definitely," he said.

"Catch me up." I moved past row upon row of Irv's inventions. "What is all this stuff?"

"Weaponry. You think General Darke is going to go down without a fight?"

I slumped into the chair across from Irv. "Isaacs said the city is decimated. His tech emptied Rise One. Three other Rises crumbled to the ground."

Irv didn't look up from his work. "That leaves at least fifteen left to remove. And their Thinkers. And then the General." He spared me a glance. "Trust me, you're going to need weapons."

"Trek—"

"Doesn't have a fraction of what he needs to do this," Irv interrupted. He brandished one of his tech tools at me. "And your voice will do a lot, but not enough. You need me, Jag."

"I know that," I said quietly. "I've always needed you."

What I couldn't say was still heard. Irv nodded slightly, acknowledging my nonverbal apology. I shouldn't have taken him with me on the mission into the Goodgrounds, not when he was scheduled to infiltrate the Association.

I cleared my throat. "So, you been down here all this time, or what?"

"About seven or eight months," he said casually. "Jeffries appointed me Director after his promotion."

I choked. "Director?"

"Tech like this doesn't go unnoticed. Someone had to authorize the production schedule. Turns out Jeffries wanted Rancho Port to be known for something. We thought it would be the tech." He pushed his glasses up so I could see his eyes. "Sorry about the capsule, brother-man."

I choked. "You knew about that?"

"We got you out as fast as we could."

"*We?*"

"The Insiders. Xander and I coordinated the escape, the day after I took command of the city." He heaved a sigh and replaced his glasses. "Not everything went according to plan."

"Xander died."

"And you got caught," he said. "But at least you were out of that capsule. Jeffries had been promoted, and I got Rancho Port." He kept working on his tech, welding this or sparking that.

I wish he'd look at me again. "What's going on here?"

"Stick around, and you'll see for yourself."

"I heard all your people are asleep."

"You heard?" Irv paused in his welding.

"I've got a mind reader on staff." I leaned back and chewed on my thumbnail.

"Where's the rest of your 'staff'?" Irvine asked.

"I sent a team to Grande to check on Laurel Woods, who manages an underground—"

"I know who Laurel Woods is," Irv said. "We've been working together for months."

A flash of annoyance shot through me. As the cracking leader, I should've known all this. If Irv was a Director, why hadn't he notified Indy—who had been leading the Resistance while I'd been detained—two months ago?

"Great," I said, my voice hollow. "We'll send word to them when we launch the attack, yeah?"

I wasn't really asking, but Irv said, "Yeah," anyway. He finished working on his gadget and set it in a row of identical weapons. "My people wake up between four and six," Irv said, grinning. "The night show is fantastic."

Irv never was a liar. The night show was spectacular. The people slowly got up, at all different times. Some went jogging. Some slept in. Some made breakfast, and some stood on balconies and sipped coffee.

Near nine, most people left their apartments and went to work. By work I mean that they went to different buildings and performed jobs like making soap and sewing clothes. Some worked in the fields, preparing the ground for planting. Some collected water, some canned food, some fiddled with tech like Irv.

I stood in Irv's monitoring room with Vi, Raine, Gunner, Thane, and Isaacs, watching. Their emotions blended with mine, but it didn't matter, because we were all feeling the exact same thing.

Shock.

Sure, I'd imagined what a free society might look like. It wasn't this. In my dreams, there was unrest. Disease. Destruction.

But this society, these people, operated almost like the brainwashed. Irv hung out in the back of the monitoring room, his arms crossed. Several minutes into the whole they-all-perform-a-job-they're-good-at thing, he spoke.

"So, what do you think?"

What do I think? I thought. *What do I think?*

Truth was, I didn't know what to think.

"It's unbelievable," Raine said. "Do you tell them all which jobs to do?"

"At first I did," Irv said. "I matched everyone with a job I thought they'd be good at, based on their Citizen profiles."

"And then?" Gunn asked.

"Then I let them pick," he said. "People are more productive when they're working a job they like. Some kept the same job, but as I interviewed each person, some adjustments were made. Most jobs have been filled, and those that aren't get done on a rotational basis."

"Wow," I said, unable to think of anything more intelligent to say. I turned to Irv. "So what do you need us to do?"

The next five days were a whirlwind of activity as I oversaw what Irv had planned and, with Raine, carried out interviews with possible Resistance recruits. Gunn and Vi were assigned to gather as much tech as possible, as per their technopathic abilities, and I didn't get to see my girlfriend very much.

By the end of the fifth day my nerves were frayed. "Well?" I snapped at a possible recruit. I took a deep breath as Raine pinned me with a glare.

We needed people to manage communications, people to help transport the tech, people to bring and prep food. The list went on and on. We'd fulfilled nearly all the assignments and sent the willing recruits to Thane for further instruction.

I let Raine finish the interview with the man and extend the invitation for him to join us on the tech transportation team. Our plan was to leave at nightfall, with a midnight stop-off in Grande. We'd make it to Freedom by daybreak.

After the man had his instructions and left, Raine put her head down on the silver table and closed her eyes. We hadn't slept much over the past few days, and I didn't even have the energy to breathe. Good thing it was an involuntary action.

I would've fallen asleep if an alarm hadn't shrieked. Outside the door the communications hub went wild with flashing lights. A couple of engineers rushed into the room to receive the message.

I didn't care. The world could come to an end, and I'd be fine. At least then I'd get to sleep.

Vi entered the room, and shook my shoulder. "Jag, wake up. This is important."

I opened one eye to look at her.

"Darke has left Freedom. So has Zenn. Intelligence says Zenn will be back in the morning, but Darke won't be back until tomorrow night."

The thrill of opportunity shot through me, breaking through my exhaustion. "Nice," I said.

"We're leaving early," Vi added.

"Define 'early,'" I said.

"One hour."

My groan mimicked Raine's.

One hour later I was on my hoverboard, face braced against the wind that howled through the sky. It began to pour, and my hair was slicked to my forehead within seconds. Water weighed down my clothes, and the driving rain made talking without a cache impossible.

Maybe for the first time, I wished I had an implant. I pulled my jacket tighter and endured the silence within myself. We hit the outskirts of Grande just as the rain tapered off. Laurel sent her team into the sky before I could say anything.

"Take the lead," I told her, as if that was the plan the whole time. She smiled sweetly, looking very much like Vi. "How's Saffediene?" I asked in an attempt to regain my leadership role.

"She woke up the first day," Laurel said. "She's made a nice recovery. Irv had just sent a shipment of medical supplies, so that helped."

"How come you didn't tell us Irvine was Director of Rancho Port?" I asked, looking over her shoulder as if something more interesting was happening behind her. "Indy's been looking for him for almost a year."

"I didn't know Irvine was lost," Laurel said.

"Right. Don't people bring *news* when they come through your underground?" I let my board rise as I inserted a new charge pack, unwilling to continue this conversation if Laurel was going to lie to me.

Laurel matched my ascension. "Plenty of news travels through the underground. My daughter's sacrifice for one. My older daughter's death." Her voice chilled like the wind. "But sorry, I didn't know his status was in question."

"I didn't know he was a Director either," I said.

"Maybe you should take that up with him."

"Maybe I will," I said, just to be spiteful. She knew how to make her words hurt; that comment about Ty's death unsettled me. I'd been close with her; she'd taught me subtle mind control and sacrificed everything to get me the best voice coaches.

Laurel flew away, settling into a conversation with Thane. Vi joined me. "What did you say to her?"

"Nothing," I muttered.

"You made her mad," Vi said.

"How can you tell?"

"I've seen that look many times," she said. "Trust me, she's upset."

"Sorry," I said automatically.

Vi laughed. "I don't care. I like anyone who can make my mom mad."

* * *

"He's there," Vi said, confirming Zenn's presence in the city of Freedom. The barrier was down, and I itched to get inside and see how much damage Isaacs and his team had done.

My patience won out, and I sent Trek, Starr, and Saffediene in first. All were former Citizens of Freedom, all were well versed in playing both sides. They could get a read on the situation and communicate with the Resistance before we flew in and announced our presence.

I watched the trio fly toward the ocean, as per our plan. They'd come in over the water as if they didn't know the barrier was down, find Zenn, and cache us his coordinates and status.

Five minutes became ten, and Raine sighed. Next to her, Irvine whispered something that made her smile. He handed her a tech gadget, and together they watched something on the minuscule screen.

I paced. Back and forth, back and forth. My doubts escalated as more time passed. Maybe Zenn was already gone. Maybe he'd hurt Trek and Starr—but Saffediene? I didn't believe he'd hurt her. She'd said they'd kissed. Zenn doesn't kiss just anyone. She'd meant something to him, and I wasn't above admitting that's why I sent her with Trek and Starr.

"Jag," Gunn said. "They've got him. Western Blocks."

Zenn

50.

Before I could call or wave to Trek and Starr, a fierce pain coursed through my body. Hot and crackling, it felt like I'd touched a live techtricity portal.

I slipped off my hoverboard, free-falling, before another layer of pain added to the sparks still flowing through my muscles. This time the ache was dull, and came from my legs.

The ground beneath me felt damp and cold. But nothing was as bad as seeing Trek and Starr lean into my line of sight, their faces filled with anger. Trek's mouth moved, but I couldn't hear what he was saying through layer upon layer of my pain.

Starr stepped aside, and the real torture began.

Saffediene came into view, her eyes filled with worry but her mouth set in determination. She bent down until her lips met my cheek. Tears coated her lashes.

"What have you learned, Zenn?" she asked in a whisper, her mouth next to my ear. I remembered how that mouth felt against mine, and the agony inside me doubled.

"Free or functioning?" she pleaded, desperate for an answer I couldn't give.

I didn't answer—and not because my voice had stopped working. Because, despite my decision to rerecord the transmissions, I still didn't know.

51.

"Let's fly," I said, dashing to my hovercraft and leaping on board. The others followed me into the sky, and we lifted over the towering wall.

I landed next to Trek, who stood a few paces away from a fallen Zenn, holding Starr's hand. Trek had no emotions to speak of, nothing for me to use to form an opinion of the situation.

Saffediene knelt next to Zenn, weeping into his chest. Her genuine sadness rose into the air, painting the scene in muted colors. Everyone else stayed back, ready for me to take the lead.

So I did.

I moved forward and put my hand on Saffediene's back. She stood, wiped her tears, and retreated to Raine's side.

I looked down at Zenn. The old familiar feelings of betrayal and disgust resurfaced. Zenn looked terrible, like he hadn't slept in days and eaten in longer. He wore the same dirty jeans, the same handed-down jacket as he had when I'd last seen him.

He didn't look like a Director of anything.

Zenn pleaded with his eyes. His mouth moved. No sound came out. Vi dropped to his side and stroked an errant piece of hair off his forehead. "He said he destroyed the transmissions he made."

She spoke with tenderness; her touch broadcasted her love for him. I understood it, really I did, but her adoration of him still sliced through me.

"He left the remains in Rise One," she said. I waved my hand, indicating for someone—anyone—to go check. With regret, I realized that Zenn used to be my number two. He would've gone to check for me. And if not him, then Indy.

As it was, Raine nudged Gunn and they left to confirm conditions in Rise One.

"He was going to fly back to Arrow Falls," Vi continued. "To make new transmissions that would gradually awaken the people." She looked at me with those beautiful, change-able eyes that were filled with tears for her "sweet, wonder-ful Zenn." "They have a meeting tonight, after Darke returns from Castledale."

"Zenn doesn't need to go to Arrow Falls," I said, refusing to let Vi's emotion for Zenn infect me. I knew she loved me; I wouldn't be threatened by her lingering attachment to Zenn.

"Irvine has recording equipment," I said. "If Zenn is seri-ous, he can make new transmissions, right here, right now." I motioned Irv forward. "Isn't that right, Irvine?"

"Sure thing, boss-man."

I knelt next to Zenn and looked him straight in the eye. "Well, Zenn. It's time to find out who you really play for."

Zenn

52. The fury in Jag's eyes unnerved me. He looked mad enough to kill me. Or at least mad enough to try.

I already felt dead inside. First from the gentle way Saffediene had begged me to answer her question. I detected forgiveness in her voice, like I could salvage my relationship with her, even if I thought functionality should prevail over freedom.

Then when Vi acted as intermediate between me and Jag, I died a little more. Seeing her show emotion because of me reminded me of all we'd been through together. That history doesn't go away overnight, and it doesn't vanish simply because we fall in love with other people.

She would always be my best friend.

Insider Tip #10: Have a trusted confidant who has your back. You'll need them when you least expect it.

And oh, how I needed Vi right now.

Jag's statement hung heavily in the air, awaiting a response. I tried to nod, but my body didn't obey. I tried to speak, but again my voice failed.

"He's serious," Vi said, still playing my spokesperson. "But he needs medical attention first."

Jag tore his gaze away from me and left my line of sight. A moment later Irvine Blightingdale crouched next to me, his cold fingers pushing against my forehead, neck, and ribs.

Something hot blazed against my wrist, and then liquid ice flowed through my veins.

"You'll go to sleep for a while, Zenn," Irvine said in a deep voice that reminded me of my father's. "When you wake up, we'll be ready to record." Irvine left, taking Vi with him. I stared up at the sky, unmoving, waiting to fall asleep, alone in my grief and pain.

That is, until Saffediene slipped her hand into mine. "I'm here, Zenn. You'll be all right."

* * *

When I woke up, Saffediene was by my side. Her eyes were closed, and her skin reflected the glow from the p-screen on the wall.

I lay propped up in a bed. Without the flickering light from the p-screen, the room would've pitched into darkness.

I tried to speak, but only managed a low gurgling sound. The pain was gone, replaced by this drugged condition where everything felt too bright and moved too fast. I couldn't decide which was worse.

Irvine entered the room. "Hello, Zenn. Good to see you awake. We're ready to begin recording."

Ready to begin recording? I couldn't even talk. I gestured to my throat, trying to communicate the problem with Irvine.

"No problem," he said. He tapped his finger on the computer beside my bed, and I felt the tension in my muscles ease. "Try it now."

"Thanks," I managed to say. "How'd you do that?"

"Tech," he answered.

"Irv has a piece of tech for everything," someone said from the doorway. I'd know that voice anywhere. It haunted me in my quiet moments, and it chased me through dark tunnels. It accused me of abandoning Vi, of turning traitor.

And it was right.

"Hey, Jag," I said.

He regarded me coolly. He couldn't figure me out, and I hadn't made it easy for him. Half the time I didn't know what I was doing, or why.

I was lost. Others had always advised me. My father. Thane Myers. Jag Barque. Van Hightower.

And now Ian Darke.

I had never directed myself, set my own course. I'd been doing what everyone told me to do for years and years and years.

Jag watched me wrestle with myself, a doubtful glare on his face. "What?" I asked him.

"You've got some weird vibes," he said. "Are you doing this or not?"

I wanted to say yes, because it would make him happy.

I wanted to say no, because General Darke would be furious if he found out.

I wanted to go back to sleep so I didn't have to choose.

In the past I'd always done whatever it took to keep Vi safe. Anything and everything to protect her, to ensure her survival, to keep her as my own.

But she was already safe. And she was with someone else now.

How was I supposed to make decisions without her as my motivation?

I glanced at Saffediene and was struck by the beauty of her freckles. Could she be my motivation?

Why did anyone have to be my motivation?

I needed to decide what *I* wanted, not what I wanted because of someone else. I needed to classify what I liked, what I didn't like, what I believed, what I didn't, what brought me joy, and what didn't.

I reached out and traced my fingertip along Saffediene's cheekbone. She startled, waking and searching my face for an explanation.

"I'm sorry, I didn't mean to wake you," I said softly. I wished Irvine and Jag weren't here. But my wishes rarely come true.

Saffediene didn't respond verbally. She closed the distance between us and kissed me. Then I really, really wished Irvine and Jag weren't watching.

I vaguely heard their footsteps as they left.

"I'm sorry, I'm sorry," I murmured against her mouth. She kept saying, "I forgive you. It's okay," in between kisses.

Warmth grew inside me, expanding until it pushed out my fear and doubt. Finally, with my lips raw, I gently extracted myself from Saffediene's embrace.

"Saffediene?"

She snuggled into my side. "Hmm?"

"Why do you like me?"

A long pause followed, wherein some of my doubt crept back in. I struggled to keep it at bay.

"Is this a trick question?" she asked.

"No," I said. "It's just . . . No one's ever liked me before. Not the real me, at least. And it seems that you do. I'm just wondering why."

"You don't see yourself very clearly, do you?"

I don't see myself at all, I thought. *I don't know who I am, or what I'm doing, or why.* "No," I said, "I don't."

She propped herself up on her elbow and looked me straight in my eyes. "The first time I met you, your conviction struck me like a weight to the chest. Every word was spoken with complete and utter confidence. You had an answer for all my fears, all my doubts. I remember thinking that you had everything figured out."

I barked out a laugh. "I'm really good at lying."

"That wasn't a lie. No one's that good."

I am, I thought, and I really was. The real question was: Had I been lying to myself too, all this time?

"Zenn," Irvine called. I stiffened, not sure I could record

new transmissions. Not sure I believed the words that I'd need to force out of my mouth.

"I believe in you," Saffediene said. "I believe that you'll find yourself. Just go in there and say the first thing that comes to your mind."

Irv adjusted the dials on his equipment, twisting one way and then the other. He wouldn't look directly at me, and Jag wouldn't look anywhere else. He stared at me, his twisted smirk saying, *Let's see what you have to say.*

I sat as still as possible, looking at the bandages on my knee and ignoring everyone. I tried to organize what I might say on the transmissions, but nothing jelled.

Then Irvine hooked something to my throat. "Good luck," Jag said as they both left. Now I had no one but myself to account to.

I remained silent for a few minutes, trying to find the right words to start. They didn't come. The equipment blinked, encouraging me to speak already. I knew Jag and Vi and everyone else were waiting in another room, waiting to hear what I'd say.

I was waiting too.

I thought of Saffediene, and how she remembered every

detail of the first time we'd met. I felt bad that she hadn't made that big of an impact on me, but I was determined to make it up to her.

I believe in you. Her words raced through my mind.

I opened my mouth. "Citizens of Freedom, it is time for you to wake up. This is the last brainwashing message you'll hear. That's right, brainwashing. And it stops here, now. Today."

Jag

53. I sat in a darkened room, watching the day fade into dusk. Zenn's voice still floated in my head, full of conviction.

As much as I didn't want to admit it, his words were perfect. The transmissions were perfect, and they'd been cycling through the feed for the past five hours. Irv had the security in Rise Twelve operating at full capacity, and he and Trek had the communication lines open again.

But I waited in silence, without a cache, in Ian Darke's house. Vi had come with me, and I'd managed to convince her to stay upstairs while I spoke with Darke.

I imagined what I might say to him, how I might incapacitate him. I had nothing. With Freedom in ruins and on the brink of a new, free society, Darke didn't seem so intimidating anymore.

Sure, there were more Directors to overthrow and more cities to unbrainwash, but now I knew it was doable. Now I knew we had the resources, the personnel, and the experience to actually carry it out.

I'd dispatched my traveling team a few hours earlier. They were headed to the friendliest cities—Harvest, Cedar Hills, Grande, Mountain Dale, Baybridge—with copies of Zenn's recordings. I'd laced my voice over his, and then Gunn had as well. The power of our three voices could wake the dead.

People everywhere would soon come out of the mental fog they'd been in their whole lives. We'd establish laws, teach correct principles, and let the people govern themselves. I almost smiled.

My parents had died in defense of freedom. I'd been working for years to see the birth of a free society. I felt a crack in my barriers. I'd let Vi in, at least a little bit. It hurt, but feeling something and experiencing life with someone else was better than feeling nothing and being lonely all the time.

I was so wrapped up in my thoughts, I didn't notice someone enter the house.

"Well, hello, Jag," Ian Darke said, his voice smooth and low. "To what do I owe this honor?" He cast his eyes around the room. "And where's Director Bower?"

I steepled my fingers under my chin. "He's detained."

"Is he dead?"

My stomach tightened, but a smile stretched my lips. "Perhaps." I'd let Darke think what he wanted, especially if it played in my favor. "Sit down. We need to talk."

Darke moved to the chair opposite me so swiftly, it was as if my voice had influenced him.

Interesting, I thought. Darke should have extensive protections against voice and mind control. I wondered if his personal tech security had been corrupted. I wondered if he knew.

His security was down, Vi confirmed. *He just switched it back on. He'd turned it off to save energy during his travels.*

Did he get what he wanted in Castledale? I kept my eyes on Darke while Vi and I held our mental conversation. I had no personal tech security to keep Darke out of my head, but I didn't care if he eavesdropped on my convo.

No, she said. *Can you feel his emotions?*

No, I said. *He's folded those away.*

He's worried, Vi said. *At least he was when he arrived.*

Thanks, babe, I thought. *Stay upstairs, okay?*

She didn't answer, and I knew she'd do whatever she wanted, even if that meant storming downstairs at any moment.

"Here's what's going to happen," I began. "The Resistance owns Freedom now. I've already sent my people to every city in the Union." A lie, but Darke didn't need to know I didn't have the manpower to fly to every city in the Association. "By morning we'll control two out of every three cities. You're finished." My words settled in the room, heavy with threats.

I'd had plenty of experience with Directors like him, and I didn't expect him to respond. When he didn't, I added, "The cities we won't own will come around once they see our superior way of living."

"Sounds like you have everything worked out," he said. "But I'm sure you know I'm not simply going to mount my hoverboard and fly into the night."

"What are you going to do?" I asked.

Jag! Vi shouted in my head, and I flinched at the panic in her tone.

"Sounds like your team has discovered what I'm going to do." Darke stood up, his fingers pressing buttons along the wrist-port band on his left hand.

I jumped to my feet. Vi's voice echoed in my head, but with no new information. I sprinted for the door, shouting, "Lock down!"

Irv's tech leapt into action, securing all of the room's exits, locking Darke inside. His rage followed me into hall, propelling me toward the stairs. My heart pounded as loud as my footsteps as I flew up them.

"Vi!" I barged into the bedroom where she had been camped out. She stood at the window. Terror flowed from her.

I joined her at the window, and she gripped my arm. My fear matched hers as I took in the scene outside.

The sky was filled with fire, with men on hoverboards, with taser blasts.

With death.

Time clicked by in breaths. *One, two, three.*

"Let's go," Vi begged. "Jag, come on!"

I tore my gaze from the scene outside. "You said Darke didn't get what he wanted." It sounded like an accusation, but it was a plea. I wanted Vi to tell me I was hallucinating. Something to make the men outside be Resistance members.

"He didn't get the tech," she said. "He got an army." She bolted into the hall, screaming behind her, "Come on!"

I took one more look out the window. I looked toward the Rises. Bright lights flashed along the top of Twelve, signaling that they were under attack. I sprinted after Vi, my fear solidifying into fury.

* * *

"Straight up," I said to Vi. "Please, Vi. Fly straight up."

She glared at me. "I can help."

"I know that," I said. "But I do not know how to live without you. Please. Straight up."

"You're going straight up too, right?"

"Right," I said.

"Fine." She stepped onto her hoverboard and launched herself up. I followed her, climbing above the chaos raging through the Rises several miles away. She stopped a few hundred feet in the air, and I paused next to her.

Fire leapt from the roof of several Rises, the numbers of which I didn't know.

"Two, Six, Nine, and Ten," Vi said.

"Six and Nine," I repeated. "That's bad." Zenn had gone back to his old flat in Rise Nine to set up a home base. Thane, Trek, and Irv were operating their communications hub and tech production out of Twelve. Isaacs had gone with them. Starr had gone back to her old flat in Six to establish an infirmary, taking Raine, Gunner, and River with her.

Laurel and Saffediene were part of my traveling team, and I'd dispatched them to Harvest to gather refugees who were willing to fight. They'd be gone until morning.

Darke had brought hordes of people with him. They all

wore black, making them almost indistinguishable against the night sky. When their tasers discharged, white hot light marked their position.

My people had tasers too. Protective gear. Hoverboards. My spirits lifted as I realized we had the same equipment, the same drive to win.

I leaned into my board, pointing it toward Twelve. Vi followed, her voice in my head. *What's your plan?*

Communicate with Zenn, Starr, and Raine, I thought. *Let them know what's going on, and let them know that we're meeting at Twelve.*

She didn't answer immediately. A few minutes later, she thought, *Done. Jag, what are we going to do?*

"Fight back," I said out loud. "We're going to fight back."

The scene on the roof of Twelve was organized noise. I didn't see Trek or Irvine, but Thane was issuing directions to small teams of people.

"Status," I barked as he sent a group of five men into the sky.

"Jag," he practically sighed. "There you are." He gripped my hand in a shake that lasted only two seconds. He hugged Vi in a fatherly gesture. "As soon as we saw Darke's army, Zenn made new transmissions and Irv sent them out over the lines. He asked anyone who wanted to fight for a different future to come to Rise Twelve. The Rise is choked with people."

"Nice," I said. "Keep talking."

He held up his hand for me to wait as he gave a destination to another group, this one all women. They wielded tasers, and determination flashed in their eyes.

"I'm sending out the groups. Trek and Irv have outfitted them all with protective gear and tasers, and Starr blitzed over from Six to help organize them into groups of five by like talents."

"Like talents?"

"Starr can read minds incredibly well. She's putting people with flying skills together. People with math skills. People with problem-solving skills. The leader of each group brings me a paper." He took one from a man in the next group. "Based on their noted skill set, I give them a section of the city to defend." He turned to the group and assigned them the prison camp in the south orchard. "Detain the prisoners by force if necessary," he told them before they lifted into the air.

"We've recalled our traveling teams. Hope that was okay," Thane said as he scanned the paper for the next group.

"Sure, fine," I said, surprised he'd practically asked. I

clutched Vi's hand and watched as Thane sent out team after team after team. Pride welled inside me at the efficiency of my Resistance. From Irvine to Starr to Trek to Thane, everyone had risen to the task at hand.

"Where do you need us?" I asked after Thane had sent another team to Rise Six to put out a still-smoldering fire. "And what's Zenn's status?"

"Why don't you go find out?" Thane said. "He's in his flat in Rise Nine. And do something about the fire while you're there. Trek just said we've assigned all the volunteers."

"How many?" I asked.

"Thousands."

"How many did Darke bring?"

"A lot more." Thane's voice pinched with worry. "Clones, most of them."

"You stay here," I said. "Work with Irv to keep the transmissions flowing. Maybe we can create a frequency only Darke's clones can hear. Can we brainwash them that way?"

"I don't know," Thane said. "I'll talk to Irvine." He disappeared down the stairwell, leaving me and Vi on the roof.

The smell of ash and burnt metal filled the air. The city flickered with flashes of tech and flame. We launched from the shallow lip of the roof and aimed ourselves toward Rise Nine.

"You know the flat?" I asked Vi.

"Yeah," she replied, the first words she'd spoken in twenty minutes. She led me to the balcony, and we both pounded on the glass door with our fists.

Laurel opened it not two seconds later, her face drawn. "Jag," she said. "Thank the stars." Laurel gathered Vi into a hug and drew her into the flat. Her relief at seeing her daughter alive was touching, but we didn't have much time for that.

Raine and Gunner hovered in the corner near the kitchen, watching the flashes of fire outside. "Where's Zenn?" I asked, noting his absence.

"You just missed him. He left to record another set of transmissions," Laurel replied. Her voice held no tone, no emotion. "I came over after Starr went to Twelve to help with the volunteers."

I frowned as Vi asked, "Another set of transmissions?"

"Irvine thinks he can isolate the feed to be heard only by Darke's army," Laurel said. "He needed Zenn to record the new transmissions."

How did Irvine communicate with Zenn? How had he known to go? "Why Zenn?" I asked. Something didn't sit right with me. My voice was four times what Zenn's was. Gunner's at least double. "Who asked for him?"

"Irvine," Laurel repeated.

"Are you sure it was Irv?" I felt sick. "We were just at Twelve. Why couldn't Thane have done the transmissions? I was there; I could've done it. We've been gone, what? Five minutes?" I started pacing. "Something isn't right. When did Zenn leave?"

"I don't know," Laurel said. "Ten minutes ago?" She stepped next to Raine and Gunn and looked out the window.

"Who asked for Zenn?" I asked, knowing it hadn't been Irvine. "Who brought the message?"

"Saffediene," Laurel said. "She said the message came in while she flew past Twelve on her way here. She went with Zenn."

Vi gasped. "No," I said.

Could they abandon us now? Would they?

Should they? Could they? Would they?

Everyone looked at me. Gunner and Raine. Vi and Laurel.

"Let's fly," I said. "Gunner, you get to Twelve and report to Thane. Tell him to check on the transmissions there. Send anyone you can to help us look for Zenn and Saffediene."

I was surprised my hoverboard achieved any lift what with the sinking feeling in my stomach.

Zenn

54.

I followed Saffediene until she
turned away from Rise Twelve
and flew toward the western
wall. Something wasn't right—had she lied to get me out of
my flat so we could run away? Now?

I called after her, but she didn't turn. Her blond hair
streamed loosely behind her unwavering back. I stalled in
midair, a war brewing inside me. I could fly away amid the
confusion. Leave. Find a tiny apartment in a tiny city and live
out my days with Saffediene by my side.

I could join the troops Ian Darke had brought back with

him, though I knew there'd be no going back to the Resistance after that.

Or I could fly to Twelve and see where my talents were most needed.

Saffediene had said she believed in me. That I used to speak with conviction. I'd recorded the transmissions to urge people to make their own choices. All around me, people had done exactly that.

But Saffediene had made this decision for me. "Zenn?" She hovered in front of me now. "Come on."

"Where are we going?"

"Someplace safe," she said.

"I can't abandon the Resistance," I said. "Not again." I swung my hoverboard away from the wall and faced the fighting before me. "We can't leave."

I'd left before. I'd left Vi to face the hovercopter pilot alone, when I was thirteen.

I'd left Blaze standing in that alley to await his death.

I'd left Jag without a contact in the Goodgrounds.

I'd left Vi to attend training with the Special Forces.

I'd left my brother in Castledale, and now I didn't know where he was, or if he was still alive.

I'd left my father's memory in the recesses of my

mind, never thinking about him, never doing anything to find him.

I'd left Saffediene in an electro-net, and all my friends to fend for themselves during the last battle.

I would not be remembered for those acts. I would not be the person who simply left when things got really hard.

"It's not who I am," I said.

Saffediene hovered next to me, silently crying.

"I will fight," I said. "Because it's the right thing to do. Because it's what I believe in. Because I want to."

"I love you," she whispered. "Because you fight for what you believe in. I just thought you believed in us."

"I do." I didn't tell her I loved her, because I wasn't sure if I did. I knew I wanted to spend more time with her. I knew she could be as important to me as Vi once was.

"But some things are bigger than two people," I said. "We leave now, and we'll always regret it." I reached for her hand, and she let me hold it. "Trust me, I know. I've turned my back on my friends many times. I've always regretted it."

"Zenn, I just want you to be safe."

"You don't need to worry about me," I said.

"I'm scared." She drifted closer to me, and I threaded my fingers into hers.

"Me too, Saffediene." I leaned in and kissed her. "Me too."

I pulled away and took a deep breath. "But today, Saffediene, we have to face the future. Today, we fight."

"Okay," she said. "Okay."

We flew toward the Rises, our tasers drawn and activated, as a scream pierced the sky.

A figure dropped in front of us, a streak of pale skin and dark hair.

"Vi!" I cried, even as the darkness swallowed her.

55.

I watched Laurel fall through the sky in slow motion, her scream stretching into thin ribbons. The sound of it would never leave me.

Someone screamed Vi's name, and the timbre of it startled me from the shock of witnessing a Resistance member's death.

"Zenn," I said. Saffediene stood next to him on her own hoverboard. They both watched the disappearing form of Laurel Woods.

"Thane, it's Zenn," I said, mostly because he was the closest person to me. Vi hovered several feet away, her mouth open as she stared into the sky that had swallowed her mother.

I circled down and stalled in front of Zenn. "Zenn, look at me."

He raised his shell-shocked eyes to mine, and a shudder rippled through his body.

"She knew the risks," I said as the others joined me. "We all know the risks, right?"

A sob escaped from Saffediene. Vi nodded, along with Raine. Thane stood there, looking at me without moving. I'd never seen someone hold so still, especially while riding a hoverboard.

"We're all needed," I said, looking at my friends. Their talents were catalogued. Practiced. Coveted by the Association. "We all have something valuable to contribute." I looked at the people flying around me. I thought of those who had volunteered to fight for freedom only a few hours after listening to Zenn's messages.

"This is what we've been working for," I said. "This is the night we win. The night we take back the control from those who have kept it from us for lifetimes." My voice sounded with pure authority. "Tonight, this night, we instate a free government."

I looked at each of them as I spoke. Vi nodded; Thane too.

Raine looked worried, but pressed her mouth into a thin line of determination.

Saffediene was still crying, but Zenn said, "Tonight, we fight."

"Two groups," I commanded. "Thane, you're with me. Raine, take Saffediene to Rise Twelve. Report to Irvine about Laurel"—my voice caught, but I quickly cleared it away—"Laurel's fall. Zenn, Vi, I want you together." The words meant so much. I knew Zenn understood what I really meant. He nodded. "Vi, tell Zenn about his dad." I ignored the hope and worry coming from Zenn when I said that.

"We'll go get Darke," I said, "and meet up with everyone at Twelve when this is over."

No one questioned my directions. Raine flew away with Saffediene, and I turned my attention to the guards nearest me. "Stop this," I said, employing my most powerful voice. "Go home." They flew away without a second thought. Thane smiled grimly at me, but I felt no satisfaction.

"Vi," I said. "Do what you need to do." I didn't look at her. "Zenn, keep her safe."

I watched Vi and Zenn zoom away, desperately hoping that wasn't my final good-bye with the girl I loved.

Thane and I flew into the fray, and I used my voice at every opportunity. Thane did too. We'd managed to ground a dozen enemies in just a few minutes. Someone above me dropped his taser, and it discharged against my board. Waves of techtricity streamed through me and my board, causing my back to arch and my board to stall.

Again I saw Laurel falling through empty space, but this time my face replaced hers.

I clenched my teeth against the pain but could do nothing as my board fell. I landed on something hard. Someone kicked away my useless board. When I opened my eyes, I was looking straight at Thane Myers.

He'd saved me. Again.

"Thank you," I breathed out, my heart still pounding hard with the fear of free-falling. "Can we fly double on this thing?" I eyed his standard-issue board.

"We have no choice," he replied. "I'll navigate. You order people around."

Thane was a good flier. He maneuvered us through streams of guards, and I commanded hoverboards to quit, leaving Darke's clones stranded in the air.

The Citizens of Freedom then tased, bound, and took the prisoners to the camps Irvine had set up near the orchards.

I told people to go to sleep. I told them to go home. I told them to join our side. I said whatever felt right at the moment.

It seemed like Thane flew forever, from one end of the city to the other, again and again. And still there were guards and clones to command.

On the third trip north, Thane brought his board to a full stop. Darke stood in front of us, his hoverboard humming with energy. He folded his arms and regarded the two of us.

I stood in front of Thane, anger burning through my body. Thane put his hand on my shoulder and whispered, "Patience."

I didn't have much of that. Thane had been fighting from the inside for twenty years. He had untold stores of patience.

"Leave," I said. "Leave now, and we won't kill you."

Darke threw his head back and laughed. I fingered the tech along my belt, wondering if any of it would kill him. I fought against the urge to throw everything I had at him.

With the last of his laughter hanging in the air, I plucked a tech grenade from my belt and launched it toward him. He raised both hands and shoved them toward me.

The tech grenade reversed direction and landed between me and Thane on our hoverboard. Thane kicked it away, and it exploded in the air. The surge of energy forced us upward, and I dropped to a crouched position so I wouldn't fall again.

"That was not patience," Thane said. "Let him make the first move."

We hovered above Darke in the sky now. "Nice try," he said, ascending to our level. "Did you really think I'd let you overthrow my Association with a few tech grenades?" He drew closer and closer. "Did you really think I'd return unassisted?"

"Your clone-guards are almost defeated," I said, gesturing to the almost-quiet sky. "We've nearly got them contained now."

Malice glinted in his dark eyes. "All of them?"

Sudden fear struck me, struck me hard. Darke touched his temple. "One thought, and I'll have another five thousand clones here in under five minutes."

I didn't detect any deceit. He really had more clones.

Before I could respond, a cheer rose up from the crowd. It sounded wild and free, and I knew my Resistance had won.

"I've instructed them to regroup at Rise Twelve," Thane murmured in my ear.

I nodded slightly, glad one of us had a cache to keep in contact with the group. Rise Twelve would be the best place for our troops if Darke was rallying for another attack.

No one seemed to want to make the first move. I exercised my patience, and waited for Darke to act. With his personal tech security systems on, my voice wouldn't do much. My tech gadgets could be used against me. So I waited,

> waited,

> > waited.

The pressure in my chest pinched tighter and tighter with every second. I opened my mouth and screamed in an attempt to release the pressure inside.

The hoverboard under my feet lurched. I stepped back to regain my balance, expecting to bump into Thane.

But he wasn't there.

He was flying through the air, straight toward Darke, his hands outstretched. Thane hit Darke full force, clenching his hands around Darke's throat. Together, they landed on Darke's hoverboard, which shimmied and started to tip sideways.

My fingers fumbled along my belt, desperate to find something that would incapacitate Darke, but leave Thane unharmed.

The two tangled together, wrestling against one another. "Jag!" Thane yelled. "Jag, now!"

I struggled for a solution, but I seemed frozen. Everything happened so fast, and their hoverboard tilted and tipped, yet they stayed on.

"Jag!" Thane screamed.

Jag, Jag, Jag, Jagjagjag! My name sliced through the night.

My fingers closed around a spherical object. Darke threw a punch. Thane's head snapped back, and he slid from the hoverboard as I launched the grenade.

The resulting explosion filled the sky with bright yellow light that illuminated Thane's slack face as he fell into the depths of the night.

Zenn

56.

"Tell me about my dad," I demanded as soon as we flew away from Jag. "Vi, tell me."

She looked me straight in the face. "He died in Rancho Port—helping Jag to escape."

The air left my lungs. Dead. My father was dead. Part of me died with her words. "When?" Though it didn't really matter, I needed to know.

"A few days before they brought Jag to Freedom," she said. "About six weeks ago."

Just over a month. One month. Shame filled me. I should've looked for him. I'd had the resources in Freedom.

I'd had the leeway. But I didn't. I was afraid of finding him, afraid of that familiar pride I'd find in his eyes for the things I'd done, afraid of telling him about the mistakes I'd made.

I flew as if in a fog. I spoke without thought. The battle raged around us, despite my voice-controlling clone after clone to descend to the ground and freeze. Despite Vi's mind control and the line of guards she sent to the camps, where they'd be detained.

"Zenn, it's not enough," Vi said, and her voice shook with frustration. "I have to do something different."

She stepped from her board to mine, lacing her arms around my waist. I instantly snapped out of the *my-father-is-dead* haze. I looked down at her, and found the fear in her eyes so unsettling.

She'd looked at me this way before. When we'd snuck to the Abandoned Area. When Ty had disappeared. When I'd told her I was leaving for the Special Forces. We'd been there for each other for years, through fear and loss and heartache.

"I love you," I said before I could stop myself.

"I love you too," she said. "Please stay with me. Don't drop me."

I didn't understand what she meant until her eyes rolled back into her head and she slumped against me. The guard flying toward us suddenly jerked, climbing above us on his hoverboard. He smiled coldly at me before he started firing on the three officers that were flying with him.

And then I knew. Vi had given herself in order to control others. *Please stay with me. Don't drop me. I love you, love you, love you.*

I lowered her to the board and crouched over her still form. I would stay with her until the end, whenever that may be.

I navigated the board through the fray, following the guard as he annihilated those around him. When taser fire hit my board, I ignored the pain in my chest even though the heat reminded me of the fires I'd seen on the propaganda vids. The crackle of flames sounded in my ears though the night sky wasn't filled with fire.

Something sliced through my right arm, but I pressed my bleeding wrist to my side and kept navigating after the guard. I leaned over Vi's body and voice-ordered anyone who got too close to turn themselves in at the camps.

I glanced at Vi's body. Drops of blood decorated her face. My heart leapt in fear—had she been hit? Then I realized the blood was dripping from a gash that ran from my wrist to my elbow. The pain was held at bay by the adrenaline pumping through me. My board bucked, sharp heat exploded in my chest, and in the distance, I heard someone call my name.

It sounded like my father, but I knew that was wishful thinking. I ignored the voice—and the pain rising through my body—and kept following the guard. Minutes or hours later the officer finally turned to look at me. His chest heaved with the effort it took to breathe. I knew exactly how he felt. I pressed my hand to my heart and felt a sticky warmth there.

"Go," he said, and then his body crumpled to his board.

I could barely support my own weight. I couldn't get enough air. Vi was soaked with blood, and so was I.

"Rise Twelve," I croaked.

"Whoa. Are you guys okay?" a girl asked.

"She took control of someone's body," I said as we hit the roof hard. I rolled onto my back, still cradling Vi in my arms. My breathing was ragged and sounded wet. "She told me what she was doing. She told me not leave her." I sucked in another breath and looked into Starr's eyes. "I didn't leave her."

"You need medical attention," Starr said. "Go get help; I'll take care of Vi."

I shook my head, which felt detached from my body. "No, I'm staying with her. She asked me to stay with her."

"Go get Fret," Starr said to someone I couldn't see.

"Yes, Fret. I need to see my brother." I sighed as another

grenade exploded nearby. Its light illuminated two people riding one hoverboard, but I didn't give them much thought.

My legs, my arms, my face—nothing even hurt. I had Vi. She loved me. Jag had charged me with her care. His trust meant more than my life, which I felt slipping through my fingers like water.

Fret held his fingers to my throat. "Brother," he said. "We need to get him inside."

"How'd you get here?" I asked, unable to move.

"I brought over two thousand people from Harvest. Trek contacted us. We now have more Insiders than Darke has clones."

I didn't respond. My head hurt too much and I didn't know what to say.

"Please, Zenn—"

"Did you know Dad is dead?" I blurted out. I turned my head toward him and found the truth in his downcast eyes. "You did. Why didn't you tell me? In Castledale, you could've told me."

"I didn't want to be the one to bring him up," Fret said. "I regret it. I'm sorry."

"That was—" I cut off, afraid to voice what I truly thought. That Fret was a coward. That he'd known Dad had loved me more. That he should've told me, no matter what.

A cheer rose from the crowd in the sky. I didn't share their joy. I felt so, so tired.

"I miss you," I said. I coughed, and tasted blood. Fret had done a lot for the Resistance. Father had never seen the value in Fret's contributions because Fret had no talent. I hadn't either—until now. Fret's influence—however small—over thousands of people had brought help to Freedom. Help when we needed it most.

"I miss you too, brother," he said. "You'll be okay, you'll see." His voice cracked on the last word.

Another grenade explosion brightened the sky. I saw someone fall. "Take Vi inside," I whispered. "Please."

Vi woke as Fret attempted to remove my arms from around her. I still couldn't move. She leaned over me, tears filling her beautiful eyes. "Zenn, oh no. Please." Her hands hovered above me, not quite touching me, but flitting around like they wanted to.

"I love you," I whispered again.

She bent closer and kissed me quickly on the mouth. "You're my best friend," she said. "I can't—you can't—" Then her tears fell, splashing against my face and neck. She cradled my face in her hands.

At her touch, I closed my eyes and focused on breathing. It was so, so hard.

* * *

Around me, people seem to be crying. Raine and Gunn. Trek and Fret. Jag.

Saffediene howls into the night, and strangely it's Vi who comforts her. She's sobbing too and hugging Saffediene like if she lets go, they'll both shatter.

In the dark, I smile. I feel like I've come home. Saffediene was right. No matter what I've done, I can come back to these people and they'll forgive me. Because they're my friends. I've been through so much with each of them, experienced some of the best times and some of the worst. They accept me. And I finally know which society is better.

Finally, I am free.

Jag

57

The conference room in Rise Twelve has seen better days. The sun streams into the room, and the table is filled with bottles of water and bags of food. It's lunchtime, and I've gathered everyone for a debriefing before we send traveling teams to key cities in the Association.

"Our losses include River Isaacs, Thane Myers, and Laurel Woods," I say, my voice tight with emotion. "I will file a full report on Thane's death, as he gave his life to spare mine and to ensure the success of this mission."

Next to me, Vi stares straight ahead. "Zenn Bower died," she says. "Flying with my additional weight was difficult for him, and he took many hits before we made it back to Rise Twelve."

I squeeze her hand, but it's not enough to ease her grief. I've felt the pain of losing two parents in the same day, and there is never enough happiness to fill that void. Not now, not ever.

And with the loss of Zenn too? I suspect Vi will never heal completely. Sure, time dulls the pain, but there's always something that brings it back to the surface. She has me. I'll help her keep that pain at bay. Blaze and Pace had done the same for me many times. *Both my brothers are dead.* I grip Vi's hand too tight as the breath leaves my body. I will have to learn to rely on her for the comfort Blaze and Pace once gave.

I meet her eyes, and she raises her eyebrows in a silent question: *Are you okay?*

I might never be okay, but I simply nod. For now, I'm still alive.

And we won.

Irvine weeps silently into his hands, once again reminding me that our victory has a steep price. I'll never get to explain myself to Indy. Never get to say good-bye. I clear my throat in an attempt to push back the grief at losing her without making things right between us.

"Traveling teams will leave tomorrow at first light," I say.

"Who feels like they can volunteer for these missions?" I'm through assigning, and I don't expect anyone to raise their hands.

But Saffediene does, immediately followed by Mason Isaacs. They catch each other's eyes, and I know they'd rather be anywhere but here. One lost a boyfriend, the other a daughter. I assign them the coastal northwestern cities. It's the longest mission available.

Surprisingly, Gunner volunteers too, with Raine's hand raised as high as his. They get seven cities to visit and instruct. With Gunn's voice, I know everything will be taken care of.

"Irv," I say. "Will you and Trek stay here? Maintain the transmissions and start the clean up?"

He nods, his eyes still rimmed with tears.

"Won't you be here?" Gunner asks.

"No," I say. "Vi and I will take the Mountain Region out west. Right, babe?" I look at her and find gratitude in her expression. She needs to go home, away from this city where the most important people in her life have died. She needs to sleep in her own bed, and sit on Zenn's front steps, and skip rocks in the lake like she used to with Ty.

"Yeah, sure," she says. "I want to go back to Seaside anyway. I'd like to visit my sister's grave."

"I'll come too," Fret Bower says. "I want to erect a memorial for my brother and my father in the Goodgrounds."

I swallow hard, purposefully not looking at the empty seat next to me where my second-in-command—my once-best-friend—Zenn—should be sitting. I cannot imagine anyone but Zenn writing me notes and sliding them across the table. I cannot thank him enough for giving his life to the Resistance. For dying so Vi could live.

"It's settled then," I say, unable to contain the tremor of pain in my voice. "The three of us will go together."

acknowledgments

Wow, a third book! What an adventure this series has turned into. From *Possession*—which was written as a stand-alone—to *Abandon*, I can't thank Anica Rissi and Annette Pollert enough. The whole crew at Simon Pulse is an absolute joy to work with.

Michelle Andelman is one of my biggest champions, and this book wouldn't have even been written without her.

I appreciate all the questions and conversations about my writing and books from my friends and family. You are all made of awesomesauce! Especially Adam, my patient husband, and my kids, who have eaten more home-cooked meals this year than ever before.

The life of a writer is filled with roller coasters. For making the ride fun: the Baconistas. Seriously. I'd be dead in the water without you. For encouraging me to get back in line for another ride: my critique group. You guys are awesome listeners. For reminding me that roller coasters are at carnivals and carnivals are supposed to be magical: my blog readers. Your support is priceless. Thank you, thank you!

I love getting e-mails and Facebook messages from readers who love this series. You always make me smile—and I hope *Abandon* is the ending you were hoping for.

about the author

Elana Johnson wishes she could experience her first kiss again, tell the mean girl where to go, and have cool superpowers. To fulfill her desires, she writes young adult science fiction and fantasy. She lives in central Utah, where she spends her time with many students, one husband, and two kids. Find out more at elanajohnson.com.

LET
THE
SKY
FALL

SHANNON MESSENGER

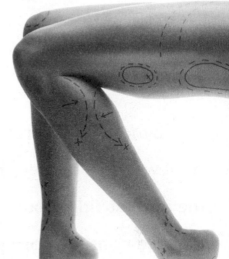
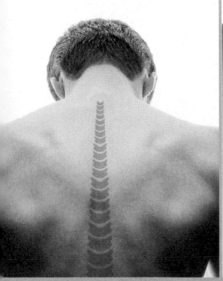

SIMONTEEN

Simon & Schuster's **Simon Teen**
e-newsletter delivers current updates on
the hottest titles, exciting sweepstakes, and
exclusive content from your favorite authors.

Visit **TEEN.SimonandSchuster.com** to
sign up, post your thoughts, and find out what
every avid reader is talking about!